MOTHER KNOWS BEST

BORIS BACIC

© 2024 by Boris Bacic

All rights reserved. No portion of this book may be reproduced mechanically, electronically, or by any other means, including photocopying, without permission of the publisher or author except in the case of brief quotations embodied in critical articles and reviews. It is illegal to copy this book, post it to a website, or distribute it by any other means without permission from the publisher or author.

For the woman who gave birth to me. Thank you for silently enduring your pain so that I could have the life I do. Your resilience has been a stepping stone in my journey, and I'm eternally grateful for your support.

Contents

Prologue	7
One	11
Two	15
Three	23
Four	33
Five	39
Six	51
Seven	59
Eight	69
Nine	79
Ten	91
Eleven	103
Twelve	111
Thirteen	119
Fourteen	129
Fifteen	135
Sixteen	145
Seventeen	151
Eighteen	159
Nineteen	167
Twenty	173
Twenty-One	181
Twenty-Two	193

Twenty-Three	203
Twenty-Four	207
Twenty-Five	215
Twenty-Six	223
Twenty-Seven	229
Twenty-Eight	239
Twenty-Nine	243
Thirty	249
Thirty-One	257
Thirty-Two	263
Thirty-Three	273
Thirty-Four	281
Thirty-Five	289
Epilogue	299
Final Notes	305
More Thrillers by the Author	307

Prologue

Adam can never relate to the people around him talking about the unhealthy relationships they have with their mothers. He'd listen to his friends' horror stories about moms from hell manipulating their children to make them feel like crap, abusing them when they were kids and later gaslighting them about it, deflecting all criticism when confronted about it years later and refusing to take responsibility for their actions, and so on and so on.

The hate they speak with always makes the tension in the room palpable. Only hate for a parent can go as deep. When the need for love and attention is betrayed, we go into the polar opposite.

Adam listens and nods for two reasons. The first one is that he knows that, at the end of the day, those same people will paradoxically continue to give those evil moms chance after chance, hoping they'll change—which will never happen.

As human beings, we're programmed to constantly seek the love and attention of our parents, even when it's clear they won't give it to us. It's easier for us to hope that will change than to accept things the way they are.

It's the one aspect of life that can't be replaced, no matter how loving our partner is or how many children we have. That's why we keep coming back, even when it makes us feel like the same, powerless kids that were abused by those parents.

Adam knows all this in theory, but that's about it. He's lucky enough to have a good relationship with his mom, which is precisely the second reason why he nods.

He doesn't truly understand what it means to have a toxic parent. He mostly remembers the good stuff from his childhood. His mom has always been supportive and protective, but not overly protective so as to make a weakling out of him.

When he first called to tell her that he had a new girlfriend and that they would like to come for a visit, his mom went out of her way to make Beth feel like she had always been a part of the family. When he broke the news that he and Beth got engaged, his mom couldn't have been happier. When they married, his mom gifted them so much money they were able to pay off their student loans. Adam didn't even know his mom had saved up that much, and although both he and Beth were reluctant to take it at first, they only agreed because his mom assured them that they needed it more than her.

Beth, having been raised as someone who was taught to believe she would hate every moment she'd have to spend with her mother-in-law, finds herself surprised by the woman's kindness, even to this day.

Adam knows he's really lucky to have such a loving and supportive mom. Some people would go as far as to call him a mama's boy, but he doesn't care because he knows that those same people who call him such names yearn for a relationship like that one deep down. Since they don't have it, it's easier for them to hide behind the façade of deprecating humor.

Adam has never considered the possibility of his relationship with his mom changing.

Then one day, he gets a call that will change his life forever.

ONE

The call comes on a warm, August Friday. Adam has just returned from work at the university. Teaching physics is fun, but it can also become repetitive at times. This monotony is only worsened by the deadpan expressions and yawns of uninterested students.

A pleasant smell emanates from the kitchen, but he can't identify it until Beth says, "Lasagna will be ready in fifteen!"

Adam smiles. The weekend is ahead. He and Beth don't have plans. Maybe they'll go to the movies tomorrow, have some friends over, depends on their mood. Adam loves simple weekends like those. No stress, he gets to unwind from the workweek, and he gets to dedicate more time to his beautiful wife.

Beth walks out of the kitchen and wraps her arms around Adam's shoulders. "Hey, you." She gives him a peck on the lips. "I missed you."

"I missed you, too," Adam says.

Dating for two years, married for one, and they still behave like a couple of teenagers. Similar to how Beth was told she would hate her mother-in-law, Adam was told by his male friends and relatives that he would hate marriage.

You're getting married? Big mistake. It's not too late to run.

You've been married for how long? A few months? Wait a few years until you start hating your life.

"How was your day?" Adam asks.

"Uneventful." Beth saunters back into the kitchen. "Oh, before I forget, your mom called."

"What did she want?"

Something clatters in the kitchen at the same time as Adam asks the question, and the lack of response from Beth tells him she hasn't heard him. He walks into the kitchen to see her taking out the plates and silverware. The oven is roaring. The top layer of the lasagna inside it is sizzling. The edges have already begun turning brown.

"Looks good, honey," Adam says. "What did my mom want?"

"I don't know." Beth shrugs. "She told me to tell you to call her back."

"Okay. Can it wait until after dinner? Did it sound like it was important?"

"Oh, you know her. Nothing ever sounds urgent with her even when it is. She could have called while she was in the middle of a warzone, and I wouldn't know what was going on until I heard the gunshots in the background. And even then, she'd probably be like, 'Oh, it's nothing, Bethany. Don't you worry your pretty little head about it.'"

Adam cracks a smile at that. His mom is good at making it seem like a severe situation isn't so severe, just so she won't worry anyone. How she's able to stave off panic with such a convincing act still baffles Adam. Despite telling her for years not to hesitate to tell him when she's in trouble, she never listens because she never wants to be a bother, especially now that Adam is married.

Adam figures she'll retreat even further when he and Beth have a baby. He doesn't want her to do that, though. He wants her in his life, to be there and to experience the happiness that he and Beth are experiencing.

"Guess I'll call her now, just in case," Adam says.

"Okay, babe." Beth puts on her mitts and is carefully cracking open the oven.

Adam is already in the living room, dialing his mom's number. She picks up on the second ring, but it's not her voice that greets Adam.

"Hello?" a soft, feminine voice speaks.

"Uh, hi." Adam is taken aback. "I'm sorry, who is this?"

"My name's Eleanor. I'm a nurse at Saint Mary Hospital."

Nurse? Saint Mary Hospital?

An iron ball drops to the pit of Adam's stomach. A nurse who is in possession of his mom's phone. That can only be bad news. Something happened to his mom. What if she's dead and the nurse is about to tell him that?

Oh God. Not like this. Please.

His mind races to the last conversation he had with his mom. It was three days ago when he called to see how she was doing. She had been fine, or at least sounded like it. Her voice had been slightly croaky. What if something had been wrong and he just failed to register it because of her expertise at hiding things? She had talked about going out for coffee with her neighbor Blaire, and Adam had talked about work.

Take care, Mom. Love you, he had said.

Love you, too, sweetie. Say hi to Bethany, she had replied.

That is going to be their last conversation, Adam thought. The years they had to experience together gone, just like that. She would never live to see Beth and Adam buy a house. She would never see the birth of her first grandchild, or bask in the joy of getting to spoil him.

"Is this Adam?" Eleanor asks, snapping Adam back to reality but only by a little. The majority of his consciousness swims in the nightmarish world where his mom is gone, where he needs to prepare for the painful funeral, where there's a mourning period, where...

"Yes, it is," Adam blurts and realizes how shaky his voice is.

Is my mom gone? he wants to ask, but there's a lump stuck in his throat.

"Adam, I'm afraid your mom had an accident at home." *Oh no.* "She broke her hip while going down the stairs and had to be hospitalized."

"Okay..." Adam says.

She might sense his agitation because she says, "She's okay, but do you think you can come here any time soon?"

But Adam isn't listening anymore. All he's heard is *she's okay.* Nothing else is important. The rest of the conversation goes in a blur, but Eleanor doesn't let him go until she's sure he understands all the details. She can probably hear how distressed he is, so she makes him repeat all the relevant information.

When Adam lowers his phone and turns around, he sees Beth standing in the kitchen doorway, staring at him.

"What happened?" she asks, and he repeats everything the nurse made him remember.

His mom has fallen down the stairs and broken her hip. She's been hospitalized, and she's okay, but they need to go there now.

"Oh my God," Beth says. "Let's go there right away."

Adam doesn't protest. The rumbling in his stomach caused by the savory smell of lasagna on the kitchen table has long since disappeared, replaced by a tight knot.

He can eat once he's made sure his mom's okay.

Two

His mom lives one state away from Oregon, in Casper, Wyoming, so he and Beth hop on the first available flight. The entire time, Adam keeps staring out the window at the converging clouds below. Beth notices his worry, so she squeezes his hand and says, "Hey. It's okay. She's fine. The nurse said so, right?"

"Yeah, but it's the complications I'm worried about. When older people break their hips, they often die," Adam says.

"Your mom's built like a tank. You really think a flight of stairs is going to be the end of her? Besides, she's only fifty-four years young."

That evokes a smile out of Adam. Looking at her, he's reminded that, whatever happens, Beth will be here for him. For better or for worse. The beauty of the moment is marred by a different dark thought that looms in his mind.

His mom is okay now, but she won't always be. This was a close call, a warning before she gets her ticket punched. It could happen tomorrow—or next year, or in a decade. It's impossible to tell.

The pain of losing his dad still feels too fresh, even though he died when Adam was still only seventeen. Ever since then, anxiety has been following Adam around. At night, he often thinks about what will happen when his mom dies, which prompts him to have difficulty breathing.

He thought that the dark thoughts would at least help him brace himself for the day when it would finally happen. The panic attack that he suppressed—and is still suppressing—told him how wrong he was. All he does is wear himself down while the pain remains fully radiant.

Right now, Beth's words keep the panic at bay. *Your mom's built like a tank.* If she's as tough as she presents herself to be, she's going to outlive him *and* his kids, and maybe even his grandkids.

****

When they arrive to the hospital, Beth asks Adam if he wants her to go with him or if he would rather have some privacy.

He tells her it's okay if she wants to stay in the waiting room. He knows how much Beth hates hospitals, ever since she lost her dad to terminal cancer. She's had her fill of clinics for two lifetimes, and coming with him here is already more than Adam could have asked for.

"But your mom will think I'm inconsiderate," she says.

"Not at all, babe. She'll understand. She knows what you've been through." Adam gives her a kiss. "I love you. I'll be back as soon as I can. Buy something from the vending machine if you like."

The young nurse who works at the reception is polite but slow. She shuffles down the corridor too slowly for Adam's natural gait while talking about the treatment the hospital has given to his mom. Worse yet, she occupies the middle of the corridor, so Adam can't even overtake her to lead the way.

When they reach the room where his mom is staying, the nurse gestures and says, "She's in here. We've given her some painkillers, so she's sleeping most of the time, but I think she's awake now."

"When is she going to be discharged?" Adam asks.

"We're still waiting for the doctor to take a look at the x-ray, but if everything is okay like we think it is, she'll be okay to leave tomorrow. Are you and your wife going to be taking care of her?"

"What?" The question takes Adam aback.

The nurse gives him a despondent look that says, *you poor thing, you don't know.* "She broke her hip. She lives alone and will be unable to do anything on her own for the next month at least, although it will probably be much longer until she's fully independent again."

"Oh, damn." Adam looks down. "I don't think I can do that. My wife and I live in Oregon. I'd need to quit my job to move here."

"Does she have any other family members we can call?"

"It's just me."

The nurse offers a thin-lipped smile. There's nothing she can do for him here. "Well, I'll let you think about everything. In the meantime, feel free to go inside and see her."

"Thank you."

The nurse leaves, and the corridor is filled with silence and Adam's rampant thoughts. He's going to need to talk to Beth later, and that's really the only thing he dreads. If it were up to him, he'd be okay with his mom staying with them until she's fully healed, but the apartment he and Beth are renting is small, and they need their privacy.

He can't think about that right now, so he grabs the doorknob and pushes the door open. The first thing that hits him is the medicinal smell. It's been in the air ever since he first entered the hospital, but it's a lot more potent here.

His mom is lying in bed, watching the TV mounted on the wall. She's the only patient in the room; all the other beds are empty.

At the sound of the door opening, she turns her head and cracks a wide smile. She looks small, pale, withered, not at all like the strong woman Adam knows. Not for the first time, he realizes how frail his mom is. She's been vibrant her entire life, and while those traces remain, they're drowned out by her weakened state.

"Oh, hi, sweetheart," she says with a croaky voice.

She raises one hand to greet him. The gaudy bangles and bracelets that hang off her wrist jingle like bells. Adam is surprised they let her keep those things on. His mom is inseparable from the jewelry she wears. She always wears them on her wrists and around her neck, and the accompanying rattling noise has become somewhat of her trademark.

He doesn't know where she got them. He doesn't even know if there's a symbolic meaning to them. He just knows the pieces of jewelry are older than even him. He'd tried asking her about them, but the answer he got was vague, and he hadn't cared enough to pry.

"Hey, Mom." Adam approaches her bed.

He wants to bend down and hug her, but he's afraid of hurting her, so instead, he takes hold of her hand. She squeezes back, but it's a feeble grip.

"How are you feeling?" he asks.

"Peachy." She grins.

"Mom." Adam gives her a stern look, a polite way of saying *cut the crap and be honest*.

His mom's smile droops slightly, and she rolls her eyes. "I'm fine, Addy. In a little bit of pain, but other than that,

I'm perfectly okay. I'm waiting for the doctor to discharge me so I can go back home."

"From what the nurse has told me, you'll need someone to take care of you for the next few weeks."

"Nonsense. I told you; I'm feeling fine. I'll be on my feet in no time."

Adam clenches his jaw. His mom is nothing if not stubborn, and he wonders if this is the right time to be arguing with her. He locates a nearby chair and drags it to the bedside to sit in it.

"Where's Bethany?" his mom asks.

"She's in the waiting room," Adam says. "You know how she is about hospitals."

"That poor girl, forced to be here because I was clumsy. You two didn't need to fly out here for me."

"What are you talking about, Mom? Of course we did. You're hurt, and we wanted to make sure you're okay."

"You worry too much, Addy. It's going to give you wrinkles."

They sit in silence for a little while until Adam asks. "So, what happened?"

His mom groans. "I was taking dirty laundry downstairs. The pile I carried blocked my view, and I missed a step."

"Jesus."

"Don't worry, it happened when I was close to the bottom." She lets out a shrill chuckle. "And the laundry softened my fall."

"Imagine what would have happened if you didn't have it with you."

"If I wouldn't have had it with me, I wouldn't have fallen."

They laugh at that, his mom harder than him. If she's stressed about this entire situation in the slightest, she's not showing it. Maybe she still doesn't realize how bad it's going to be for her in the next few weeks.

"Mom, listen. We need to talk," Adam says.

"About what?" she asks.

"About what to do until your hip heals."

The door opens. Both Adam and his mom turn to see Beth entering.

"Hi," she says softly.

She's awkwardly running a finger across the tattoo on her wrist. She often does that when she's nervous.

Adam is surprised, but at the same time, he realizes he should have expected Beth to come. Her love for his mom overrides her fear of hospitals. Adam suddenly loves her a lot more right now.

"Bethany, sweetie. What are you doing here?" his mom asks.

"I came to see how you're doing. Are you in pain?"

"Not at all. I'm so sorry to have worried you. I hate being a burden to other people."

"You're not a burden, Mom," Adam says.

They spend some time chit-chatting until the nurse walks in and tells Adam and Beth visiting hours are almost over and they can return in the morning after the doctor checks up on her.

"Don't you worry about me, you two," his mom says. "You must be tired from the flight. Why don't you stay the night at my house? The keys are in my purse."

Adam and Beth's financial situation is pretty tight, especially after paying for the flight, so they're glad they don't need to look for a nearby hotel.

"Thanks, Mom," Adam says as the keys jingle in his hand.

"She looks okay," Beth says when they're out of the hospital.

Adam doesn't respond. He doesn't know how to tell her they'll have to take care of his mom for the next month or two.

THREE

The house feels weird with only Adam and Beth in it. It's too quiet, enveloped in a darkness that no amount of sunlight can dispel.

It's also too *big*, even for a family of three like when Adam was growing up. Slowly, those numbers dwindled over the years. First, it was Adam's dad who left, and then Adam, leaving the mom alone. She would be able to breathe life into any structure, whether it's a luxurious penthouse or a rundown shack, but even her aura isn't enough to fill the spaciousness of these walls.

"You okay?" Beth gently touches Adam's arm when she notices his pensive gaze.

"Yeah. I'm starving. You wanna order something?"

They only had some snacks at the airport, which boomeranged the hunger way too soon. The thought of Beth's gorgeous lasagna going cold on the kitchen table, hundreds of miles away, fills Adam with a nibble of annoyance.

Beth takes out her phone. "Sure. What are you in the mood for?"

"I dunno. Pizza?"

"Margherita?"

Adam's favorite. "Sure. Thanks, babe. I'm gonna hop in the shower real quick."

He's just delaying the conversation at this point, he realizes, but he can't help it. He's dreading Beth's reaction. He knows his wife likes his mom, but does she like her enough to live with her for the next month in the cramped apartment they're renting?

He'll have to find out tonight.

****

Some time later, Beth and Adam are sitting in the living room, watching TV. The family-sized pizza box lies open on the table in front of them. Three huge slices and a crust from one remain.

For the first few minutes after eating, they sit in silence. Beth is touching the tattoo of the strange symbol on her wrist. She's disgusted by it. When sitting at any table, she turns her wrist face-down so the tattoo remains invisible to other people. When wearing long-sleeved clothes, she neurotically tugs at the sleeve to keep the tattoo covered.

Adam loves that tattoo because it's evidence of what she survived, and he's proud of her even more because of it. He asked her once why she doesn't remove it if it bothers her so much, but she said she leaves it on as a reminder.

For the past twenty minutes, they've been chatting about random things under the quiet atmosphere of the room and the glow of the TV screen.

"I'm impressed with your mom's TV size. And it's a flatscreen," Beth says.

"She's not that old, Beth. Besides, she loves movies."

"Really?"

"Yeah. Thursdays were movie night back when I lived with her. Every week, we'd take turns picking out movies. I always went for comedies or mysteries. She chose thrillers or horror."

"You never told me about it."

Adam shrugs. He isn't the type of person to talk too much about himself unless he's sure it's going to be interesting to the other person. It caused a problem in some of his earlier relationships because the girls opened up to him while he kept his side of the court closed. He wasn't trying to hide anything; he just preferred to learn more about the other person than talk about himself.

That, and he thought he was a really boring person. He still thinks that, but somehow, to Beth, he's the most intriguing person on the planet. He'd tell her about what he considers are the most mundane details from his past—what kind of bait his dad taught him to use when fishing for salmon, the routines he had in college, even went into details about physics—and she listened with rapt fascination.

She was good at getting him to open up right from the start. He'd find himself talking so fast sometimes he'd be stumbling over his words. He'd then realize he was talking for the past five minutes, and he'd say he was sorry, only for Beth to tell him not to apologize because she enjoyed listening to him talk.

He'd just spent ten minutes talking about the theory of relativity, and she was still there, still staring at him with that smile on her face and that sparkle in her eyes. He knew then and there he'd put a ring on her hand.

Six months later, he did. The initial plan had been to wait at least eight months, and the only reason why he even waited half a year was because he didn't want to scare Beth away with such a permanent commitment. The signs were there all along, though, but he was terrible at reading them—still is—and the past experiences that burnt him made him tiptoe before popping the question.

I want nothing more than to listen to you talk to me about physics for the rest of our lives, she had told him.

"Guess I forgot to tell you about it." Adam shrugs.

Maybe it's one of those things his brain pushed down as a defense mechanism, to protect him from the overwhelming sadness that looms above him right now. The realization that his life is moving on but his mom's is stagnant. She's all alone, her duty as a parent complete, nothing left to keep her occupied.

But that's not true. His mom isn't like one of those parents who have no other interests than their kids. She has her own hobbies. She watches movies. She hangs out with people. She goes to a book club once a week.

"You said she watches horror and thriller? Wow. She didn't strike me as someone who would watch something like that." Beth leans an elbow on the backrest of the couch, tucking her knees up to her chin and facing Adam.

He says, "Oh, she's a horror freak. Name any movie, and I can guarantee she's watched it."

The conversation prompts Adam to wonder if his mom still has movie nights on her own. Does she prepare a huge bowl of buttered popcorn just like back when Adam still lived here? Does she sit on her spot on the couch while leaving his unoccupied? Does she miss watching movies with him?

It makes him melancholic.

"I like this house. The furniture and the colors of the walls are kind of old, but I like the layout," Beth says, oblivious to Adam's thoughts.

"My dad designed it with the help of a friend who was an architect."

"He had taste."

"I don't think he was aiming for that. I think he was just looking for a design that would help evacuate me and Mom out of the house in case of a fire. Guess he'd seen a lot of bad stuff at work as a fireman, and he wanted to prevent that from happening to us. Did you know most people in fires don't die from actual fires but from smoke?"

"Really?"

Adam shifts in his seat. "Yeah. Because there's so much smoke and toxic gases made by fires; people die from that before the fire ever reaches them. So, they at least don't need to experience burning alive, which is a terrible way to go because your body tries to keep you alive for as long as it can, and it just causes you immense pain until it can no longer take it. But what I think is even worse is when you actually survive something so bad, and you have these terrible burns that need so long to heal and leave you in so much pain. My dad said he once ran into a burning building and saw a kid who had burns to over ninety percent of his body. Miraculously, he survived."

Beth's look of attention turns into utter horror. It makes Adam realize, not only that he had been talking for way too long but that the topic is not appropriate either.

"Sorry," he says.

"Don't apologize. You know I love listening to you. Maybe just ease up on the horror stories before bedtime, huh?"

Beth must realize he's oversharing because he's stressed—something he always does—because she runs her fingers through his hair. She does that for a little while before leaning in to give him a peck on the lips.

"Hey, you know what I just realized?" she asks.

"What?"

"This is the first time we're alone at your mom's house."

Adam looks at her to see a mischievous grin on her face. As if to confirm his suspicions, she gently runs her fingers down his thigh.

Adam doesn't respond because he's not in the mood. Something about having sex in the house tonight doesn't seem right, which is weird, because they already did it in the past multiple times.

Beth loves the idea of having to be quiet while someone is right next door. The fact that they're in someone else's house, all alone and free to do all kinds of dirty things, as loudly as they want, plays a big factor in Beth's current state of arousal.

He can understand why. Having been raised in a cult where pretty much everything was restricted, Beth now can't get enough of some of the forbidden things. The tattoo on her wrist representing the cult's symbol is a permanent reminder of that.

She leans in and kisses his neck. He remains frozen stiff, not knowing how to tell her now's not the time. She migrates the kisses downward toward his clavicle then plants a palm on his chest and runs it down his abdomen.

Adam puts his hands on her shoulders and gently pushes her away. When she looks at him, she's flustered, but the look of lust is replaced by confusion.

"I have to tell you something," Adam says.

Beth looks like she just got slapped. Adam makes it sound like the news he's about to deliver is the worst in the world. For all he knows, maybe it is. He has no idea how Beth is going to react, and that's adding another layer of stress to the whole thing.

"What is it, babe?" she asks, notably impatient to find out.

She's pulled back from him. There's a visible distance on the couch between them, the short-lived moment of romance gone like blown-out candlelight.

"It's about my mom," Adam says, and he doesn't know how to continue.

"Okay. What about her?"

"So, the doctor said it's pretty much going to be impossible for her to do anything on her own for the next few weeks." He waits to see Beth's reaction. She nods slowly, but he detects no understanding on her face, so he continues, "She, uh... doesn't have anyone to take care of her."

"Okay." Beth nods again. "What about your Aunt Erica?"

"The two of them aren't exactly on good terms. Erica probably doesn't even know my mom's at the hospital."

"Uh-huh." Beth averts her gaze to the TV.

"Beth," Adam says to grab her attention. "I'm the only person she has left."

The way Beth's eyes are fixated ahead of her on one spot indicates she's thinking. Finally, she turns her head to Adam and says, "Even if we wanted to, we can't take care of her, Adam. She lives here, and we live..." She raises a hand, but the attempt of the gesture dies halfway up. "We'd need to quit our jobs and move here. It's just not possible, babe."

"I know. That's why I was thinking we could fly her out to our place until she's able to walk again."

If Beth is shocked or appalled, she's doing an excellent job hiding it. Adam knows what that blank-faced stare means, though. She's not in favor of his suggestion, and she's simply doing her best not to show it.

"You want her to live with us until her hip heals?" she asks.

The question sounds accusatory, something down the line of *are you out of your damn mind*.

"Just until she's better. It'll be four weeks, tops," he says.

He phrases it as four weeks rather than a month because it gives the illusion of a shorter time—at least to him. Twelve weeks of dieting doesn't sound so bad until you realize that's three whole months, an entire season.

But it won't be four weeks, and he knows it. It'll be *at least* four weeks, and most likely twice as long until his mom's fully mobile and independent again. Beth doesn't need to know that. If she hears it's going to be more than a month, she won't even entertain the thought of having his mom over. This way, he can at least get her to consider it.

"Our apartment is small, Adam," Beth says. Her hand instinctively reaches for the tattoo again, but she becomes aware of it and lets it go.

"We have an extra bedroom we're not even using," Adam retorts.

"Sure, but it's still a small apartment. I work from home most days, and I really need the quiet to focus. I won't be able to work in the living room with your mom constantly there."

Now she makes it sound like his mom is a pest that's going to be bothering them.

"We really have no other options here, Beth," he says, biting down on the trace of anger that manifests at the front of his mind.

"Why not let the hospital take care of her? They're better equipped for those kinds of things."

"Sure, if you want us to get further into debt. Do you know how much a night at the hospital costs?"

Beth looks down, brainstorming for other solutions. She's not only put considerable distance to Adam on the sofa, but she's also assumed a defensive body language. Adam doesn't remember when that happened.

"We need our privacy, Adam. Especially now when we're..."

Adam reaches to take her hand, which is stiff like that of a corpse. "I know. We can still try to have a baby with my mom in the apartment. We'll just have to be quieter."

"No." Beth shakes her head. "I'm not going to conceive a baby in conditions where I need to be quiet. I want us to be able to do it without worrying about the other person hearing us. If we're going to continue trying, we're going to do it *after* your mom leaves."

So now she's giving him an ultimatum. The anger that had manifested earlier is now blooming into something full-blown, but he still refuses to give it power. If he does, it'll take control, and he and Beth are going to get into a nasty fight, which will result in him sleeping on the couch tonight.

They don't need that. Not right now.

"Okay, fine," he says. "We can put the baby on hold."

He realizes how terrible it sounds only after the words leave his mouth. Beth gives him an unsatisfactory look as if she was hoping he wouldn't agree to the presented choice.

"Baby, it's only going to be for a month," Adam lies again. If she manages to survive with his mom for four weeks, another extra two weeks won't be a problem. "Four weeks, and then we'll fly her back home and continue with our lives. It's no big deal."

Beth lets out a deep sigh. "Sorry. It's not that I don't like your mother, you know that. She's your mother after all, and I'd be a terrible person to make a fuss about this. It's just... This is going to derail our plans and our life, and I hate it when that happens. And I really need some alone time from time to time, and the thought of having someone in the apartment twenty-four seven is just..."

"You'll have your privacy, babe. I promise. She'll be in the bedroom most of the time anyway, so you won't even notice she's here. I'll take care of everything she needs, okay?"

The anger is gone because he got what he wanted. She hasn't directly said it, but it's clear. Adam pulls Beth in for a hug and strokes her back. She's uncertain about this whole thing, but he'll make sure his wife has everything she needs for her space.

He says, "I promise we'll be back to our life in no time, Beth."

Four

"I really don't think this was necessary, Addy. You and Bethany haven't been married for long. You don't need a rodent like me to ruin your privacy," his mom chirps as Adam helps set her into bed. Her jewelry jingles.

"Don't call yourself a rodent. And we don't mind. Really. Right, Beth?" Adam looks at the doorway where his wife stands.

"Sure. You're no trouble at all." Beth smiles, but Adam knows that smile. It's the fake one she gives to other people when she's trying to cut the conversation short.

She's not indifferent about his mom staying with them. And even though they'd come to the agreement days ago, and even though Beth was very supportive of it and helped as much as she could, the fact that she's having second thoughts is undeniable on her face.

Sometimes, we think we're ready to emotionally face something until we actually face it, and we realize how daunting practice is compared to theory. It's easy to win made-up arguments in our heads when we have time to think of a response than in person when the opponent is impatiently staring at us.

The past few days have been so hectic that Adam hasn't even stopped to consider how Beth might be feeling. The somber look in her eyes makes him realize that, and he suddenly feels like the worst person in the world. He's been worried about his mom, but not his wife.

He'll have to make it up to her. And it can't be something as simple as flowers. It's going to have to be something huge, something that'll completely overshadow the way she's currently feeling. He doesn't know what that will be, though.

Beth isn't picky, and small things are enough to make her happy. Adam is sure flowers would satisfy her, but she deserves more. Maybe a nice, romantic dinner, and...

Well, just dinner. He won't be able to scatter rose petals or light candles around the apartment.

Dammit.

Guess dinner will have to do.

"As soon as I'm better, I'm flying back home. I don't want to be a burden to anyone," his mom says.

Beth quietly exits the room. Adam covers his mom with blankets and puts the TV remote on the nightstand where she can reach it.

He asks, "Do you need anything? Water or anything to eat?"

"No, thank you. You're too kind, Addy."

He smiles and turns to leave, but his mom grabs him by the wrist so suddenly that he turns back to see what she wants. She's looking at him with concern and something that looks like sadness.

"You and Beth need your privacy," she says. "Now that you've flown me all the way out here, I'll stay, but I'm going to be as quiet as possible."

"Mom, for the last time, you're no bother to us." He doesn't mean to say it so brusquely, but it comes out of his mouth that way.

Beth is upset, which bothers him, but there's also the fact that he needs to keep reassuring his mom she's not bothering them. He feels squeezed from two fronts.

One thing at a time. One thing at a time.

"We'll be in the living room if you need anything," he says and exits the bedroom.

Beth isn't out in the living room, so she must be in the bedroom. Despite that assurance, his eyes drift to the floating shelf in the foyer just to make sure Beth's keys are there.

He considers leaving Beth alone. She might need some privacy right now. Adam doesn't like to consider the idea that his wife needs to spend time away from him, but he's learned to accept her like that. He knows she loves him and loves spending time with him, but she sometimes needs a few hours to chill out from all human contact entirely.

The way she does it most of the time is by going to the bedroom, putting on her headphones, and blasting music loud enough to drown out all external noise. Other times, she takes a walk in the park.

Sometimes, she'll invite Adam to go with her. It's moments like those he feels her love more than when she shows it with affection because she's letting him into her sacred space, devoting her alone time to spending it with him.

Adam stops in front of the closed bedroom door. He dreads going inside because he doesn't know what he'll encounter. Will Beth welcome him if he sits next to her? Will she use one hand to run her fingers through his hair while browsing social media on her laptop with the other?

Or will she remain frozen stiff when he sits next to her, not telling him to leave but also not doing anything to approach him?

That seeming indifference scares Adam more than anything. He'd prefer if Beth openly showed her anger by yelling. This coldness makes him feel like they're strangers.

It gives him a glimpse into what things would be like if they ever got divorced.

Adam cracks the door open and pokes his head inside. He sees Beth sitting in the middle of the bed in the darkness. Her face is lit up by the glow of the laptop in front of her. She looks up and catches Adam's gaze for a moment before averting it back down to the screen.

Adam steps inside. He almost leaves the door open until he remembers they have a guest now. He sits on the bed next to Beth. "Hey."

"Hey." She touches his knee before continuing to type away at the keyboard.

That's a start.

"You okay?" he asks.

She stops typing and brushes her hair behind her ear. She looks at him and smiles. "Yeah. Just still trying to process that we're not alone anymore."

Adam takes her by the hand. "I promise things will not be as bad as you think. And besides, she'll be gone before you know it."

He's waiting for her hand to squeeze his, to show she doesn't just want to pull away from him. She does tighten her grip, and she looks at him with a lopsided smile.

"I'm sorry. I know I'm being a brat," she says with a shake of her head. "I guess I just never expected we'd be living with someone for that long. When we visit your mom, it's different. We stay there however long we want to stay; we leave when we want to leave. This is like…"

"Like a prison," Adam says.

She looks at him in a way that says, *that's what I was trying to say* but then quickly moves her gaze away.

"Hey." He brushes her hair. "You're not a brat. It's perfectly normal to feel this way. Okay? I know how much you value your space, and I promise my mom won't get in the way of that. She can't even get out of bed."

"Yeah, I know. I'm not bothered by it, babe. Promise. I just need to get used to the fact that she's going to be here. I'm glad we're able to help her. Really. And this might let you two catch up and bond like old times, so I'm happy for that."

The response evokes a smile out of Adam. It's moments like these that he realizes how lucky he is to have such a supportive wife. Somebody else would have said there was no way they'd let their mother-in-law live with them. Somebody else might have a terrible relationship with their MIL.

The fact that his mom is respectful enough not to cross boundaries and interfere makes that possible. Strangely, he's looking forward not just to spending time with his mom, but also to letting Beth get to know her—if she decides to do so, of course.

"So, we're cool?" he asks.

She chuckles. "Yes, honey. We're cool. "She notices the skeptical look on his face, so she leans in and gives him a kiss. "We're *cool*. I promise."

"Okay." Adam nods.

He gets up to give Beth her alone time, hopeful about the upcoming month.

FIVE

For the past few weeks, everything's been okay. His mom has started walking with the help of a rolling walker. She's still slow and unable to perform some of the things on her own, and she can't sit for too long without pain, but she's getting better.

She's started helping around the house despite Adam telling her not to over-exert herself. She's not wearing only her bracelets, but her necklaces, too, and the rattling can often be heard throughout the apartment. She keeps dismissing Adam's warnings, telling him not to worry because he's going to get age spots too soon.

It's the least I can do to repay you two for letting me stay and taking care of me, she says.

Adam doesn't like that. She makes it sound like they took her in out of charity. That's not the case, and Adam explains they took her in because she's his mother, but she doesn't want to listen.

One day, he returns from work, and immediately, a savory and very familiar smell hits his nostrils. He expects to see Beth in the kitchen, but when he walks in, his mother is there instead, pulling a casserole out of the oven.

"Mom!" he shouts, ignoring the mouth-watering sight of dinner in front of him.

She turns around to face him and takes off the mitts. "Oh, hey, sweetie. How was your day at work?"

"Mom, you shouldn't be cooking. The doctor said you can injure—"

"Oh, stop it. I feel totally fine, Addy. A few more days and I think I'll be able to do a backflip." She lets out a chortle.

"I'm serious, Mom. It's not about how you feel. If things get complicated, you're going to need more time to recover."

"If you wanted me to leave as soon as possible, you should have just said so."

Adam shakes his head. "No. That's not what I—"

"Relax, Addy. I'm just joking. I know you love your momma." She pinches his cheek and turns her attention back to dinner. "Food will be ready in about fifteen minutes. I hope you didn't eat anything before dinner."

Adam feels like he's being transported back to his childhood, and it's not a bad thing. He feels like he just came back from school on a Friday, his mom's lunch is almost ready, and he's starving. He's going to eat lunch, and he's going to hop on his Xbox to play Call of Duty with his buddies all day long because there's no school tomorrow.

The reverie is interrupted when he remembers he's an adult, and his mom is not the person who takes care of everything anymore. The roles have been reversed.

"Where's Beth?" Adam asks.

"She's in the bedroom. I swear, that girl shuts herself into that room way too much. It's not healthy. Did you see how pale she is? She needs to get more sunlight on her skin. Why don't you take her out more?"

"Thanks, Mom," Adam says, not responding to the other bevy of questions.

He enters the bedroom to see Beth in her usual position, seated in the middle of the bed. She takes off her headphones when she sees Adam. He closes the door behind him and says, "Hey, can I talk to you?"

The smile that had formed on Beth's face drops like an anchor at that question. She assumes it's bad news.

"Sure. Did I do something wrong?"

It hurts Adam to see how her first assumption is that it's her fault. Being raised in an environment where you're told you're never good enough tends to do that.

"My mom's cooking dinner," he says.

"Yeah. That's really nice of her." Beth nods.

"That's not what I meant. She shouldn't be cooking. She has a broken hip, remember? Why didn't you say anything to her?"

Beth's back stiffens, and her face grows rigid. "FYI, I did tell her not to do it, but she didn't want to listen. She never wants to listen to me."

"Well, why didn't you just stop her?"

"Stop her how? Block her from entering the kitchen? Because that's the only way I could have stopped her, and even that's questionable. Just the other day, I found her folding the laundry, and I told her I'd do it, but she insisted. I can't force a grown woman to stop doing something, Adam."

Adam raises his eyebrows. "She was folding laundry? Beth, do you realize how dangerous that is for someone with a broken hip? It wouldn't kill you to check on her once or twice a day."

He knows this is a bad, bad approach, but he can't control himself.

"Again, what do you want me to do? She's your mother. Why don't you try to talk to her?"

"She won't listen to me either. She's too stubborn."

"Well, there you have it." Beth shrugs and looks down at her laptop, indicating the discussion is over.

Such dismissal makes anger bubble inside Adam.

"These things wouldn't happen if things were done on time," he says.

He knows he messed up the moment the words leave his mouth, but it's too late to take them back, and he intends to stick to his guns until the end now.

Beth raises her head at him, a venomous look on her face. "I'm sorry, what?"

"She's folding laundry because it's been out of the dryer for too long. She's making dinner because you didn't cook. If things around the apartment were all done, she wouldn't be doing them."

Beth's face further takes on a look of incredulity. "You better be joking." Adam remains silent. "Do you know how much work I do around the apartment every day? And that's with a full-time job. I didn't make dinner for one day, so what?"

"It's more than just for one day, Beth." Adam hangs on to the last comment because that's where he has leverage. "We order a few times a week because you don't want to cook."

Beth scoffs. "I'm not going to cook just because your mom is too stubborn to know she should be resting. I'm not your maid, Adam. If you want dinner, why don't you make it yourself sometimes?"

Things are escalating fast. Beth loves cooking for the two of them—he knows that—and he's pushing it by saying she should do it often. He's making her feel unappreciated, which might result in her being fed up with cooking.

"I don't want to argue," he says when he realizes he's in too deep, but it's too late by then.

"You want some milk?" he asks his mom as he gets up.

His mom smiles. "Old habits die hard, hm?"

Adam comes back with a glass of milk and sits down. The casserole is on his plate already. He had managed to forget about the fight with Beth until he sits down and looks at her empty seat. That's when his mood darkens again.

"Addy, can I ask you something?" his mom says, and Adam knows right away he's not going to like the question because no one does so much preparation when they want to ask something insignificant—they just ask it.

"Sure, Mom," he says.

"Did you and Beth get into a fight because of me?"

Adam should have expected that question, but he didn't, and now he's caught off guard, unable to answer. He stares at his plate, the appetite slowly washed over by a knot inside his stomach.

"No. We didn't get into a fight," he finally says.

He looks up at her. She flashes him a vague smile and says, "Eat before it gets cold."

She doesn't believe him. She knows he and Beth got into a fight. The fact that she has to witness that embarrasses Adam. He averts his gaze to the plate, determined to enjoy the meal.

He takes a sip of milk first, as he always did, and then jabs a fork into a piece of the casserole. Steam erupts from the spot where the tines of his fork perforate the baked surface. He takes the first bite and...

He had been afraid he'd bite into it and find a completely different taste. Something unfamiliar and underwhelming compared to the nostalgia trip he yearned for. The plethora of tastes that floods his mouth is exactly how he remembers it.

"This is it. This is the same kind of casserole you used to make," he says.

"Don't fix what ain't broken. The recipe is from your grandmother. She made it even better than me, but you're probably too young to remember that."

"Too bad she died when I was so young."

"Yeah. She really didn't like you at first, you know?"

"Really?"

"Yeah. She used to scream at me and your dad to get you out of her room whenever you wandered there."

"But she changed her mind later?"

His mom puts a bite into her mouth. She chews, swallows, and says, "You kinda grew on her later. I came back from the store once and saw you sitting in her lap while she was reading you a story. It might not sound like a lot to you, but trust me, it was a big deal to see her do that."

"Hm."

They continue eating in silence for a few minutes before his mom speaks up again.

"Must be very important work," she says.

Adam looks up, confused.

"Beth's work. It must be very important when she had to leave the apartment in such a hurry, right before dinner."

"Yeah." Adam nods and avoids her gaze.

He still carries the fear from childhood that his mom can tell if he's lying just based on eye contact. Back when he was a kid, he thought she had a superpower to be able to do that. As an adult, he realizes she's probably able to decipher it from more than just a simple eye contact: a lack of detailed response, uncomfortable shifting, erratic movement, etc.

Adam hopes she won't read right through him, but he's somehow aware that she knows everything. She's a mother, after all, and she has way more life and marriage experience.

"Is Beth... okay, Addy?" she asks.

"Yeah. What do you mean?"

"I mean because of... well, you know." She lowers her voice. "Her past."

Adam told his mom that Beth used to be in a cult because he shares everything with her, but he's regretted it ever since because his mom has been looking at Beth like she's a patient who escaped a mental institution.

She doesn't understand that Beth was just a child back then, abused and brainwashed daily until she grew up, realized it was all bullshit, and found a way to escape. It was a tough life, and that past still haunts her. His mom has always judged Beth because of her past, even though she never openly said it.

"Yes. She's fine, Mom," Adam says, choosing not to get into the discussion.

His mom leans back and nods. "I never did that back when your father was alive. It was well known in our house that, when dinner's ready, everyone sits at the table and eats together. Storming off without so much as an apology was considered disrespectful."

Adam stares at his plate. He hears the words his mom is saying, but it takes his brain a moment to connect the dots and understand she's calling Beth disrespectful. She may be his mother, but Beth is his wife, and he isn't going to allow anyone to talk badly about her.

"Like I said, she has work to do." Adam forces himself to smile.

"I'm not just talking about dinner, Addy," she stuffs a forkful into her mouth and chews, her gaze lingering on the plate.

"What do you mean, then?"

His mom chews a moment longer, perhaps gathering her thoughts before giving her response. She swallows, jabs a piece of beef onto her fork, and says, "The apartment. It's a mess. The dishes are always dirty. The laundry, too. There's dust everywhere. A good wife keeps a home clean."

"We've been kind of busy lately, Mom." *Taking care of you.* "Things are usually clean around here."

"I understand why you're too busy to do it. You're at the university all day long. But Bethany is at home."

"Just because she's home doesn't mean she's not working. She has a remote job."

His mom still doesn't fully understand the concept of online jobs and remote work. Staring at her blasé expression, he can tell his words aren't getting to her, and he wonders why he's even trying to justify how he and Beth live their life.

"Please, don't get upset, Addy," his mom says.

"I'm not upset."

"I'm just seeing things differently. I'm a completely different generation, after all." She chuckles.

Her words are supposed to dispel the tension in the air, but Adam's annoyance doesn't let up.

"I'll clear the table." She stands up after she's done eating.

The conversation is over at least, but Adam's mind continues to replay it. He can't help but feel like his mom's goal the entire time was to get her point across and get him thinking.

SIX

His mom watches TV after dinner. She doesn't utter a word to Beth, and Beth doesn't utter a word to Adam. Right after returning home, she waltzes into the bedroom, leaving Adam and his mom in the living room.

For the first time since having his mom stay over, Adam feels like the apartment is too small. He can't go to the bedroom because Beth is there, but he also can't go to his mom's room because he has virtually nothing there that belongs to him. It would be weird for him to sit there just so he can be on his phone.

So, he's forced to sit on the living room couch with his mom and stare at the show on the screen even though he doesn't see it because his mind is hung up on the conversation with his mom, and on the fact that Beth is angry at him.

He's torn between going into the bedroom to try to talk to his wife and waiting for her to cool off. At the same time, he has to keep a straight face in front of his mom. He remembers how she once told him about her friend whose son was in a toxic relationship and ended up fighting with his girlfriend whenever he came for a visit.

She said, *That poor woman just wants to see her son for the one weekend a year that he visits, and he ruins it for her. She looks forward to making them feel at home, but they end up screaming at each other while she has to listen. It's unfair to her to force her to listen to that crap.*

Granted, Beth and Adam never had arguments when visiting his mom, but now that she's here, it's inevitable it would happen sooner or later. And now, sitting next to his mom, keeping things hidden from her seems unnatural because he remembers when he got bullied at middle school, and when he felt like life was over because his dad had died, and when his first girlfriend left him, and when his third girlfriend cheated on him because those were all the times when he came to his mom for help.

She always listened, and sometimes, that was enough. Other times, she gave him advice on what to do: a solution he already knew but needed confirmation from a person that he knew would make the right decision in that situation.

His mom comments something about the doctor actress in the TV show, but Adam doesn't pay attention. He nods and gives brusque responses while staring at the bedroom door where Beth is.

He glances at his mom occasionally. She doesn't seem to notice anything is wrong with his mood. He wants her to notice it and ask him about it. That way, the choice will be made easier: Ask and I'll answer. At the same time, the walls in this apartment are thin. If Beth has no headphones on, she'll probably hear everything, and the last thing Adam needs is for her to think he's conspiring with his mom against her.

Despite his desire to voice his worry, he swallows it down and continues blankly staring at the TV, waiting for the time to pass until he can go to bed and talk things out with Beth. His mom keeps talking, and eventually, Adam's one-word responses turn into two words, and then three, and then three with a chuckle, and before he knows it, he's forgotten about his fight with Beth, and he's talking and laughing with his mom.

He can't tell for sure, but whenever he glances at her, he sees her momentarily eyeing him in a scrutinizing manner. Maybe she did notice his bad mood after all, and this is her way of cheering him up without having to bring up the heaviness of the conversation. If that's the case, he's grateful to her for broaching the situation that way.

The impending sense of dread looms nearby, though, and it intensifies every time he looks at the bedroom door.

Eventually, his mom is the one who stands up from the couch—slowly with the help of her roller—and says she's going to wash the dishes in the kitchen before calling it a day. Adam protests that she shouldn't do it, once again emphasizing her broken hip, but as always, she doesn't listen.

It's already late by then, and Beth hasn't once exited the bedroom since returning home. Adam wonders if she ate while she was outside, and if not, if she's deliberately ignoring the hunger just because she doesn't want to step out and face him.

He notices darkness under the crack of the door, which means she's turned off the lights and gone to bed. That causes a spark to reignite his worry.

Beth never goes to sleep without Adam. She does go to bed, but she stays on her phone with the lights on until he joins her, no matter how late it is. There's only one instance when she doesn't wait for him.

When she's really, *really* angry.

At that point, Adam doesn't care that his mom insists on doing the dishes. He has no time nor desire to babysit her. All he wants is to talk with Beth and see how he can fix the situation. A flicker of relief washes through him when he enters the bedroom and sees the glow of her cell phone near the edge of the bed, illuminating her face.

He doesn't say anything at first. He gets into bed, turns toward her, and contemplates how to start the conversation. While watching TV with his mom, he's thought of what to say and replayed it in his mind over and over, but now he draws a blank.

He gently touches Beth's shoulder. She continues to remain frozen stiff, the intensity of her phone's screen intermittently changing as she scrolls. She's scrolling too fast, making Adam wonder if she's actually watching whatever's on her screen or just pretending to do so, just like he did with his mom back in the living room.

"Beth, can we talk?" he utters.

Not a great way to start a conversation. It raises the stakes before it even begins. He wishes he could be smooth like his mom in cheering other people up. Being a physics teacher transferred to his personality, too. Everything is either black or white, no gray zones or blurred lines. Either he and Beth resolve fights, or they don't.

"I'm too tired to talk tonight," Beth says coldly.

This is going to be hard, Adam realizes, because Beth talks in her "stranger" voice, as he calls it. It's the atonality with which Beth talks to him whenever she's angry that makes him call it that.

"Just five minutes and I'll let you sleep. I promise," Adam says.

Beth continues scrolling on her phone. Adam prepares to say something else in an attempt to convince her when Beth reaches toward her nightstand and turns on the lamp. She locks her phone and puts it on the nightstand before scooting up into a sitting position.

Adam's suspicions are confirmed. He knows right away this conversation is going to be difficult, and probably fruitless, because he sees the deflective expression on her face. He's already in too deep even if it means the conversation is only going to make her angrier, and they'll end up sleeping on opposite sides of the bed facing away from each other, and Adam won't fall asleep for hours because of the worry that will eat away at him.

"Yes?" Beth asks, her gaze meeting with Adam's for the first time since she got home.

"I'm sorry. I was wrong to have attacked you like that. I got angry, and I blamed you, and I shouldn't have."

Beth stares ahead of her. "Sounds like you two had fun watching TV."

Adam doesn't know how to respond to that. "We were just talking."

"So, you take your anger out on me, you have dinner, spend time with your mom, and now you come to try to talk with me when it's time for us to go to bed? Might as well take care of whatever's still not fixed since you have five minutes to spare, right?"

"No. Beth, that's not what it's like at all. I didn't wait for the last moment to fix things with you on purpose. I was just trying to give you time to cool off."

Beth sighs but doesn't say anything. For a brief moment, her features relax before resummoning the previous rigidity. She doesn't want to argue either, but she remains angry because she knows, if she lets this go too easily, Adam will know he can get away with things.

In reality, Adam isn't like that, but Beth has traumas that she's still dragging with her from her childhood. No matter how many times Adam shows her he won't take her trust for granted, a dose of skepticism remains on her side.

"I'm sorry for what I said," Adam says.

Beth softens up once more. "I might have overreacted, too."

Adam knows the conversation is steering in the right direction. Now he just has to make sure not to make any sudden veers, and everything's going to end okay.

"Your reaction was completely called for. I would have reacted the same way," he says.

"No. Not when your mom is here. I don't want her to worry about us. If she sees us fighting, she might think it's something terrible even if it's a small argument. She doesn't need the stress right now."

Suddenly, Adam loves this woman a lot more. She's putting not only Adam but his mom in front of her own needs.

"Beth, thank you for being so thoughtful, but my mom's a tough lady. You don't need to worry about her."

Beth shrugs. "She's only going to be staying here for a few more weeks anyway, right?"

Adam has forgotten there's a time limit to his mom staying with them, and suddenly, the thought of her leaving makes a nibble of uncertainty manifest at the back of his mind.

"Yeah," he says to Beth.

"What's wrong?" Beth asks when she notices his pause.

"Nothing. I just... it's nothing."

"You don't want her to leave."

Adam knows Beth is good at reading him, but the accuracy still baffles him sometimes. He whips his head toward her but doesn't say anything.

"No, I do, I just... I guess I'm getting too used to her being here," he says.

"You know she has to leave sooner or later, right? I mean, we can't live with her, especially not in this small place. And since we plan on having a new member of the family..."

"No, you're right." Adam nods, but he hates how a microscopic part of him is doing somersaults in the hopes of finding a way for his mom to stay with them. It's not possible, and he knows it. Plus, he would never subject Beth to that. And with them working on having a baby...

Beth slinks up to Adam, interrupting his thoughts, and they start kissing. He forgets all about his mom when she runs her hand down his stomach and grabs the bulge in his boxers. She stops kissing him and gives him a surprised smile, as if to say *already?*

"Maybe we can stay up a little longer," Adam says.

Seven

His mom cooks regularly nowadays. Beth and Adam have three warm meals a day. Adam is transported back to his childhood whenever he smells his mom's Bolognese, her Philly cheesesteak, and her homemade pizza (made from scratch, dough included).

The quantity of the food she makes is worrisome because, no matter how much there is, everything is eaten since it's so good. Adam has already gained a couple of pounds since she moved in with them. Beth doesn't seem terribly happy about eating that kind of food either because it's too good to resist. She asks his mom to tone it down, at least for her, and his mom nods and agrees. But then she turns right around and does exactly the same thing she's been doing.

Beth doesn't say anything to that. She just stoically keeps quiet, but from time to time, she shoots a glance in Adam's direction, silently pleading with him to do something.

If only she knew he was as powerless as her. If his mom makes her mind up about something, not even a speeding train can stop her.

One morning, Beth and Adam wake up to get ready for work when Beth says, "Hey, are we still good for date night this week?

Date night is a regular thing the two of them have every week, or at least had before his mom moved in. Ever since then, it became less frequent and then stopped entirely. They talked about it after their last fight and came to the conclusion that they have to bring date nights back because they strengthen their bond.

"Of course. We don't want to skip date night," Adam says.

"Cool. What would you like to do?"

"Hm." Adam thinks. "I vote for an escape room. It's been a while since we did one of those."

"That's a great idea."

"And why don't you choose the restaurant?"

"Okay. I'll make a reservation for tomorrow. What about your mom?"

"What about her?"

"Won't she feel left out if we go without her?"

"Beth, it's called date night for a reason. She'll understand it's just for you and me."

"Okay. As long as there's no confusion."

They get out of the bedroom to see the table set and breakfast served. It's scrambled eggs, sausages, and crispy bacon this time. His mom is pouring OJ into the glasses on the table. She's able to move a lot faster and a lot easier. Sometimes, she doesn't even use her roller.

"Good morning. I know you like to wake up at the last moment and rush to work without eating properly, so I made sure to get everything ready earlier today," she chirps.

"Thanks, Mom." Adam takes a seat.

Bethany sits across from him and stares at the food with a judgmental glower.

"Um, Mom? Beth doesn't eat this kind of food," Adam says.

His mom freezes. "Oh. And why is that?"

She looks at Beth as if to say, *explain yourself.*

"Hypertension." Adam defends her. "The doctor said she should ease up on the fatty food because of her blood pressure."

"Oh, sweetie. But you're skinny!" his mom says.

"I know. Bad genetics, I guess." Beth awkwardly brushes her hair behind her ear and chuckles.

His mom looks incredulous, like she doesn't fully understand what Beth is trying to tell her.

"Well, surely you can eat a little of what I made," she says.

"Thank you, but I'm not hungry," Beth says.

"Oh, nonsense. Come on, have some eggs and bacon. It's really good."

"Mom," Adam says sternly, but his mom is already transferring a chunk of eggs and some bacon onto the plate.

Grease is dripping off the spatula as she does so.

"There you go. Oils are healthy, you know?" his mom says.

Beth looks disgusted by the plate of food in front of her.

"Mom, she told you she can't eat that," Adam says.

"It's all right. I'll just have some eggs," Beth says.

Adam knows she's doing it just to get his mom off her back, so he remains quiet. Beth grabs a fork and stabs a piece of egg on the tines. She puts it in her mouth, chews, and nods.

"It's good," she says.

His mom seems satisfied with that.

"See? You should be cautious about listening to doctors so diligently. They can be wrong, too. These younger generations nowadays are so sensitive. Look at me. For fifty years, I've been eating food that experts today are classifying as fatally dangerous, and I'm completely fine." She walks into the kitchen where she continues to talk.

Adam leans across the table and says, "I'll talk to her. Don't worry about it."

"Thank you," Beth says as she stabs another piece of egg onto the fork.

"You don't need to eat it."

That seems sufficient to Beth. She puts the fork down and announces loudly enough for his mom to hear, "Well, I'm already late, so I should get going."

She pushes her chair back and stands up.

"Oh, already? But you hardly ate anything." His mom appears in the kitchen doorway.

"That's all right. I'm not hungry anyway. I'll be home for lunch, though," Beth says.

Up until recently, Beth has worked from home most days, save for Thursdays when she goes to the office. It's not mandatory to go to work, but employees who go there get various benefits, like break rooms, nap rooms, snacks, warm meals, etc. Adam knows that the benefits aren't the reason why Beth is working in the office. She doesn't care about any of those amenities. She just wants to spend some time away from his mom.

Although Beth hasn't said anything, Adam can't help but wonder if his mom is bothering Beth when she's working from the bedroom. Something at home is definitely bothering her to the point of getting dressed, commuting to the office, and working in a space filled with people where she would have no alone time whatsoever.

Adam takes a mental note to talk to Beth when she's back from work.

"Be sure to come on time, you two," his mom says. "I'm making my famous cheesy pasta."

Beth's smile remains frozen, morphed into a rictus. She catches Adam's gaze for the briefest moment. "Oh, actually, I just remembered I have some important meetings today. I'm going to have to skip lunch and grab something to eat while I'm out. Sorry."

"What about you, Addy? You're coming home for lunch, right?" his mom asks.

The way in which she asks that question makes Adam feel sorry for her. She just wants to have lunch with her son and daughter-in-law. She's all alone at home while they're working.

Adam hadn't planned on coming home for lunch, but now he has to. He's going to have to cancel lunch with his coworker John, though.

"Sure. I'll be here, Mom," he says.

"Hey, I was thinking," Beth says to his mom. "Why don't you take it easy for today, and I'll make us dinner?"

His mom says, "Oh, you don't need to worry about me. I'm perfectly capable of doing everything around the house. I think I've demonstrated that in the past few weeks, haven't I?"

Beth looks at Adam again. Even Adam can't tell if it's a passive-aggressive comment or a poor choice of words.

"No, we know," Beth says. "I just wanted you to try out my cooking for once."

Adam realizes what Beth is doing, and he's impressed with the subtlety. Breakfast was fatty, lunch is going to be fatty, too, and dinner probably as well, so Beth is stepping in to take control of things. Truth be told, Adam misses having an easy dinner that isn't going to leave him feeling like he has a boulder in his stomach. Something light like chicken breast and steamed vegetables.

"Okay, Bethany. That sounds like an excellent idea," his mom jovially agrees, and Adam thinks he can almost feel even the walls of the apartment breathe a sigh of relief.

"Perfect," Beth says.

"What will you make?" his mom asks.

"Um... It's a surprise."

In other words, *I don't know yet. I just don't want to eat your dinner.* As much as Adam feels dirty deceiving his mom like that, he knows she won't understand, and he has to keep his wife's health in mind, especially if they're going to have a healthy baby.

He and Beth leave the house together. Just like his mom's stay, Adam knows that he and Beth going to work together won't last forever, so he savors every moment. He doesn't want to tell Beth how much he enjoys driving her to work every morning because he knows she's going to start going to the office just to give him that feeling.

Her comfort is more important to him than his feeling of romanticism, and vice versa.

When Adam drops Beth off at work, he shouts after her to wait. He gets out of the car and spends a minute kissing her. It brings him back to when they first started dating and he dropped her off home after spending the night at his place.

"What's gotten into you?" she asks with a smile.

"Can't a guy express his love to his wife?" he asks.

"Maybe I'll keep going to the office even after your mom leaves." She kisses him. "Oh, I reserved a bank heist-themed escape room near Hawthorne for tomorrow and a table at *Vincent's* after that."

Vincent's is Adam's favorite place because they have the best steaks in the city. He knew he shouldn't have left Beth in charge of reservations because of course she would go for what he likes, and not what she likes.

"You're a queen," he says.

"Then you better treat me like one, servant." She gives him another kiss.

After dropping off Beth at work, Adam goes to the university. He doesn't have many classes today, but there's a lot of paperwork to take care of, so he immerses himself in that while drinking his second cup of coffee for the day. He realizes how much he's falling behind because there's no way he can catch up with everything today. He's going to need to do some work during the weekend, but he's determined to burn through whatever he can today.

He doesn't realize that hours have passed until he feels the ache in his shoulders. He leans back in his chair, stretches, and picks up his phone.

"Oh, crap." He immediately leans forward when he sees that it's way past lunchtime.

There's no point in him rushing back home now. He'll just grab something from the university's cafeteria and continue working.

There are two missed calls from his mom, so he calls her back. She doesn't pick up, so he leaves a voicemail.

"Hey, Mom. Sorry for not showing up for lunch. I was working and lost track of time. I'll be home for dinner tonight. Actually, can you save me some of your pasta? Thank you."

He grabs a sandwich from the cafeteria and runs into John, who says, "If you wanted to eat alone, why didn't you just say so?"

He's joking, but Adam still feels obliged to explain himself. "Sorry, buddy. Got caught up in work and lost track of time."

"Your loss. I was gonna get us ribs."

"Bummer. Hey, do you and Tara wanna hang out this weekend?"

"Can't. It's her dad's birthday."

"Next time then, maybe."

John nods before they head their separate ways. Beth calls Adam sometime later.

"Hey. Are you still at work?" she asks.

"Yeah. I have a lot of catching up to do, so I'm going to be late today."

"Okay. How late do you think you'll be? I wanna know so dinner can be warm when you come home."

She's too damn thoughtful.

"I should be there by seven. If anything changes, I'll be sure to let you know beforehand."

"Okay. Remember to take frequent breaks, babe."

"Always do. Love you. Oh, honey? One more thing."

"Yes?"

"You're going to hate me, but... I think we might have to cancel date night tomorrow. I'll have way too much work during the weekend."

"Oh." Beth sounds surprised. Adam can sense disappointment in her timbre. "Okay, sure. I'll call the restaurant."

"I'm so sorry, babe."

"Don't be. I understand you have a lot of work. We can just move it to next week, okay?"

"Yes. Please don't divorce me, baby."

She chuckles. "I won't. But you owe me big time."

"I won't fail you next time, I promise."
"I know. Love you."

Eight

By the time Adam can no longer take the ache in his neck, the sky outside has already turned orange. He stretches, checks the time, and figures he's done enough work for today. Right now, he just wants to go back home to eat dinner with his loving wife.

Tomorrow's Friday, but as much as he was looking forward to date night, he's going to be stuck working. He thinks about moving date night to Saturday instead of tomorrow, so that way they don't need to skip it this week, but there's no way he can find the time.

He doesn't want his mind to be hung up on work. He wants to give Beth and date night his undivided attention.

Adam packs his things and heads home. When he opens the door, a savory smell lingers in the air, and there's a sound of sizzling coming from the kitchen.

Adam beams. "Something smells good. What are you making, Beth?"

But just as he says that, his mom steps out of the kitchen, the jewelry she refuses to take off jingling with every step she takes, and says, "Oh, hi, Addy. You're just in time for dinner." Adam notices the wooden spoon stained with red sauce in her hand. "I'm making something special."

"Oh," Adam says, unable to come up with words. "I thought Beth was going to make dinner?"

His mom throws her head back and laughs. It sounds like derisive laughter, but it's impossible to tell what's going through his mom's head. "She's too lazy, so I'm handling it."

Adam doesn't appreciate that comment about his wife.

"She's too lazy?" he asks to give his mom a chance to correct herself.

And she does. "Well, she says she's tired from work." But then she ruins it again by stepping closer to Adam and lowering her voice, "You know, I worked a lot back in my day, too, but your dad would never come home to no dinner. It's a woman's obligation to keep her man fed."

Adam nods, unable to argue with his mom. It's not like she would listen to him anyway.

"Okay. Is Beth in the bedroom?" he asks.

"Yeah. She's been cooped up in there for an hour now. I don't think that's healthy for her. You should really talk to her, Adam."

Why is she like this all of a sudden? Is it just because he and Beth didn't come home for lunch?

"I'll talk to her," Adam says with a feigned smile before heading into the bedroom.

Beth is lying in bed, fiddling with her phone.

"Hey," he says.

She gives him a brief look. "Hi."

"I thought you were making dinner tonight."

"Yeah, I was going to."

Adam lopes to the bed and sits next to Beth. He caresses her head and asks, "Tired from work?"

"Not really," she retorts.

Adam realizes she wants to say more. A *lot* more. For some reason, though, she doesn't. Is she refraining from saying something that's going to offend him or his mom? Somehow, Adam knows that there's going to be tension tonight between him and his wife, and he knows it's somehow related to his mom.

"Did something happen?" he asks.

"Mhm," Beth says, her gaze still glued to her phone.

"Wanna tell me what?"

Beth remains silent for a little bit. "Sorry, what?"

Adam opens and closes his mouth when he notices Beth isn't listening to him.

"Can you... not be on your phone for a second?" he asks.

He expects a volatile reaction. Instead, Beth puts her phone face down on the bed next to her.

"Sure," she says perkily.

"Okay." Adam takes her hands into his. "Talk to me, babe. What's going on?"

Beth sighs. A long moment passes before she finds the strength to utter two words that Adam should have expected but somehow still finds himself shocked to hear them.

"Your mom," Beth says.

"What about her?" Adam is afraid to know the answer, but he can't keep running from it. If his mom somehow insulted his wife, he's going to have to have a serious talk with her.

"She was already making dinner when I came home," Beth says.

"Really? Maybe she forgot it was your turn."

"No, she didn't forget. She just doesn't care about what I say. I called her when I finished work to tell her 'I'll be home in twenty minutes, right after I buy all the ingredients I need for the dinner that *I'm making*.' She said okay, and when I got home, she was already cooking."

"Maybe she's upset with us for not showing up to lunch."

"Adam, that doesn't give her the right to behave like this. It's not just today either. She still mentions to me in passing how we didn't show up to Marielle's wedding two years ago. And she often gives comments about my weight."

"What?" Adam scoffs.

"Yeah. She's always asking me if I'm putting on weight on purpose and if it's trendy to be "fuller" nowadays. Then she tells me a lady should maintain a ladylike figure and that she never would have allowed herself to gain weight when she was younger because no man would love a fat woman."

Adam's jaw hangs open because he can't believe what he's hearing. Beth must be exaggerating because there's no way those words came from his mom.

"She says that?" he asks.

"Yeah, Adam. And when I tell her it's because of her cooking... and I try to say it in a positive way but also to let her know she needs to start listening to us more... she dismisses it and says it's all about our ability to control ourselves."

"What? Okay, she couldn't have said that in those words, Beth."

Adam knows he's playing a dangerous game by discrediting what his wife says, but he's too frazzled by what he's hearing to believe it.

"It's not just those things, Adam. It's always negative comments directed at me. She thinks I'm mentally unstable because of..."

"Because of your past, right?"

"There are things you don't see because she only says it when she and I are alone. She's not the same person as she is when you're here. At least once a week, she reminds me I'm running out of time to give birth, for Christ's sake!"

Adam is mute. He doesn't know what to think or say. A part of him wants to tell Beth she might be overinflating the situation, but now that the suppressed anger has started pouring out of her, he can't do so without ending up sleeping on the couch.

"Well, she isn't doing that on purpose, Beth. I mean, she's not an evil woman. I think I know her."

"I don't know if she has malicious intentions or not, but it's not pleasant. Like, at all. I have to listen to these comments day after day while she pretends to be this nice woman with you."

The sentence causes a jab at Adam, but he doesn't respond to it.

He asks. "Beth, this has clearly been bothering you for a while now. Why didn't you tell me anything?"

Beth crosses her arms and purses her lips. "I didn't want to bother you with it."

"You didn't want to bother me?"

"Adam, you can't blame me for not talking to you. If you could see yourself, how happy you are that your mom's here... I didn't want to be the one to ruin that for you."

Adam understands. Beth is in a tough position. If she tells her husband she's bothered by her mother-in-law, not only does she dampen his mood, but she also opens up doors to future fights. Whenever something small arises, Adam would be able to hold a grudge against her for ruining his time with his mom despite them not seeing each other often.

But this is different, as much as he would like to believe otherwise. If what Beth says is true, then he's going to need to talk to his mom about her behavior. He hopes she'll understand because he hates being caught having to choose between his wife and his mother.

"Yeah, but if she's bullying you, then I think I have the right to know about it, Beth. Especially if it's this serious," Adam says.

"I wouldn't call that bullying." Beth shrugs.

"Definitions don't matter here. I'm going to talk to her."

He stands to leave the room, but Beth leaps to her feet. "No!"

She steps in front of him, looking over her shoulder at the door then back at him.

"No. I don't want you to do that," she says in a lower voice.

"Beth, I'm not going to allow her to treat you like this."

He's about to brush past her, but Beth sidesteps to stop him. "If you talk to her, she's going to know I told you."

"Yes, and?"

"I don't want her to know. She's only going to make my life worse."

"Beth..."

"Please. Believe me, I know those kinds of people."

Those kinds of people. What does Beth mean by that? It's hard for Adam not to be offended by that comment. Does she mean like her mother? Because if that's the case, it's one of the worst insults she could throw in Adam's face about the woman who gave birth to him.

"I didn't mean it like that," Beth says when she notices Adam's facial expression, but the damage has already been done. "Look. I don't think she's bad. You're right. She probably isn't doing it on purpose, but she's most likely unaware of how it affects me."

Adam breathes a reluctant sigh. What Beth is saying makes sense, but he hates leaving things unresolved. At the same time, as much as the cowardly part of him hates to admit it, he's glad he gets to avoid the conflict.

Just then, his mom shouts from the living room, "Dinner's ready!"

There's a sound of plates being set on the table, and Beth and Adam exchange a look that says, "I guess we'd better go out there."

Dinner looks amazing, as usual, but too fatty. Beth doesn't complain this time. She puts meat and potatoes onto her plate. It could be Adam's imagination, but he thinks she's lost weight in the past few weeks, and that causes a pang of worry to splash him.

Only after living with his mom again did Adam realize how unhealthy her meals are. Everything is dripping with oil and grease, and its nutritional value is poor. It's tasty, but like everything in life, delicious means unhealthy.

When Beth cooks, she makes bigger portions for Adam, sure, and the food they order isn't the epitome of healthy, either, but they do everything in moderation. Adam wonders what it's going to be like for Beth when she gets pregnant. They still don't know what kind of foods she'll have to avoid, but they don't need to be doctors to know his mother's cooking is not fit for a woman in pregnancy—especially someone with hypertension.

For the first time since his mom broke her hip, elation swaddles Adam at the realization that she won't be here when Beth becomes pregnant. He'll be able to take care of her the way he sees fit, and he's going to make sure she's treated like the queen that she is.

Everyone is seated at the table, and his mom says, "Leave some room for later. I made dessert."

Adam's mood skips the resentment he's been feeling toward his mom. He fills his plate with food, sets it down, and takes the first bite. It's good, as always, but he must have taken on some of Beth's behavior because the knowledge of the unhealthiness of the meal makes it less appealing.

"What did you make?" he asks.

"Pecan pie."

Adam almost drops the fork. He avoids Beth's gaze because he's afraid of what he'll see there. Anger? Shock? Hurt?

He looks at his mom instead, who's filling her own plate with food, oblivious to what she just said.

"Mom, Beth is allergic to nuts," Adam says.

"Is she?" His mom raises her eyebrows and looks at Beth.

"Yes."

"What's wrong with you being so sickly, Bethany? You can't eat fats, you can't eat nuts. Are you sure it's not just all in your head, sweetie?"

"She's deathly allergic. You know this, Mom," Adam emphasizes every word.

He knows his mom knows it because he made sure to mention it even before they flew out to meet her the first time. She always knew it. She always followed that rule religiously. After Beth joined the family, she never put nuts in anything, ever. She even spread the word to all the relatives when Beth and Adam were invited to certain gatherings.

And yet, somehow, she's behaving as if Beth's allergy never existed in the first place.

"Well..." she says as she shifts to a more comfortable position in her seat. "I guess I forgot about it."

NINE

"Ouch," John says and then adds a small hiss through his teeth.

"Yeah. I don't know how to approach the situation," Adam says.

The two of them are sitting in the empty cafeteria, eating sandwiches. They hadn't planned on sitting together to eat. They just found themselves in the same place at the same time, and they sat down together. Then, John had asked Adam how he was doing, and what was supposed to be one sentence turned into ten minutes of raving about his life with Beth and his mom.

Only now, when Adam is done complaining, does he realize that John hasn't uttered a single word since asking that fateful question. His humongous sandwich is almost gone, whereas Adam has hardly touched his.

"Sorry, man. I'm talking your ear off," Adam says.

"You're good. I'm just thinking."

"About what?"

"About how to handle the situation. I was in a similar spot once."

"Oh yeah? How?"

"Tara and I went to a relative's birthday party, and some lady who claimed to be my aunt started preaching about how I should be treating my wife."

"Okay? And what happened?"

John shrugs. "Nothing. She kept pestering me about it, and when she went on to do the same to Tara, we left the party."

"That's not the same as my situation at all."

"Maybe, but your mom sounds a lot like that aunt that bothered us."

Adam has taken a bite out of the sandwich and is taking his time chewing it. Once he swallows, he asks, "How so?"

"Well, for one, you said your mom is really polite about everything. I think there are two kinds of rude people in this world." John raises one finger. "One: the polite rude ones, and two..." He raises another finger. "The nasty rude ones. Your mom sounds like the polite rude category."

"Mhm." Adam is taking the time while John is speaking to catch up eating.

"Honestly, I think you're in sort of a pickle because polite rude people are the worst kind of rude people. They're gonna criticize you in the worst possible ways, but they're going to do it so politely that you don't understand if they're doing it on purpose or if they're just oblivious to their comments. It makes it really hard to be direct with them."

"That makes sense, except I think you're wrong about my mom. She's not "polite rude." Adam makes quotation marks. "She's direct because of the way her generation was raised, but she means well with her comments."

"Right. But the thing is—can you say for sure she means well and isn't just disguising her criticism behind that veil of politeness?"

Adam frowns. "Of course I can say it for sure. She's my mom. I know her."

"You *knew* her as a kid, and that's the knowledge you still have about her. Children's perception tends to be distorted. If there's an adult you were afraid of as a kid, when you see them again as an adult yourself, you automatically assume a defensive stance and say "I'm not afraid of you anymore" even though there might not be anything to be afraid of at all."

Adam takes another bite of his food, choosing not to respond to John's comment.

John has finished his sandwich, and he says, "Look, I'm not trying to demonize your mother or anything like that. I just think you should consider the possibility that what she's doing is on purpose. You'd be surprised at how often that's the case."

"Well, in the worst-case scenario, I can just wait until she's healed and leaves. It won't be long now."

"How much longer is that going to be, by the way? I thought you said it was going to be around four weeks."

"No, I said at least four weeks, but I told Beth four weeks because I didn't want to tell her it's longer than that."

"It's been more than four weeks now anyway. She moved in..." John looks up as he does quick math in his head. "It'll be five weeks in a few days."

Has it really been that long? Adam could have sworn it was maybe three weeks, going into four, no more than that. Then again, his mom is walking so much easier these days. Her movement is a lot less stilted, and she's able to bend down and squat to a certain degree and at certain speeds.

She's not using the roller anymore to move around, so it sits in the corner of the living room. In fact, it has been sitting there for the past two weeks or so.

A group of students walks into the cafeteria and heads for the food line. John takes a look at his wristwatch and says, "Anyway, I should get going. I got the next class coming soon. I'll see you around. Don't stress too much, Addy."

He calls him Addy as a joke because it's what his mom calls him.

"See you, John," Adam says as his coworker stands up, picks up the papers and napkins after him, and leaves.

As much as Adam would like to say there's no need for him to reevaluate his mom, his mind unwittingly stops itself on John's words. He wouldn't have given it a second thought had Beth not told him about some of the things his mom tells her.

Now, he's in limbo, pendulating between believing she's the good woman he knew her as or accepting she might have changed. But if she did change, why would she change for the worse? Did loneliness make her bitter? Is she jealous of Beth?

Is that what this is? Every mother wants to see their child build a happy family of their own, but that also means they have to leave the nest they grew up in. Surely, his mom knows this. Surely, she's not holding grudges because of that, is she?

Jesus, what if she hates Beth because she feels like she stole Adam from her? What if the politeness she'd been displaying toward Beth all these years was fake, and Adam hadn't noticed it because they never spent long enough visiting her?

They've been living together for the past four weeks, and what if the cracks are now starting to show?

Adam doesn't want to think about that right now. Besides, he has a lot of work to do, so he needs to get back to it.

Beth calls him while he's still in the office.

"Hello?" he asks.

"Hey, babe. How's work?"

"Like watching paint dry. Are you done for the day?"

"Yeah. Rachel's in town, and she wants to go out for drinks. I just wanted to let you know I'll be home a little later. Oh, and she wants us to go to the amusement park tomorrow. Would you like to come with us?"

If he goes with them, Beth's time with Rachel would be marred by her constantly checking up on Adam to make sure he isn't bored out of his mind. He doesn't want to ruin the fun for her.

"No, thanks. I prefer some alone time every now and again."

"Alone time even from me?"

"Anyone but you."

His mom strangely pops into his mind. He squints to chase the thought away.

Beth says, "Okay, babe. I'll see you tonight. Love you."

"Love you, too. Say hi to Rachel."

After hanging up, he stares at the screen of the laptop in front of him. He pulls his chair in and continues working. He doesn't hurry because he's not in a rush to go home.

****

By the time Adam comes home, he's exhausted from work. There's no mouth-watering smell coming from the kitchen. His mom is folding laundry.

"Hi, Mom," Adam says.

"Hi, sweetie," she greets.

"Well, this is strange. I don't smell dinner." He smiles jokingly.

"I didn't make anything tonight."

Adam cocks an eyebrow. Ever since she started cooking for them weeks ago, his mom has made three meals a day for him and Beth without fail, not a single one skipped. That's why it's impossible not to be shocked at the fact that there's no dinner tonight.

"Is something the matter, Mom?" Adam asks, feeling dread coiling up in his stomach.

She looks at him briefly before continuing to fold laundry. "No, Addy. I just thought I'd let you kids have the kitchen to yourselves a little bit. I've been hoarding it all this time, and it's just not right."

Adam wouldn't have batted an eye in the past. Now, he can't help but raise his guard, wondering if there's a meaning behind his mom's behavior. Maybe she just realized she was in the wrong for cooking dinner yesterday when Beth should have done it.

In the end, he decides he doesn't have the strength to guess whether his mom is angry or not. Besides, if she is, she's in the wrong.

"Bethany is still not home. Is she working this late?" his mom asks.

"No. Actually, she said a friend of hers is in town, so she's grabbing a drink with her. She'll be home later."

His mom stops folding laundry. "A drink? Alone? This late?"

Adam doesn't respond. He knows better than to get into an argument with his mom about something like this. He would tell her it's perfectly normal for girls to go out for a couple of drinks, and she'd tell him she never did it back in her day and his dad would never allow her to go alone, and how, nowadays, only "certain kinds of girls" went out drinking alone on Friday nights.

The defensive stance in his mind catches Adam off guard. He's starting to realize that, either Beth is influencing his opinion of his mom, or she's been here for too long and it's starting to affect him by making him irritable.

"I guess it's just you and me tonight. Wanna watch a movie or something?" Adam asks.

"I'm good. I think I'll call it a night earlier."

"Mom, you sure you're okay? You sound sad."

"I'm fine. I always get like this when it's the anniversary of your dad's death."

"Oh, shoot. Is that today?"

"Tomorrow." His mom has finished folding laundry, so she walks over to the couch and sits down, letting out a huge sigh. She asks Adam, "You don't honor that day?"

Adam feels a pang of shame. No, of course he doesn't honor the day that brought him so much sadness. Even after all these years, every year, when the date comes, he feels like he's been transported back to the past and is reliving his dad's death again.

Sometimes, if he's lucky, the date rolls by without him noticing until it's already a few days late. So no, he doesn't do anything special on that day, and he has no intention to.

"Why would I do that, Mom? I'd rather celebrate his birthday." Adam shrugs.

Right after saying that, he realizes that's a lie, too. He doesn't want to celebrate his father's birthday when he's not around. It would remind him what he's missing out on, and that in turn would be no better than doing something for his death day.

"Wait, do you do something for that day?" Adam asks as he plops on the couch next to his mom.

She takes a long moment to respond. "I go to his grave, put some flowers on it, light a candle, and I..." She puts a hand over her mouth. Her face remains relaxed, but Adam can sense her fighting tears. When she speaks up again, her voice has gone up an octave. "I then go home, and I make hot wings because it was his favorite meal. And I watch football."

"You watch football?" Adam asks in disbelief. "You don't even like sports, Mom."

His mom regains her composure. "No. But he did. I usually just let it play in the background. I still don't understand those rules. It's just a bunch of men tackling each other and running after a ball like headless chickens. I don't get what the big deal is."

Adam still doesn't fully understand it either. For his dad, it was about supporting the Seattle Seahawks and being happy when they won. For Adam, it was about spending quality time with his dad. It didn't matter that he didn't have a favorite player. The only reason why it mattered when they lost was because it would mean his dad would swear and spend the next hour or so analyzing the game and pointing out what they could have done better.

Once Adam's dad died, so too did Adam's desire to watch football.

"Hey, Mom. Listen. How about we do something in Dad's memory tomorrow?" Adam asks.

"What did you have in mind?"

"I don't know. Let's see what there is."

Adam takes his phone out and looks up games taking place in the near future.

"Oh, look. There's a baseball game tomorrow, and it's close by. Wanna go?" he asks.

"I don't know, Addy. Why don't we stay home, and I'll make us some hot wings?"

"It's gonna be good to get out of the house a little. You and I still haven't had our mother-and-son date, and you've been here for a while. Come on, we can buy the overpriced hot dogs and beers they sell at the stadium."

His mom looks like she's weighing her options, but a ghost of a smile tickles the corners of her lips. Eventually, she shrugs. "Okay, let's do it."

They watch TV a little bit until his mom decides it's time to go to bed. Adam has completely forgotten to have dinner, so when he breaks out some bread and peanut butter, his mom shoos him out of the kitchen and tells him she'll make the meal for him. She ends up splicing together a peanut butter, jelly, and banana sandwich, and it's heavenly.

By the time Adam slinks into bed, he hears the front door opening and closing, followed by shuffling footsteps, and a muffled voice.

"Oh, Bethany, it's you," his mom says.

"Yes, it's me. Who else do you think it could have been?" Beth chuckles.

"I don't know what to think. Only burglars come home this late. Burglars and... well, certain types of women."

It's like there's instant tension in the air. Adam waits for the ominous silence to pass. The conversation that ensues is a muffled blur of imperceptible words. Beth's voice is louder compared to his mom's.

Oh no.

Adam gets out of bed and approaches the door. He leans his ear against the wooden surface to eavesdrop. By the time he does so, the conversation is over, replaced by an angry patter of footsteps approaching the door.

He doesn't have time to move before the door opens, revealing an angry Beth standing in front of him. Adam opens his mouth to ask her what happened, but she pushes past him into the room. Adam looks out into the living room just in time to hear the door of his mom's bedroom clicking shut. The light under the door's crack is engulfed in darkness, and it's as if she's never left her room.

Adam closes the door for more privacy, just because he's not sure if his mother will be eavesdropping.

"What happened, Beth?" he whispers.

"Nothing," Beth retorts as she's taking off her clothes to get ready for bed.

"Beth, come on. Did my mom say something to you?"

"I don't want to talk about it. I had a wonderful night with Rachel, and I'm not going to let that goddamned witch ruin it for me."

The words *goddamned witch* come out as a hiss, which takes Adam by surprise. He's never heard Beth talking about his mother that way, but he doesn't have it in himself to get angry at her. If it was anybody else, he would have told them off right away, but it's not anybody else.

It's Beth. His wife. The woman of his dreams and, hopefully, one day, the mother to his child.

"Beth, just talk to me, babe," Adam insists, but Beth isn't listening.

"I'm gonna take a shower and brush my teeth. I'll be here in ten minutes," she coldly says.

The anger is gone from the contours of her face. That's probably the worst part about it. When anger dissipates, pain emerges, and that's exactly what he sees on her face right now.

He knows there's nothing he can do. Even if he tries to make her feel better, she's just going to deflect it. The best thing he can do right now is to leave her to cool off. Hopefully, by morning, she will have forgotten about the whole thing.

That doesn't mean the problem will be solved, though. It will only be patched up with a flimsy Band-Aid, and the rot beneath it will continue to grow until it's purged from their home.

Ten

Sometime during the night, Beth presses her body against Adam's. She flings an arm over his chest and sleeps that way. In the morning, she's still snuggling up to him. For a little bit, Adam fears that Beth will remember she's angry when she wakes up, but when she opens her eyes, she's her usual, perky self.

It would be a bad idea to try to talk to Beth about what happened last night, so he lets it go. If the topic arises in the future, he'll be sure to handle it, but not when she's in such a buoyant mood.

His mom is in the living room, watching the TV on mute. She hasn't made breakfast this morning.

Now it's becoming weird. He understands that she hadn't made dinner yesterday because she was in a bad mood, but this morning? Something is going on. She must have heard Beth complaining to Adam, and now she's avoiding cooking to let Beth do it.

Sure enough, the moment Adam and Beth step outside, his mom says, "I didn't make breakfast because I thought Beth would have liked to cook for once."

She's talking to Adam, and even though Beth pauses to look at her, his mom never once breaks eye contact with her son. Her comment confirms Adam's suspicions. She's heard them complaining, and now she's being spiteful.

His mom's tone conveys kindness, but the context of the words communicates disrespect, so Adam doesn't know what to think.

There are two kinds of people. The nasty rude and the polite rude.

Staring at her and unsuccessfully trying to read her face, Adam realizes that John was right. His mom is the polite rude kind. For the first time in his life, he's wondering if his mom isn't as innocuous as he's believed her to be.

Beth doesn't seem to be paying attention. She's already closed herself in the bathroom, not dignifying his mom with a response. Not even a *good morning*.

"Mom." Adam gets closer to her and whispers, "Beth is in a bad mood today, so can you, like...?"

He's waiting to see if his mom is going to take a hint. She's staring at him but doesn't say anything. Also, Beth is not in a bad mood—or at least she wasn't when they woke up—but things changed really fast these days. Beth could be in a really good mood, only for his mom to shoot it down in an instant.

"Can you just..." He's looking for the right way to phrase the question. "Be nice to her today?"

Damn.

That's the wrong thing to say, and he realizes it when his mom frowns.

"What are you trying to say? I'm *always* nice to her," she says.

There's a sound of flushing in the bathroom, followed by the tap running.

No, you're not, and she can confirm it.

"I know, but she's been kind of sensitive lately. I think it's the hormones," Adam says.

His mom continues staring. "If she has a problem, she should go see a doctor, and not have us tiptoe around her.

You're the man of the marriage, Adam. Why don't you sit her down and talk to her?"

"That's not how it works, Mom. Listen, can you please just be careful with what you say to her today? Please. Just for me."

For a moment, it looks as if she's going to acquiesce. But then she leans back in the couch and says, "I don't think I'm doing anything wrong that Bethany should be offended by."

It's too late to continue the argument then anyway because Beth steps out of the bathroom.

"What would you like to eat?" Beth asks.

"I'm fine with anything, really."

"I'll have some cereal. Do you want some, too?"

"Sure."

With his peripheral vision, Adam notices his mom's mouth pulling into a judgmental grimace, and Adam can practically read the thoughts in her mind: *Cereals are for kids.*

"What would you like? I can make you some eggs if you like," Beth says.

"No, thank you. I think I'll wait for lunch."

"Speaking of lunch, I'll make something for us today so you can finally try my cooking for once."

His mom tries to smile.

Beth makes cereal for herself and Adam, and they eat without his mom for the first time in a long while. He gets a glimpse into what their life used to be like while they were living alone. Since the dining table is by the wall in the living room, it's impossible not to become aware of his mom sitting on the couch and watching TV.

The meal with Beth also reminds Adam the two of them haven't traveled anywhere in a while because he instantly pictures the two of them eating burgers at a diner they stopped at on their road trip. Once his mom flies back home, he'll save up money to book a trip for them.

Beth has always wanted to go to Alaska, so he might surprise her with flight tickets as soon as he can afford them. It's probably the last chance they'll have to go anywhere before Beth gets pregnant. After the baby comes along, vacations will be impossible for a while.

After breakfast, Adam brings out his laptop and gets to work. He still has a lot of things to catch up with and doubts he'll be able to finish it by the end of the weekend, which means the extra work is going to bleed into his work week.

While he's working, Beth goes grocery shopping for lunch while his mom cleans the house. Adam tells her not to put too much strain on her hip, but as usual, she doesn't listen.

Beth makes turkey burgers for all three. By the time lunch is ready, Adam has managed to complete a significant amount of work, but he still has a long way to go. He figures now's as good a time as any to take a break.

"Looks amazing, Beth," Adam comments when Beth brings out the tray with burgers.

"Why thank you," Beth says.

Adam looks at his mom, hoping she'll have enough decency to compliment her daughter-in-law's cooking, but she doesn't say anything. She just stares at the platter nonplussed as if thinking she could have done it better.

Beth takes out one burger for each plate. Even when it's directly in front of his mom, the woman looks like the meat might come to life and crawl out of her plate.

Adam ignores the bratty behavior and takes the first bite. It's heavenly.

"Nice work, babe. This is really good," he says with his mouth full.

He steals a glance in his mom's direction, in his mind urging her to go on and start eating, because he notices Beth impatiently waiting for her reaction. His mom takes the burger into both hands and inspects it from every angle.

Adam expects her to find some flaws. His appetite is suddenly waning.

"I thought you said you can't eat fatty foods," she says finally, just as Beth takes the first bite.

Beth rapidly chews and swallows so as to reply to his mom. She puts a hand over her mouth as she says, "Turkey meat is actually not fatty."

"Then why does it look so greasy?" She's no longer trying to hide the disgusted look on her face.

"It's juices from the meat," Beth says.

"Hm."

By then, both Beth and Adam have started ignoring her as they tuck in. Adam is almost done with his burger, and he can already tell he's going to grab another one. He wants to compliment Beth's cooking because the food is not only delicious but also doesn't leave him with a heavy feeling in his gut, like after his mom's cooking.

His mom brings the burger closer to her face. Her nostrils flare as she sniffs it (What the hell is wrong with her) and takes a nibble out of it. She retains a sour expression while chewing, chewing, slowly chewing, and the entire time, Adam and Beth are anxiously awaiting her verdict.

She swallows and then realizes the eyes that are plastered to her. She puts the burger back on the plate and pushes her chair back. "I'm actually not very hungry."

"But you didn't even eat breakfast," Adam says.

"If you don't like the burgers, I can make you something else," Beth offers.

"No, thank you, Bethany, it's okay. I'll make some wings later. You're very kind to have tried to make lunch."

Beth squares her shoulders. She looks ready to fight, but his mom has already turned around and is sauntering back to the living room couch. Adam squeezes Beth's hand in a silent attempt to say, "Don't. It's not worth it."

Beth's lips are pressed tightly as she looks at Adam. Finally, her gaze gravitates to her plate, and she continues eating.

That was a close one.

The tension remains in the air, though. Just one small push and there would be another fight in the house.

Adam tries to enjoy the meal, but he no longer has an appetite because his mom's words are bouncing in his skull like tennis balls off a wall, and they're making him angry.

You're very kind to have tried to make lunch.

The hell is that supposed to mean? Once again, Adam can't figure out if his mom is purposely being condescending or if it's just her way of talking. She's never talked to Beth like that before, so what's going on?

Maybe the fact that she's getting older is making her more stubborn and more difficult to deal with.

Maybe it's just because today is the day Adam's dad died and she has a lot going on inside of her.

The incident is forgotten soon, and Adam goes back to work. Beth prepares for her hangout with Rachel.

Meanwhile, his mom prepares for the baseball game Adam has booked for them. By then, Adam realizes he's been working enough for today, so he closes his laptop. He doesn't move it from the dining table because he'll continue working tomorrow.

"This is sort of exciting," his mom says. "You know, your dad took me out to watch a baseball game when we first started dating."

"That must have been nice."

"Well, he kept shouting the whole time that the players were incompetent, and I ended up kissing him to make him feel better that his team lost. It was the first time we kissed."

Beth comes out of the bedroom, and she looks dashing. She's put on just enough makeup to make her prettier without it being glaringly obvious. She's wearing a red shirt that she wore on their first date and jeans.

"Ready for your friend date?" Adam approaches and plants a kiss on her lips.

She notices his mom checking her outfit in the mirror, so she asks, "What's going on?"

"We're going to a baseball game. It's the anniversary of my dad's death, and I figured since you're going out with Rachel, I might as well go out with my mom."

Beth's face is fixed in a frozen half-smile as her eyes flit from his mom to Adam. She asks, "Can I talk to you for a second?"

They head into the bedroom. Adam closes the door behind himself.

"Is something wrong?" he asks.

When Beth turns to look at him, he already has his answer. She's not angry. She's furious. She's just doing everything in her power not to let that emotion run rampant.

"I thought you were supposed to work today. What's going on?" she asks.

"Right. I was going to, but then I remembered today's the day my dad died. And since you're going out with Rachel..."

"Okay. It's just... You canceled our date night because of work, and now you're taking your mom out. You do realize how this looks from my side, don't you?"

Adam knows exactly what Beth is trying to say. In her eyes, he's prioritizing his mom over his wife.

He says, "I hadn't planned on things happening this way, babe. My mom was just really sad about my dad being gone, so I wanted to do something for her to make her feel better."

"I see." Beth looks down.

No longer angry, she looks defeated. Adam knows that look. It's when she gives up on trying to provide arguments because she feels like it's going to be pointless. The next right thing to do for Adam would be to apologize, but he knows that's going to be pointless, too, because the words are going to be hollow compared to the betrayal that Beth feels.

"Baby..." he starts.

"How much longer is she going to be staying here?" Beth asks.

The question surprises Adam, but it also reminds him that his mom can't stay with them forever. Not that he wants her to either. He's starting to become fed up with the constant stress, so it's almost time for his mom to go home.

Almost, but not yet.

He says, "Just a little longer. She still needs some time to heal. We'll take her to the doctor in two weeks to do an x-ray, and if everything's okay, we'll send her home, okay?"

"Two weeks?!" Beth's face grows taut. "Adam, she's been living with us for over a month."

"She just needs a little more time."

Is Adam saying that because he really thinks it, or is his desire for his mom to stay overshadowing rational thinking?

"She's completely fine. Don't you see her? She's doing everything around the house."

"She's prone to being injured right now, Beth. She needs a little more time."

"You always put her in front of me."

That sentence causes another painful jab to Adam's chest. He feels like the statement is unfair. He always does everything in his power to put Beth first, but he also tries to be reasonable.

"What? Beth, where is this coming from?" Adam asks.

Beth has crossed her arms and is staring nowhere in particular.

"I always put you first, babe. What are you talking about?"

"No, you only say you do. Ever since she's moved in with us, you've done nothing to stand up for me."

"That's not true, Beth. You think this is easy for me? I'm constantly caught in the crossfire of you two fighting. I'm sick of it. She's an old woman. It wouldn't kill you to show just a little bit of goddamn understanding."

Adam doesn't mean to let anger take control like that, but he can't help it. He's been holding everything inside of him for too long, and now there's a crack in the dam, releasing a torrent of all the stale emotions out of him.

It's not Beth's fault directly. It's not even his mom's fault. It's the culmination of everything piling for weeks and Adam sweeping it all under the rug. All this time, he's been trying to accommodate both his wife and his mom, and he's had it.

His emotions are important, too, but they are being neglected, and now it's manifesting in the form of a desire to say all sorts of nasty things to Beth and his mom—things he knows he's going to regret the moment the anger lets go, but things he so badly wishes to say just to see their faces twisting in pain.

Beth turns around and raises her hands to her forehead as if staving off a migraine. The little whimper that escapes her mouth makes him realize in horror that she's crying.

The anger is instantly gone, and what remains is a lingering sense of defeat. He's failing as a husband and as a son. Mostly as a husband, though, which is seen in his wife shuddering.

"Beth..." he starts but can't find the rest of the words.

The moment his fingers graze her back, she whips around and says, "No."

Her face is tear-stricken, her makeup ruined. It's all his fault. Adam has ruined Beth's makeup in the past, but it was the good kind of ruining. This is the first time he's made her cry when she's ready to go out.

Beth rummages through her purse and locates a pack of wet wipes. She cleans her face off, wiping the makeup. Thirty minutes of hard work in front of the mirror lost, all because of Adam. The guilt that envelops him squeezes him like an anaconda, crushing the bones in his body.

Beth sniffles, blows her nose, and says, "I'm already late. I have to go."

Her voice is shaky when she says it.

"Beth."

"No. Please, just stop. There's nothing to talk about, so don't even try it. Have fun at the game. I'll see you tonight."

But Beth is already out of the bedroom. She puts her shoes and coat on and storms out of the apartment before Adam can say anything else.

His mom has seen the whole thing, but she doesn't say anything. Perhaps she notices Adam's distress and knows it would be a bad time to comment. Instead, she gives him a warm smile and says, "I'll be ready when you are. Take as long as you need."

Eleven

Try as he might, Adam can't make himself enjoy the game. He's watching the players give their best on the field, and he's listening to the crowd applauding and cheering, but he feels like he's sitting in a small bubble excluded from that universe.

Every once in a while, he checks his phone for messages or calls from Beth, but there's nothing. He wonders if she's having fun with Rachel or if their hangout turned into Beth complaining about Adam and his mom.

His mom seems to be having fun, though. She's clapping along with the crowd. She talks to Adam from time to time, and he responds as best he can, for her sake. Sitting on the bleachers next to her, he sees a woman who's completely different than the one when Beth is around. This woman is full of life, buoyant, kind. The one who's around Beth is...

Adam doesn't even want to think of the word, but *evil* comes to his mind.

Goddamned witch, Beth's words reverberate in his mind.

The crowd lets out a long "oooh" because a batter has just made a third strike. The player throws his bat on the ground in anger and walks toward the benches.

"That's a shame," his mom says. "Your dad would have shouted at the man if he were here. He'd say something like, "My dead grandma can play better than you.""

She lets out a chortle. Adam feigns a smile at that.

"Addy, you've been awfully quiet today. Is everything okay?"

"Yes, Mom. I'm fine." Adam nods.

His mom gives him a scrutinizing look before turning back to the game, but her enthusiasm seems subdued. A moment later, she leans closer to him again. "Is it Beth? Are the problems between you two worrying you?"

"No, Mom," Adam lies.

"Then why was she so angry when she left?"

Adam doesn't feel like talking about it, and yet somehow, it pours out of him. His mom seems to still have the ability to make him open up to her, just like when he was a kid.

"She and I were supposed to go out today, but I canceled our date because of work, so she sees us coming to this game as me prioritizing you over her," he says.

His mom pulls her head back in surprise and says, "But that's ridiculous. She's going out with her friend, so why is she getting angry?"

Adam shrugs. They don't talk for a minute before his mom decides to speak up again.

"Adam, are you happy in your marriage?"

The question surprises Adam so much that he has to look at his mom to make sure he heard her right. "What? Of course I am. Why would you ask me that?"

"It's just that you two seem to be fighting a lot lately. No mother wants to see that. If she's making you miserable, you need to either talk to her or get a divorce."

Going for the jugular right away.

"She's not making me miserable. I'm very happy with Beth."

"I just call it like I see it, sweetie. No need to get upset. Whenever I see the two of you, there's some sort of tension. And I hear you arguing in your room often. I know you think I don't hear it, but I do. I just choose to stay out of it."

Adam hadn't been upset before she said that, but he is now. The main reason why he and Beth are fighting so much is precisely because of his mom, so who does she think she is, giving him advice?

He forces himself to calm down. It's not his mom's fault. No matter what Beth says, it's not his mom's fault. She hasn't done anything wrong in this case. It was all Adam's fault for canceling the date and then taking his mom out instead of Beth. Of course she'd feel betrayed.

"It's very easy to fall into the habit of things, Addy," his mom says.

"What does that mean?"

"It means you could be unhappy in a marriage without even knowing it."

"I'm not unhappy with Beth," Adam emphasizes again.

"Okay, sweetie," his mom says, and she backs off.

She doesn't believe him, but she wants to avoid fighting. That makes him angrier for some reason. Why doesn't she just say what's on her mind? If she has something against Beth or thinks she's not the right woman for her son, she had ample time to say so before they got married.

The rest of the game goes by in a blur. Although Adam is in a foul mood, his mom seems to have had fun. She talks with joy in the car, and eventually, Adam forgets all about their conversation at the stadium.

When they're close to home, though, his mood plummets like an anchor again because he remembers that he still has unresolved issues with Beth.

He hopes to be able to talk to her about it tonight.

****

By the time Beth comes back home from her hangout with Rachel, it's late. His mom is sleeping, and he's in the living room, watching TV and waiting for her to come home. The way she smiles at him upon returning home tells him he might catch his lucky break with her tonight.

She sits on the couch, kisses him, and tells him all about her day. She apologizes for getting upset earlier, but he assures her it's not her fault but his. She asks him how the baseball game went, and he conveniently skips the part where his mom told him he should either solve the problems or get divorced.

Looking at Beth, he's able to see past all the problems they've had recently. He loves her more than anything, and he could never divorce her. He doesn't see himself growing old without her.

He sees them in a big house in the suburbs, raising kids, and having a big dog as a pet. He sees himself and Beth growing older and seeing their kids off to college. He sees himself and Beth visiting their grown kids for Thanksgiving or Christmas. He sees...

He sees himself dying earlier, just like his dad. The kids live out of state, the dog they bought is dead, and Beth is left all alone in that big house. Suddenly, she's no longer Beth but his mom, and she falls down the stairs and breaks her hip. One of her kids takes her in, and that's when problems with their marriage start.

"What's wrong?" Beth asks.

He shakes his head. "Nothing. It's late. We should probably head to bed."

Beth's lips curl into a conniving smile. She leans across him, kisses his neck, and says, "It's Saturday. We don't have to go to bed early."

It's been over a week since they last had sex, and Adam is more than eager. He pulls Beth into the bedroom, closes the door, and they slink under the covers.

Foreplay isn't even needed. Beth moans, and as much as Adam wants to remind her to be quiet, he doesn't want to ruin the mood. To make matters worse, the bed is squeaky, so they have to go slow. Beth seems to like having to be quiet.

Her breathing grows rapid. She's close, and...

There's a knock on the door. It's so abrupt that Beth's panting turns into a gasp of shock. Both heads turn to the door in anticipation.

"Addy? Can you come help me with something for a moment?" his mom says.

As if on cue, the jingle of her jewelry resounds on the other side of the door.

Come on, not now.

Adam's mind is spinning, searching for something to say that will make his mom go away for just a little longer. It's already too late by then. The moment of passion is over. Beth has already scooted away from Adam and is pulling the covers over her body.

"Just a second, Mom!" Adam says then turns to Beth. "I'll be back in a minute. Okay?"

He gives her a juicy kiss before getting dressed. His erection is all but gone by then. He opens the door just enough for him to sidle out of the room. His mom is standing in the living room.

"What's up, Mom?" he asks.

"Can you come here for a moment?" She motions for him to follow him into her room.

"What is it?"

"Can you move my bed so that it's aligned with the wall? It looks crooked like this."

Adam can't believe what he's hearing.

"You want me to move the bed?" he asks just to confirm he hasn't misheard her.

"Yes."

"Mom, it's past midnight. Why would you care about this now?"

"It really bothers me that it's not standing properly. I mean, look at it. The left side of the headboard is a few inches away from the wall."

"We really shouldn't be moving the bed right now, Mom. The dragging will wake up the downstairs neighbors."

"Oh, it'll just be a second. Come on, sweetie. Help your momma out."

Adam can stand in her bedroom arguing with her why moving the bed now is a bad idea, but the tingling in his penis is urging him to get back to Beth.

"Fine," he says.

He moves the bed to the way his mom wants it to be.

"All good?" he asks.

"It's now a little too much. Can you move it back just a bit?"

He does so.

"Okay. Now forward just a tiny bit more."

He does that, too.

"Okay, perfect," his mom says.

"All right. Goodnight, Mom." Adam returns to the bedroom.

Beth's not on her phone, and the room is engulfed in darkness, which is bad news. He doesn't lose hope as he slides under the covers and presses up against her. He kisses her shoulder, her neck, her cheek, and slowly, she rolls over to face him.

She puts a hand on his cheek and says, "Let's do this tomorrow, okay? I'm really sleepy all of a sudden."

The words are like a cold shower. She's punishing him because his mom interrupted them. He has it in his mind to accuse her of that before he stops himself. Why start another fight this late? In the end, what can he do?

He faces the other way and falls asleep with the tingling still in his crotch.

Twelve

In the morning, Adam is extremely irritable. Beth is still sleeping when he gets dressed and walks out into the living room. His mom is already up, watching TV. He can never tell when she wakes up because she does it so quietly, but she's always up before him and Beth.

"Good morning," she says.

"Morning," he says back.

He had hoped to get some privacy while working, but that's not happening. He contemplates going to the university. No one's going to be there today, so he'd be able to get work done. He also wants to avoid being around Beth and his mom because he's afraid he might say something he's going to regret later, all because he's sexually frustrated.

When his mom moves her hand and produces a long, irritating rattle of her wrist jewelry, Adam knows he has to get out of the apartment. For some time now, the sound of those stupid things making noise makes Adam want to rip those things off his mom's neck and wrists and toss them out the window.

Why in the goddamn hell is she even wearing those damn things?

"Where's Beth?" his mom asks.

Isn't it obvious?

"She's sleeping."

"Still?"

He doesn't care about defending Beth today, but he counters his mom just for the sake of countering her. "It's

Sunday. It's not like she has to wake up earlier or something."

His mom gives him that all-too-familiar look that says she disagrees, but she doesn't say anything to voice those thoughts. He can practically imagine what's running through her head.

A woman shouldn't be sleeping late. A woman is supposed to have breakfast ready for her man. A woman should always be busy.

"Do you want breakfast?" his mom asks.

"No thanks. I'm gonna head to the university to get some work done."

His mom raises an eyebrow. "On a Sunday morning?"

I'll be able to focus better.

"It won't be for too long," he says.

"Do you have anything you'd like me to make for lunch?"

"You choose. I don't really have a preference."

He's already put his laptop in the bag and is taking the coat off the hanger.

"All right, Addy. Remember to eat something while you're there."

"I will."

He won't. The cafeteria of the university is closed today, and he doesn't know of any good places along the way where he can buy breakfast. He will get coffee and some snacks from the vending machines at the university before he starts working, though.

The only person who's on-site today is the security guard. He lets Adam in and comments something about him being a workaholic. Adam gives him a brusque nod before heading into the building.

He's only been here on the weekend a few times, either when there was an educational event going on or when he had catching up to do grading work. He could never get used to how dead the hallways feel on a lazy Sunday morning. He likes it, but there's something daunting about it at the same time. As if the world has disappeared and he's the only person left on earth.

Those moments of solitude would be interrupted by an occasional door opening and closing, and footsteps drawing closer and farther. As much as Adam wanted to believe he's the only one who's willingly coming to the office on his days off, it would seem slacking is a common human trait.

He doesn't work for too long, but he does get a lot of work done. A lot more than at home where there are constant interruptions when either Beth or his mom want to talk to him. Mostly just his mom, though.

He doesn't get angry at her because of it since she doesn't understand it takes him a while to regain his focus after being interrupted.

It seems that even the university makes it impossible to dodge interruptions entirely, though. Adam hears footsteps approaching his office and then a knock on the door.

"Come in," he says, thinking it's the janitor or the security guard.

The door swings open, and John smiles at Adam.

****

It turns out John had forgotten his wallet in his office, so he came to pick it up. When he saw Adam's car in the parking lot, he decided to pay him a visit. The two end up talking for half an hour, mostly about Adam's predicament.

"I don't know what to do about it," Adam says.

"Well, the reason why this is even happening in the first place is obvious," John says.

"And what's that?"

"You have two *women* in a small apartment. Don't you know how spiteful women are toward each other? Especially mothers-in-law. There isn't a woman in this world who has a good relationship with her mother-in-law."

"Beth had a good relationship with her. And then everything just changed."

"Your mother was probably just pretending for your sake. Every parent hates to see their child snatched up by a stranger."

"But Beth isn't a stranger. Besides, aren't parents supposed to be happy that their child is happy? What kind of a selfish parent would sacrifice their kid's happiness for their own?"

John shrugs. "You'd be surprised at the kinds of parents that exist out there."

"Not my mom. She's not like that."

"You say that, but the stories you tell me confirm otherwise."

"That's not true."

"Oh yeah? Then why does she keep forcing Beth to eat fatty food despite her hypertension? Why did she make pecan pie even though she knew Beth was allergic?"

"That's not—"

"Why does she keep deriding her and making her feel like she's not a good enough woman by her standards?"

Adam doesn't say anything back to that because he has no counter-arguments to provide.

John puts a hand on Adam's shoulder. "Look, man. I understand she's your mother and you love her. I say kudos to you for having such a close relationship with your mom. But I have to agree with Beth on this one. The signs are right there, dude. Your mother is being evil on purpose."

Adam doesn't allow himself to agree. He doesn't want to. It's his mom they're talking about. The kind and loving woman who gave birth to him and was supportive throughout his entire childhood."

Except, some of the things she did weren't all that good. Maybe the intentions were benevolent, but they had a negative impact on Adam.

Like how she taught Adam to always call her to let her know if he was going to stay out later than intended.

Like how she always waited for him to come back home, no matter how late it was.

Like how she insisted on knowing about his sex life and teaching him to have outdated standards.

Like how she guilt-tripped him into coming home every birthday so they could celebrate it together because she subtly sent the message she was too lonely on that day, and how she called him every year at midnight, sharp, to wish him a happy birthday.

That last one haunted Adam well into his relationship with Beth because then Beth couldn't plan anything for his birthday. One year, he felt so guilty about his mom spending his birthday alone that he planned on spending half a day with Beth and then flying out and spending the other half of the day with his mom.

He would have done it, too, until Beth told him it would be physically impossible and he'd be dead tired. She had told him it was okay and that she wanted him to spend the birthday with his mom, but that wasn't what he wanted. He wanted to be with Beth.

Even for his wedding, they had flowers that his mom wanted because she thought lavender looked better.

It was always about accommodating his mom rather than accommodating himself.

It's like he had been in a cult all his life, and now his eyes are being opened to the harsh reality that his mother is not as perfect as he thought she was.

"I should head home," John says. "I got a birthday I need to head to today."

"Another birthday, John?"

"Yeeeaaah." John extends the words despondently. "Some kid. I don't even know who he is, to be honest."

"Well, good luck with that."

"Thanks. I really hope you find a solution to your problem. If you ask me, though, you just gotta send her home, and everything's gonna go back to normal."

Adam nods. "Yeah. Thanks for listening to me."

"Anytime."

It takes him a long time to collect his thoughts and get back to work. When he finally does start to focus, he gets a call from Beth.

"Yes?" he answers.

"Hi, honey. Your mom says you're at work?" she asks.

"Yes."

"Okay. When do you think you're coming home?" She sounds normal, as if last night never happened.

"I don't know," he says.

He does, but it gives him petty pleasure to screw with Beth because he's still angry.

"Okay. Do you think you'll be home for lunch?"

"Probably."

He will. Again, it gives him satisfaction to not be straight with her.

"All right. Well, I'll see you then. Don't overwork yourself, babe."

"Sure. See you later."

The conversation makes him want to stay even longer at work, despite his back aching from sitting all morning, despite starving. He ate a few Snickers bars and drank coffee, but it was nowhere near enough to keep him satiated. He sure could go for a juicy steak right about now.

At 1 p.m., he feels burnt out, so he packs his things and heads home. When he arrives, his mom is not in the living room, and there are no sounds coming from the kitchen, but a pleasant smell permeates the air.

He sees a steak on the table set for two. In the middle of the table is a lit candle.

"Mom?" he calls out, but she doesn't respond.

"She's not here." Beth cracks open the door and steps outside.

She leans against the doorframe with one hand, and Adam's jaw drops to the floor. The bathrobe she's wearing is open, revealing red laced lingerie underneath it. It's barely enough to cover a small portion of her body.

"I want to make it up to you for last night," Beth says as she steps toward him.

She lets the robe drop to the floor, revealing her body in all its glory. She runs her hands down his chest and gives him a kiss. She smells of something floral, a perfume she wears on special occasions only because she knows it turns him on.

"Your favorite," she confirms.

"Where is...?"

"Out. I gave her money to go out and told her you and I needed some quality time. We have the apartment all to ourselves for at least a few hours." She whispers into his ear, "You can do to me whatever you want."

That sentence is more than enough to drive Adam off the edge. He doesn't care about holding petty grudges anymore.

He cups Beth's pert breast and imagines tearing the lingerie off of her. He kisses her violently, moving down to her neck, to her clavicle. She's thrown her head back and is running her fingers through his hair, moaning.

"Aren't you glad you came home for lunch?" she asks.

He's too turned on to respond. He's already gently pushing her toward the bedroom as he's kissing her.

She places her hands on his chest and asks, "Do you want to eat first?"

He looks at the steak on the table, and it looks nowhere near as appetizing as Beth does.

"Fuck no," he says as he leads her into the bedroom.

Thirteen

Everything seems fine for a few days. Beth is in an okay mood, and she and his mom aren't getting into any fights.

They hardly talk to each other. If his mom makes a meal, Beth orders or makes something for herself. No derisive comments are thrown. They seem to be staying out of each other's lanes, and as much as Adam would like for the two of them to have a good relationship, he feels that it's best right now for them to avoid each other.

Adam knows it's time for his mom to go home, but he doesn't say anything. He's waiting for Beth to ask about it, but he's not initiating anything, and he can't tell why. Is he so afraid of his mom going back home?

Whenever he wants to tell her he'll buy her a flight ticket and drive her to the airport, she does something that prevents him from doing so. Either she makes his favorite meal or tells him she's in pain from her hip.

Sometimes, Adam wonders if she's deliberately doing those things to buy herself more time. She must know she has to go home soon, too. So why isn't she saying anything about it either? She always talks about how she doesn't want to be a burden, and yet, she doesn't seem to mind living with her son and her daughter-in-law in the small apartment they're renting.

A few times, Adam tries to be subtle about it. He asks about the house and whether it's a good idea to leave it unattended for too long. His mom says there's nothing to worry about, not taking his hint in the slightest.

As the days go by, Beth's mood changes. Adam talks to her, but she doesn't want to voice her feelings. He knows it has something to do with his mom. He even asks his mom if she has any idea why Beth is angry, but his mom shrugs. She's lying. He's sure of it.

Then one day, he comes home to hear raised voices in the living room.

"What's going on here?" he asks.

Beth has been shouting at his mom, but when she sees Adam, she stops.

"Nothing," Beth says.

"It's obviously not nothing. Either of you want to open up?" Adam asks.

This is the first time he's actually addressed the elephant in the room openly with all three of them present.

His mom is first to speak up. "Beth is just a little upset these days. I'm worried about her hormones, Addy. You should take her to the doctor."

Beth crosses her arms. "My hormones are fine."

She's red in the face. Furious, Adam realizes. Things can get out of hand very fast if someone says the wrong thing at any point during this conversation.

Beth looks like she wants to say something else, perhaps to hurl a devastating insult at his mom, but she's biting back on the urge—because of Adam most likely.

Even now, when she's so upset, she's putting Adam in front of herself, choosing not to say what she really wants to say.

His mom says, "I'm trying to give you the benefit of the doubt. If it's not your hormones that are making you so rude, then it's just your personality. Is that what you're trying to say?"

Beth looks like she got slapped. Adam can hear in his head a fictional audience going *oohhh* to indicate what a blow his mom has delivered.

"Excuse me?" Beth asks.

She looks like she's about to unleash a torrent of the most colorful curse words. Adam's feet are firmly rooted to the floor, his entire body tense in anticipation. But Beth doesn't say anything to his mom even after that.

"Mom. That's enough," Adam says sternly.

She looks at him with an admonishing gaze. He shrinks under it because he remembers what it was like when he was a kid and she said no about something. Except, he's not a kid anymore. He's an adult, and his mom no longer gets to decide what's best for him.

"Please, Adam," she says. "There's no need to get upset. I haven't said anything because I didn't want to upset you, but some of the things Bethany does are disrespectful, to say the least."

"You can't be serious," Beth says. "You hit me over the head with a frying pan!"

Adam turns his head to his mom. "Mom, is this true?"

His mom ignores Beth and continues, her voice incongruously calm compared to Beth's. "She's been nothing but rude to me ever since I got here. She avoids me. She thinks my food is disgusting—"

"I never said your food is disgusting! I told you I can't eat that food!"

"—she thinks I'm trying to separate you two, she—"

"I do not!"

"Enough!" Adam booms.

Silence fills the air. He's the one who's angry now—with both of them. The weeks of bottling things up have culminated in an outburst he can't control.

"We are going to lay this to rest right now," he says. "You two have been at each other's throats long enough."

His mom gives him a somber smile. "Addy, I'm sorry, but I can't help you here. This is a problem you have to resolve with your wife. I'll always be happy to offer advice to a person who's willing to listen."

Before either Beth or Adam can respond, she spins on her heel and strides into the kitchen where she starts washing the dishes. She's pretty much just said *this is a you problem* and left Adam and Beth to think about it.

Polite rude.

"Adam. Can we talk for a moment?" Beth asks.

She doesn't sound angry anymore even though the ruddiness of her face conveys otherwise.

"Sure."

They head inside the bedroom.

"I've fucking had it with that woman," Beth says the millisecond the door is closed. Adam opens his mouth, but Beth interrupts him. "I've had it with her. I'm not going to take this anymore. All she does is make me feel like trash."

"Beth—"

"She hit me over the head with a fucking frying pan! She physically assaulted me, for Christ's sake!"

Adam is tempted to ask if she's sure about it, but he doesn't want it to seem like he's gaslighting her.

"I'm just trying to resolve this as peacefully as I can," he says.

"Of course you are. You've been trying to stay out of this ever since she got here. If my mom so much as thought about doing something like this to you, I'd be yelling insults at her the very next moment."

"With all due respect, Beth, you can't compare your relationship with your mom to what I have with mine. I mean, you hate your mom. It's easier for you to go with the violent route, but I care about my mom. You know, honestly, I sometimes feel like you're jealous that you don't have that loving relationship and you're unconsciously trying to sabotage what I have because of it."

Beth's eyes widen then grow narrow, and it's in that moment that Adam knows he messed up.

"Okay." Beth nods. "In that case, since I'm such a problem for you and you refuse to take a stand for me, I'm going to sleep in a motel. And I'm going to stay there until she leaves," Beth says.

"Beth..."

"No. We're done with this topic, Adam. You obviously care about your mom more than you do about me. I swear, when I'm around her sometimes, I feel like I'm back in that fucking cult I ran away from because she does the exact same things to me as them." Her voice cracks at the end. "I'm leaving."

Those words help Adam understand that not everything is all cut and dried like he initially thought. Beth has escaped one nightmare, only to relive it again because of his mom. He doesn't want to have that.

"Beth, wait. We have to talk about this."

"There's nothing to talk about until you decide who you're going to side with. I'm really sorry, but your mom is an evil fucking woman, and I'm not going to tolerate her anymore. And I'm really sorry that I have to do this, but it's either her or me."

She turns around, making it clear that the conversation is over. Adam now really does have an ultimatum, one that he has to fulfill in a short amount of time. He can't sleep on it; he can't renegotiate. It is what it is, and he's forced to choose between Beth and his mom.

He already knows who he's going to choose, he just doesn't know how he's going to tell his mom it's time for her to go home. He doesn't have the luxury of practicing his speech either. In a way, that makes things easier.

Take away all the other choices, and you at least don't have to vacillate between options.

Adam leaves the bedroom and heads into the kitchen. His mom is there, washing the dishes.

"Mom, can we talk?" he asks.

"Sure, Addy. What's up?"

"I want to talk about Beth."

"What about her?"

"There are some... things you're doing that are making her feel bad."

"Oh?" His mom soaps up a plate and scrubs it with a sponge. "She's just sensitive. She should probably go check her hormones out, Addy. Those things can be nasty. Especially for her age. She hasn't given birth to a child yet, and that might be messing with her body extra."

Adam lets that comment slide because he wants to focus on the bigger picture.

"That's not how we treat family members, Mom. I know you might not like Beth, but she's family. She's my wife."

"Oh, Addy. I never said I don't like Beth. She's very dear to me. I just think she needs to change her behavior in certain matters."

"I love Beth the way she is, Mom. I think she's treated you with nothing but respect ever since she met you."

"That's questionable."

"You're the one who constantly makes her feel bad about herself. She keeps telling you she can't eat greasy food, and you keep making it. You know she's allergic to nuts, and you make a pie with them. And this entire time, she's been holding it all inside of herself because she didn't want to hurt you or me, and she didn't want to cause a problem for anyone."

Adam wishes they'd had this conversation weeks ago. Maybe things wouldn't have gotten this bad. The way his mom continues to wash the dishes without skipping a beat tells him it wouldn't have changed a thing because she'd never see it was her fault.

"Mom, I'm going to ask you something, and I need you to be honest with me," he says.

"Of course, Addy. What is it?"

"Did you hit Beth?" he asks, and the anger once again bites him hard.

"Of course not." His mom frowns.

"Then why did she tell me you did?"

"She's angry, Addy. Angry people say lots of things that make no sense."

She grabs a dirty frying pan and soaps it up. Adam wonders if that's the same frying pan she used to hit Beth.

"She said you hit her with a frying pan," Adam insists.

"Really?" his mom asks.

She could not care less about this conversation.

"Yes, Mom. Really. Why would Beth say something like that?" he asks.

His mom makes a face, but she doesn't respond to his question.

"Mom," Adam says more sternly this time. "Did you hit her or not?"

"Of course not, Addy. The frying pan was on top of the fridge, and it fell on her head."

Adam looks up at the top of the fridge.

"Mom, why would the frying pan be on top of the fridge? And how would it fall on her head out of nowhere?"

His mom gives him another silent response. She continues to rinse the pan. Adam is biting down on his frustration. He feels like he's talking to a wall.

"Mom," Adam insists. "Beth is my wife. I don't want to have to choose, but if you force me to, then Beth will come first."

She stops washing the dishes and turns to face him. The look of anger on her face almost makes him recoil.

She says, "I gave my life for you."

That sentence has become like a mantra to Adam because, throughout his childhood, he kept hearing that sentence. Sometimes it was said benevolently, uttered by a mother proud of her sacrifice. Other times, it was to remind him of his place, that he's here and alive only because of her willingness to put him before everything.

Over time, Adam started to see his mom as something close to a divinity. He learned to fear her and to respect her. She was his Jesus, and her sacrifice demanded eternal gratitude.

Now that he's an adult, the veil is lifted, the strings of the puppets visible. She's a master manipulator. She's done things for him, yes, but she's also taken a lot from him, and she keeps doing so.

But she will never see it.

"Mom, I think it's time for you to pack your things," Adam says.

"Excuse me?" His mom raises her eyebrows.

"I'm going to book your flight home tomorrow."

He feels the need to say something else, something like *I'm sorry*, but he doesn't because the words won't mean anything.

His mom looks like she's about to fight back. She inhales deeply through her nose and then exhales. She flashes Adam the most insincere smile he's ever witnessed from her.

"Okay. That's fine." She walks past him out of the kitchen.

Adam senses passive-aggression coming from her.

"I don't want to be a burden to anyone anyway," she says.

That's when he's sure she knows exactly the impact her words have.

Fourteen

Adam is woken up in the early hours by shuffling in the living room. His mom spends the next whole morning packing her things. Adam wonders if she's doing it as slowly as possible on purpose to instill a sense of guilt in him.

Either way, it's working.

Adam and his mom haven't spoken to each other since yesterday's fight. She hasn't even made breakfast this morning, a subtle way of letting him know she holds a grudge against him. Adam has the desire—no, the *need*—to go out there and try to strike up a conversation with her, to tell her how sorry he is for what he said yesterday.

It doesn't matter how many times he tells himself it's not his fault and that he's only doing what he's supposed to as a husband to protect his wife. His mom has years of experience manipulating people into feeling guilty.

Things that had been buried in the past for a long time are now resurfacing, and they're hitting Adam with the force of a thousand hammers. He remembers his mom doing things that seemed innocuous at the time but now have a different connotation to them. He remembers feeling sad for her all those times, only to realize she was playing victim just to guilt-trip him.

Most of all, he remembers all the times she was cold like this. He dreaded those moments because the responsibility he felt for her was so potent it made him cave and apologize even if it wasn't his fault, just to make her stop behaving like that.

He thinks he might be so triggered by her right now that he sees her every action as having an ulterior motive, but he'll be unable to see things differently until she gets away from him and gives him time to cool off.

Beth is still here, but she's on edge. She's only left the bedroom once today to go to the bathroom and to get a snack from the kitchen. The entire apartment feels like a minefield.

"All right. I'm all packed, I think," his mom finally says when it's almost noon.

Nobody has said a word until then. There's still time before the flight, and every minute ticks on slowly. Adam is eager to get his mom out of the apartment and onto the plane. He knows that guilt is going to visit him in the future, most likely as soon as he says goodbye to his mom, but there's nothing he can do to lessen that feeling.

She's in the wrong, and attempting to talk to her will only result in his hopes getting crushed when he sees a cold response from her. Either way, visiting her once a year will suffice, both for his and Beth's mental health.

"We still have time before the flight. Wanna go grab something to eat?" Adam asks.

He knows the answer before he even asks it.

"Not really hungry," she says.

"It's gonna be a long flight, and you haven't eaten anything," Adam says.

"I'll eat something when I get home. If I have something in the fridge. If not, I'll go out to buy groceries."

There it goes again. Adam clenches his jaw but doesn't say anything. His mom doesn't want a solution. She wants to be a victim just so Adam can feel bad. Adam is on the verge of telling her it's not going to work, but he doesn't because he sees no need to further strain their relationship. Just a few more hours, and she'll be gone.

That time does come an eternity later, and Adam helps his mom load her things into the car. Beth stays at home. She doesn't even come out of the bedroom to say goodbye to his mom. He becomes upset with her because of it, but he knows better than to raise it as a problem.

On the drive to the airport, Adam and his mom don't speak. He tries to strike up a conversation with her, but she's not talkative. He feels like a fool for even trying, so he remains quiet the rest of the way.

At the airport, their goodbye is cold and formal. His mom hugs him aloofly, says, "Bye, Addy," and checks in without giving him another look. Adam watches her leaving, hoping she'll turn around at least once, just to give him one final glance before departing.

She doesn't. Her pride and her stubbornness are more important to her than reconciling with her son. So be it.

Adam makes a mental note in his mind to not forget this feeling. He wants to hold on to the anger for as long as possible, to show her she isn't the only one who can hold a grudge. Deep down, he knows he won't last.

Not like her. She has him beat by years of experience, and there's no way he can keep up with her in that regard. Even as he sits in his car, he can feel the emotion deflating, replaced by an emptiness he hasn't felt since his father died.

He knows he's going home to an empty home. Except, it's unfair to say it's empty. Beth is there. Beth is his home. That lifts his spirits a little, enough to pull him out of his melancholy. He doesn't know what awaits him when he gets home. His mom is gone, sure, but he and Beth will have to deal with the fallout of her actions.

Adam dreads opening the apartment door because he doesn't know what he'll find inside. For a fleeting moment, he contemplates not going inside at all, which is impossible, of course.

He finds Beth lying on the living room couch, playing on her phone. *Lying*, not sitting. She hasn't done that in a long time. Ever since his mom has been with them, he realizes. The current position she's in also makes him realize how stiff she must have been the entire time while his mom was here.

He can't help but wonder if his mom has maybe made Beth feel bad for lying on the couch in her own apartment and playing on her phone in her own free time. The poor thing must have been a lot stiffer with his mom around than he realized.

When Beth kept telling him she couldn't take it anymore, he understood the words, but he couldn't visualize what she really meant. Now that he sees the way Beth is relaxed, the way her face is slack, the way her foot wags left and right, he understands.

She puts down her phone and gets up into a sitting position when he enters, and she says, "Hey."

Adam sits next to her, but now he's the one who's stiff because he doesn't know what to expect. Beth puts a hand on his thigh.

"Are you okay?" she asks.

She's giving him a compassionate look, gauging whether he's sad now that his mom has left. All the trouble she's been through while his mom was here, and she still has the empathy to worry about Adam rather than herself.

He thinks about her question for a moment. From the moment his mom left, he has entered a sort of vacuum. He thought he'd feel bad about his mom leaving, but he feels like a weight has dropped off his shoulders. The realization makes him crack a smile. When he looks at Beth, his grin widens.

"I'm okay," he says.

She smiles back then caresses his cheek. She leans toward him, gives him a kiss, and sets her head on his chest. He finally has his old Beth back. Things can go back to the way they were before his mom came into their lives. They can finally continue where they left off and work on the baby they've always wanted.

Adam smiles and closes his eyes. The world feels right again.

Fifteen

"You've been different lately," John says to Adam while they're eating lunch at the cafeteria.

Adam shrugs. "I don't know. Things have been okay between me and Beth, so maybe that's the change you're noticing."

"As soon as you got rid of your mother, things got better, huh?"

As much as Adam hates to admit it, that's exactly what happened. His mom moving in with them was like a domino effect, and the stability in Adam's life was the final toppled piece. Now that his mom is back home, the effects are being reversed.

He and Beth spend way more time together, making up for the lost weeks. Beth is her usual, perky self again. Adam had even forgotten that's who she was before his mom moved in with them. They're a lot more intimate, and if things work out okay, Beth might come out of the bathroom with a positive pregnancy test one of these days.

Not only has his marriage improved, but Adam feels like he has more breathing space in the small apartment. He doesn't come home from a long day of work, expecting the first thing that greets him to be, "I made you dinner, Addy."

He didn't think it bothered him at all, but now that his mom is away, like getting out of a toxic relationship, he's able to see all the things that he's been suppressing.

"I guess you were right about my mom," Adam says.

"Told you. I know those kinds of people," John says.

"It's just, she does it in such a convincing manner. I'm still having a hard time believing she's doing it on purpose."

"Well, some people can surprise you even after twenty years of knowing them. Either way, it's not your problem anymore. She's there, you and Beth are here. You get to choose if and when you're going to visit her."

"Yeah."

"And she really hit Beth with a frying pan?"

"That's what Beth says."

"Do you believe her?"

"I didn't at first, but I do now. It doesn't look like something my mom would do, but I can never tell with that woman anymore."

Adam hasn't spoken to his mom since he dropped her off at the airport. He sent her a text to ask if she'd arrived safely, and she responded with a curt *yes*. She was firm about behaving like a brat, but Adam didn't allow himself to fall into that trap this time.

He didn't cave, and he didn't ask for her forgiveness because she was the one who should be apologizing. To Beth first, and then to him.

I gave my life for you.

"Have you heard they started firing professors at the business sector?" John asks.

"What? Here at our university?"

"Yeah. There's word there's gonna be a massive layoff in every sector."

"Oh, come on. This is the worst time for it to happen. Beth and I are trying to have a baby."

"Look at it this way: At least, it's not happening when Beth is pregnant. Then you'd really be in trouble."

"Well, are they saying anything concrete about it? Where did you hear it from, anyway?"

"A guy I know was one of the unlucky ones." John scrunches his lips.

To say that Adam is panicking is an overstatement, but he does feel an unpleasant inkling latching onto him. He hopes the layoff is just a rumor and nothing more. He decides to change the topic before he can allow himself to fall into the machine of overthinking and coming to irrational conclusions.

"Hey, now that my mom is no longer here, do you and Tara wanna come over for game night this weekend?" Adam asks.

"I'll have to let you know. Not sure if Tara has anything planned out for us."

"Another birthday?"

"Probably, yeah."

"This is like, the tenth birthday you're attending this year. How many relatives could Tara possibly have?"

"Way too many."

"Well, from what you told me, a lot of them are old, so when they die, the number of birthdays should decrease."

John shakes his head. "That's not gonna save me. Tara has a dead grandmother whose birthday they still celebrate."

Adam pauses. "You mean the anniversary of her death, right?"

"No. I mean birthday. Anniversary of death, too, but also birthday."

Adam considers for a moment how a birthday without the birthday person is supposed to look.

He asks, "You just can't have a weekend that goes by without hanging out, can you?"

John makes a face. "That's what I get for marrying an extrovert."

As John walks away, all Adam can think is, *Thank God Beth isn't as extroverted as Tara.*

****

When Adam opens the apartment door, silence greets him. He still needs time to get used to the lack of noise and smell emanating from the kitchen. Sometimes, Beth cooks, but these days, they've been ordering instead.

He hates admitting it, but he misses his mom's cooking. With that comes the idea of calling his mom to check up on her. He then remembers that he promised himself he'd continue to stay angry at her because of her behavior. One of them has to step up, but he has no intention of it being him.

But then sometimes, other invasive thoughts come to him. What if something happens to his mom and the last goodbye they've had is the cold one at the airport? What if she dies believing he's angry at her and he never gets the chance to rectify those mistakes?

Whenever that happens, he occupies himself to dismiss those thoughts. At night, the panic about something happening to his mom is still there, but it comes with a lot less potency.

"Hey, babe." Beth walks out of the bedroom and wraps her arms around him. She gives him a kiss and says, "Do you want to order something? Or would you prefer we go out to eat?"

"Actually, I was thinking, do you think you could make your burgers?"

He expects her to say she's too tired to cook, so he's surprised when she smiles and says, "Of course, baby."

"Really?" he asks.

"Yes, really. Believe it or not, it's never a problem for me to make you your favorite meals."

"Thanks, Beth."

While Beth is in the kitchen, Adam sits on the couch and tears open the envelopes he grabbed from the mailbox one by one.

"How was work?" Beth calls from the kitchen.

"I had a little scare. John says there are mass layoffs happening at the university."

"What?"

He thinks Beth didn't hear him, and he's about to repeat himself, but then Beth shows up in the living room, and there's a look of utter shock on her face. "They're firing people?"

"They *fired* people in the business sector. John says they might fire some more from other sectors, but it's just a rumor."

"Oh. Okay," Beth says, but she doesn't look convinced.

Her worry elevates Adam's already present anxiety.

"Let's not worry about it right now, okay?" Adam asks as he opens the first envelope.

It's the electricity bill.

"Okay. But what if it happens?" Beth asks.

Adam shrugs. "Then I'll look for a job elsewhere. There are plenty of universities and schools in town. Someone's bound to hire me. Plus, you have your job. That's going to help keep us afloat until I get back on my feet."

He's opened the water bill and the internet bill.

Beth brushes her hair behind her ear and nods. "Yeah. Yeah, you're right. We'll worry about it after it happens."

Adam has thrown all the open envelopes on the table and is opening the last one, "Don't worry about it, honey. If they fire me, they have to give me a nice severance package. And that means—"

His sentence abruptly cuts off when he looks down at the envelope. His body feels like it's been plunged into an ice bath. The corners of his vision grow dark.

"That means what?" Beth asks.

But Adam can't respond from the lump formed in his throat. Beth walks back out into the living room.

"That means what, Adam? What's that?" She points to the envelope.

He looks at her, and getting the words out is a Herculean task.

"It's an eviction notice."

The apartment is mute for a long time. Beth and Adam stare at each other in horror, neither moving. She's ultimately the one who breaks that freeze.

"What?" she asks, but the word comes out as a meager *wh*.

She walks up to Adam, and together, they read the notice of eviction. They skim through the legal stuff, but their eyes linger on the most important item on the list: They have 60 days to move out.

"No. This isn't right. It can't be right," Beth says, snatching the paper from Adam. "This has to be a mistake."

"It has our names on it and the correct address. I don't see how it can be a mistake," Adam says.

"Why would they evict us? This makes no sense. We haven't done anything wrong. We haven't caused any problems. Could some of the other neighbors have complained about us? Maybe it's the old woman next door. It's gotta be her."

Adam stands up. "Let's calm down for a moment, Beth. Maybe you're right. Maybe it's a mistake or a scam. Let's call the landlord and see what's going on. Okay?"

"You're right. I'll... I'll do that right away." Beth nods fervently.

Adam puts his hands on her shoulders. "Babe, I need you to calm down first, okay? Everything's going to be okay." He slides his hands from her shoulders to her cheeks.

She exhales a deep and exasperated sigh then throws herself into his arms. He holds her for a minute, and then she pulls back and says, "Okay. I'm going to call now."

She sits on the couch and dials the number. She's restlessly tapping her foot on the floor and biting her nails while she waits with her phone pressed against her ear.

"Hi. Victor, is that you? It's Beth." Her voice is high-pitched like that of a kid in trouble. "Adam and I just received an eviction notice in our mail, and we wanted to know what's going on."

Adam hears murmuring on the other end, but he can't discern the words. Every now and again, Beth says *uh-huh* or *yeah,* but she never shows relief at any point during the conversation. He knows that means bad news.

"Okay, thank you. Bye," Beth says as she hangs up.

"What did he say?" Adam asks, impatient.

"He wants to sell the apartment. That's why we're getting evicted."

"What? Where's that coming from? We've been in this apartment for years."

"He says the market is ripe for real estate sale, and he wants to earn from it."

"Unbelievable."

They don't say anything for a while. Beth sits, and Adam stands, their eyes plastered to the termination of tenancy notice on the table, silence lingering in the air.

"Adam, what are we going to do now?" Beth asks.

Once the initial panic has subsided, Adam's mind starts working overtime in problem-solving mode.

"We'll find a new apartment, that's it," he says.

"But we've been in this one for so long. All our things are here."

"Then we'll just move them." He sits next to Beth and takes her by the hands. "I know you're attached to this apartment, but remember how we always said we can't wait to get out of it?"

"I know, but we don't have anywhere to go. The prices for renting are much higher than they used to be. Where would we even go?"

"We'll find a bigger place, one that's going to accommodate you, me, and our future baby. This apartment is not suitable for a family, anyway. We said that a lot of times, remember?"

"Yes, but... I just thought that if we moved out, we'd do it on our terms. Like this, we're cornered."

"Maybe that's a sign. Who knows if we ever would have moved out on our own? Like this, we're moving on to bigger and better things. And we're doing it together. No matter where we go, always together."

Adam's words seem to have calmed Beth down. She smiles at him. Maybe she realizes he's right, that it's not about where they are but the fact that they're together.

"Okay. Together," she says.

Adam kisses her. She lays her head in his lap and starts crying.

Sixteen

"Termination of tenancy? That's bullshit," John says.

"That's what I said," Adam replies.

They're eating calzone today. The inside is hard and cold, but the greasy crust strangely reminds Adam of his mom's cooking.

"This thing is greasy as hell. Look at this." Adam raises the calzone to reveal a napkin soaked in oil.

John frowns. "It's always been like that. We've been eating it for years, and you're just now noticing?"

Adam doesn't say anything to that. He takes another small bite and lays the calzone back on the plate. He takes a clean napkin to wipe the grease off his fingers. He doesn't feel like eating any more of it.

"Well, what are you gonna do now?" John asks.

"Nothing. Beth and I are gonna look for a new apartment," Adam says.

"And the landlord doesn't want to budge about continuing to rent?"

"Nope. He apparently got a good deal from the buyer."

"And you and Beth can't buy an apartment of your own yet?"

"No way. We're drowning in debt, and there's no way the bank would give us a loan. Plus, if the layoff rumor is true and I lose my job, we'll be in even more trouble."

"Hm. Well, Beth has a remote job. If worse comes to worst, you can always move in with your mom." John lets out a cackle.

Adam knows it's a joke, but he doesn't find it funny in the slightest because his mind is already conjuring dystopian future memories: Adam and Beth living with his mom. Beth miserable, crying all the time, complaining about how she hates her life there. Not working on having the baby anymore and their marriage deteriorating until Beth one day leaves Adam, all because she can't stand living with her mother-in-law.

No. He'd sooner rent a small apartment for the rest of his life, even if it meant not inheriting the house from his mom.

"What?" John asks when he notices Adam's blank stare.

"Bad joke," Adam says.

"Sorry."

Adam waves him off. "Ah, don't be. It's just me still being sensitive because of my mom."

"Have you talked to her since she left?"

"No. She hasn't even tried texting."

Adam wishes he could say it doesn't bother him, but it does. Very much so. He's had such a close relationship with his mom all his life, and it crumbled into dust in a matter of weeks. He's not only struggling with that knowledge but with his identity, and his mom's, too.

All his life, he believed his mom was one kind of person, and now his eyes are open to an entirely new plane of possibilities, none of which are optimistic. To top it all off, he never once stopped to imagine what his life would have been like if he and his mom were on bad terms. That was never even in the cards.

The only way he thought they'd ever stop communicating was if she died, so this whole thing took him by surprise.

"Why don't you try calling her instead? I mean, you're clearly bothered by it all," John says.

"I'm not." Adam tries to play it off as nothing significant, but he can tell John sees through him.

"How was the grandma's birthday, by the way?"

"As boring as it can be. I always end up drinking so I don't lose my mind around Tara's relatives."

"And what birthday will you be attending this weekend?"

"Tara and my friends are gonna be hosting their dog's birthday."

Adam waits for the punchline that never comes, so he says, "I would have thought you're messing with me, but if you attended a dead grandma's birthday, I don't see why a dog's birthday would be impossible."

"I wish I was joking, but I'm not."

Adam stares down at his half-finished calzone and then says, "Well, I should head back. Got one class soon."

"All right. Don't stress too much, man."

****

Beth is sitting in the living room when Adam comes home. The laptop is on the table in front of her, and she's leaning so close to it that she looks like she's going to be sucked into the screen. She's clicking at something, the white glow of the screen illuminating her face.

"Are you defusing a bomb?" Adam asks.

Beth's reply comes a few seconds late. "What?"

"It's just you're focused so hard. What are you doing?"

Beth sighs and leans back into the couch. She runs her palms down her face and exhales loudly. "I've been looking for an apartment all day long. Adam, there's nothing."

"What do you mean there's nothing? There's gotta be something. There's a bunch of apartments just in this area, Beth."

"Yeah, but the prices are all too high. We'd be paying double for an apartment smaller than this one."

"You've gotta be kidding me. Okay, there's gotta be something cheaper."

"There is, but it's gonna be a total dump."

"Well, we don't really have a choice right now, Beth. I'm gonna take a look."

Adam pulls out his cell phone.

"I've been checking the ads all day long, Adam. There's nothing."

Adam doesn't respond. He thinks he knows what the problem is. Beth is used to the luxury of this apartment. It's small, but it's fancy, and it's hard for her to move into a downgrade. Adam thinks she probably dismissed a lot of good candidates right from the thumbnail image

He sits next to Beth and, together, they browse real estate websites for apartments they can rent. Hours pass. It was around 6 p.m. when Adam returned home from work. Now it's already 8 p.m., he's hungry, irritable, and hasn't found a single suitable apartment.

Beth was right. Everything that's within their price range is either a total dump or so far out of town that Adam would end up spending way more gas money to get to work than he would on rent.

"This is hopeless," Beth says.

They've both stopped searching for the moment. Beth is nervously touching her tattoo. Adam doesn't want to say anything because it would be words of discouragement, and neither of them needs that right now.

"This apartment is small, but it's in such a good location. I can't believe we have to move," Beth complains.

Adam looks at her, trying to detect traces of redness in her face so he can stop her in time from breaking down.

"I'm not happy about it either. Let's leave it for tonight. Let's go out, have a nice dinner, and worry about it tomorrow."

"Adam, we don't have the money for a fancy dinner."

"We still do."

"But what if you lose your job and we can't find a cheap enough apartment?"

"Then at least we'll know we ate good before it happened."

So, that's what they do. They dress nicely, and they head out to the same restaurant where they canceled date night weeks ago. Adam orders a steak, and Beth gets Caesar salad.

"Your mom would have had a stroke if she saw me eating this," Beth says.

Adam gives a dry laugh, but he finds nothing about it funny because, more and more, he's starting to believe that between him and his mom, he's the one who's going to have to cave in.

Seventeen

On Monday, an announcement is made by the university president. It's such an important announcement that classes are canceled and all staff are required to attend the meeting.

Adam is on edge. He's grateful he took the weekend to unwind from work, but the stress of other things is constantly here, looming just above him like a dark cloud brewing up a bad storm.

There's a lot of unrest among the staff. Murmurs fill the auditorium. Everyone suspects it's about the layoff. The few people who aren't looped in the whole thing are chatting worry-free with each other. Adam finds John, and the two take the seats closest to the front row that aren't occupied.

When the president walks in, the room goes quiet for the most part, save for the few oblivious ones who are still chatting. In a way, the staff of the school are the same as the students when put in the same seats. They turn off their brains and do only what's required of them.

"May I please have everyone's attention?" the president asks.

Adam is already silently sitting in his seat, anxiously watching the president, waiting for the others to settle down, too. There's no need for the president to ask more than once. Unlike the students, the school staff are adults, and they listen to instructions.

John whispers, "Man, this guy's grown old. Been a while since I've seen him, but he has a lot less hair than last time."

Adam is steepling his fingers, but when he realizes how clammy his palms are, he wipes them on his pants. The murmurs have stopped now. The auditorium is engulfed in silence as everyone waits with bated breath for the president to make his announcement.

The president clears his throat, and it makes him sound frail and scared.

He says, "I won't skirt around the topic. I'm sure you've all heard of the layoffs that have been happening at the university lately. Unfortunately, unfavorable decisions have been made by the higher-ups, so we have to let some people go."

There are gasps and more murmurs before the president raises his hand to silence them.

"I know, I know. I'm not happy about it either. Trust me. I've had to go through our entire list of employees and see who we can go without. We need all of you, we really do, but my hands are tied."

Adam doesn't like anything about the speech the president is giving. It's just him talking about how he's not to blame and making excuses for axing employees. It's clear this is unpleasant for him and he wants to get it over with as soon as possible.

The door opens, and secretary Ava Wilkins walks in carrying papers in her hands. She's a heavy-set woman with hair tied into an oversized bun. She approaches the first row of seats and starts distributing copies to each person.

The president clears his throat again. "On this paper, you'll find a list of employees who will continue to work for the university. If you don't find your name on the list, it means you won't continue working with the university. If you have any questions about your severance package or reasons for getting fired, you can talk to Secretary Fatima Wilkins."

John leans toward Adam. "Too many people to fire, I guess, so he's taking care of us like cattle for the slaughter, huh?"

Adam's hands remain clammy, no matter how much he wipes them on his pants. His heart starts to beat faster as the secretary moves up the rows, getting closer to him.

Next to him, John keeps trying to talk to him, but Adam isn't able to listen. How can John be so relaxed in this moment? Does he care that little about his job? The voices of the university staff are louder now, and the president can't calm them down, no matter how many times he tells them to be quiet.

Things are getting out of hand. Panic is overflowing as the people reading the papers realize they don't have their names on them. Some of them complain aloud. One of them has approached the president and is vigorously gesturing to the paper while the president shakes his head.

The voices are so loud Adam can hardly hear himself think. The secretary is in front of his row now, distributing papers. He feels like he wants to jump out of his skin.

The sweat that coats his palms is icy. The secretary's face is blasé as she gives out each paper. If she's feeling any emotions toward professors getting fired, she's not showing them. For all Adam knows, this is just another task she needs to do, after which she'll go back to sitting behind the desk, taking calls, and drinking coffee. She might mention in passing how the professors have been fired and, oh, how tragic it is, but anyway, have you heard Amelia is having an affair with the groundskeeper?

When the secretary finally reaches Adam and gives him his paper, he grabs it a little too feverishly. She doesn't notice it or care because she's already moving on to the next person. Adam skims the list of employees. Next to him, he hears John sighing.

"Phew. Still here. A little disappointed, though. I really could have used a severance package and time off of work," he says.

Adam has finished reading the names, so he flips to the other side. The list goes on. With each row that brings him closer to the bottom of the page, his heart sinks deeper. When he reaches the end and his name isn't there, he flips the paper and starts reading again.

He rationalizes in his mind how it can't be possible he got fired because he's one of the most hardworking professors at the university and how he hasn't done anything to warrant losing his job. If anything, he deserves to keep his job more than John.

His heart skips a bit when he finally sees his name on the list, nestled in the middle. It's only for a moment because it's not his name but a person named Ada.

Adam can feel John's gaze on him, that fake, hopeful gaze. He doesn't care whether Adam got fired. He gets to keep his job, and it's every man for himself at the university, it seems. Adam has finished reading the list four times already. The last two times, he went through each letter of each name individually, even tracing each row with his finger.

He isn't on the list.

No matter how hard he tries to conjure up his name from thin air, he's not there. His heart rate slows down. His body relaxes. A sense of defeat overtakes him, and he feels utterly deflated and spent. He's staring at the paper knowing full well the words on it aren't going to change.

By then, the auditorium settles down for the most part. Some people are chatting with each other as if nothing had happened, content that they weren't hit by the layoffs. Others are sitting catatonically like Adam, staring at one spot—mostly at the paper.

"If you see your name on the list, you have not been fired. If your name is not on the list, you're no longer going to be employed here," the president repeats.

John's hand touches Adam's shoulder. "I'm sorry, man. It's not going to be the same without you."

He's talking like Adam's dead and already buried. He's not. He's still a part of this university. Except, he's not going to be soon.

Years of working here will have been for nothing. Once he's out the campus gate, he'll never be able to return. The security guard will treat him as a stranger and, if he gets too close, a trespasser.

The next hour goes by in a blur. He doesn't remember much about how he got to his car and started driving home. He stares blankly ahead at the road, wondering if this is all just a bad dream.

I'm no longer a university professor, he thinks.

A loss of identity comes with that realization. For years, Adam has taken pride in being a professor. He loved it when people asked him what he does for a living, and he responded with, "I teach physics at a university."

What's he going to say now? I *used* to teach at the university? I'm looking for a job right now? I'm searching for the right opportunities?

Then comes the thing he dreads even more.

How am I going to tell Beth?

She's going to flip, he's sure of that. The worst possible scenario that they feared has come to pass. What are they going to do now? Everything will have to be put on hold. The baby, saving money for a house, all of it will be replaced by other things. Beth and Adam will go into survival mode, where their primary concern is going to be whether they can afford to pay their bills and buy groceries.

Adam wants to call Beth, to tell her the news and be done with it as soon as possible. He's afraid of doing it over the phone, though. He wants to be able to see her face when he says it so he can determine whether she's angry, sad, shocked, or something else.

When he enters the apartment, he immediately calls out to his wife.

"Beth?"

The apartment is quiet. Beth might be out for lunch or—

The bedroom door swings open, and a surprised Beth steps out. She smiles. "You're home early, babe."

Heat flushes his face. He needs a moment to find his tongue. Something is stuck in his throat, making it impossible for him to speak.

Beth has already noticed something is wrong because her look of pleasant surprise is replaced by worry.

"I—" Adam starts, but his words are choked.

Beth doesn't wait. She runs toward him and wraps her arms around him. He doesn't need to say anything because she understands. Not that he would be able to anyway because he starts crying harder than he has in years.

He cries because they are getting evicted. He cries because he got fired. He cries because everything he and Beth planned is crumbling right before his eyes.

Most of all, he's crying because he misses his mom.

Eighteen

Adam is ashamed to look at Beth. She's been nothing but supportive ever since he got fired, but he feels like he failed the two of them.

He's been applying for new jobs for a week now, but none of the employers have called back yet. Beth doesn't seem to be stressed about Adam being unemployed. Not yet, anyway. Maybe she's trying to hide her panic in front of him, but if anything, she's enjoying having him at home.

Stress usually works in a way that it creates a rift between married couples. For Beth and Adam, it seems to be working the opposite way. Beth often comes up to him and asks for cuddles, and they even have sex a lot more often.

"Careful. If things continue like this, I might decide to stay unemployed," Adam jokes.

He misses working at the university already. He wasn't the kind of person who romanticized his job. He loved almost everything about it. Sure, there were some things he didn't do as enthusiastically—like paperwork—but every job came with downsides to it.

He's trying to look ahead at the opportunities that might be waiting for him. He has a severance package that will help keep him and Beth afloat for a while, but there's a constant, silent reminder of a countdown. He's not panicking yet, but the closer the timer gets to zero, the more the anxiety will grow.

Since Adam is hunting for jobs, Beth is the one looking for an apartment. They don't have much time left. A little over two weeks. Adam still doesn't know if they're going to be kicked out on the exact date mentioned in the tenancy termination papers or if the landlord is going to be slightly flexible and understanding of their situation.

He doesn't want to allow himself to believe they have the freedom to choose.

Another week goes by. Every day after that seems to pass in a heartbeat. The countdown to their eviction is almost here. After that, the countdown for the end of Adam's severance package will continue.

They went to view some apartments in the past few weeks, but even the ones that were the right fit price-wise had something faulty with them. If the apartment didn't have an infestation or a leaky ceiling, then the landlord was a real piece of work and made insane demands of his tenants. One in particular stood out because he carried a list with him.

I expect you to answer your phone whenever I call you. You have to pay rent exactly on the date we agreed on. I'll be here personally to pick it up every month and inspect the apartment to make sure you haven't stolen or broken anything. You can only decorate the apartment with things that have been run by me first. No smoking in the apartment. Guests are allowed only during the weekend from 5 p.m. to 11 p.m. If anything breaks down, you have to pay for it.

Beth and Adam exchanged a look before Adam interrupted the guy. He sounded like he wasn't even halfway done with the list. They told him they weren't interested and bolted out of there.

Things are not looking good for Beth and Adam. He's still jobless. He went to a few job interviews, but none of the employers called him back. His severance isn't going to last much longer either. Once it depletes, their savings will start to deplete, too, and they're already meager enough as they are.

"Any luck finding a suitable apartment?" he asks Beth when she gets out of the bedroom.

"Nothing. Any luck finding a job?" she asks.

"A few potential positions, but they never called back."

"What is it about employers not being able to construct a simple rejection email? It's just plain rude to keep candidates hanging."

"I know, right? One time, back before you and I met, I applied to work at an online school to teach English. Whenever I logged in to check the status of my application, it just said 'It's being reviewed.' It stayed like that for months, and then I got an email from them saying they needed teachers, so if I'm interested, I should apply. Stupidly, I did, and guess what the website said."

"That your application is being reviewed?"

"Yeah."

"Unprofessional behavior from a company." Beth shakes her head.

She sits on the couch next to him and stares blankly at the black TV screen for a minute. She's playing with her tattoo again.

"Babe, I think you really should remove that tattoo," Adam says.

She looks at him in surprise.

"It doesn't bother me. I just think it unnecessarily bothers you," he says.

"The memories get intense sometimes, but I have to remember."

"You don't need to punish yourself like that."

"It's not punishing. I want to remember where I came from. To know how strong I had to be to survive such a thing."

She finds solace in knowing she's survived worse than this. Adam smiles at that.

"What are we going to do, Adam?" she asks.

It's the first time Adam hears worry in her voice since he got fired from the university. He doesn't know if she's been holding it in her all this time, or if the stress is finally starting to get to her now that they're days away from being homeless.

"We'll keep looking. That's all we can do. We just need to find an apartment for now, and then we'll handle my job later on."

Beth seems unconvinced. "I just don't understand why nobody is calling you back."

"It's a tough market, I guess."

"Yeah, but there are so many schools in our city. I can't believe none of them need a physics professor."

"I guess the layoffs have been happening en masse. I read about it online."

Just then, Adam's phone starts ringing. He picks it up and hastily looks at the caller ID on the screen. These days, he's hoping it's numbers he won't recognize because he expects employers to call him to schedule an interview.

His eyes grow wide when he sees who's calling him.

"It's my mom," he says.

He knows it's not terribly important to Beth, but it is to him. His mom is calling him after weeks of not communicating with him at all. Beth would know how weird it is for him to go days, let alone weeks without talking to his mom on the phone, and yet, she seems nonplussed at this piece of information.

If anything, she looks irritated. She stands up and says, "I'm going to continue looking for apartments in the bedroom."

She's still angry at his mom, and Adam doesn't blame her. His own resentment has waned, though. He can hardly even recall why they stopped speaking in the first place. Right now, he's just glad his mom is calling.

He waits until Beth is in the bedroom and the door is closed before sliding the button on the screen to answer. He brings the phone to his ear and utters a tentative, "Hello?"

"Hi, Addy," his mom says in a perky voice.

Adam hadn't been sure whether his mom would be cold and distant, but now that she sounds like her old self, he's slowly creeping out of his bubble toward the unknown outside.

"Hi, Mom," he says.

"How are you? How are things at home?"

It sounded like, "Are things getting better now that I'm gone?" but Adam knows he's exaggerating that in his mind.

He hesitates. "Things are... okay. Beth and I are fine and, you know. Things are good. How are things on your end?"

It's a weak attempt at getting the attention off of him, one that his mom recognizes right away.

"Are you sure everything's okay, Addy? You don't sound too good. Is everything fine between you and Bethany?" He hears a familiar jingle in the background, but it does nothing to annoy him this time.

"Yes, Mom. Everything is okay between us."

He wants to add *but*, but his Mom beats him to it.

"But?"

Adam bites his lower lip. She's really good at reading him, even hundreds of miles away, just by hearing his voice. She's a mom, and moms know their children better than they know themselves. That's at least what his mom always tells him.

"To be honest, things are not so great, Mom." Adam sighs.

"What is it? Talk to me, sweetheart. You know I'm always here to help you and Bethany."

Has she forgotten about how their last interaction ended? Has she chosen to be the better person and turn a blind eye to it? Adam is suddenly overcome by shame over how he behaved toward his mom while she lived with him and Beth. He owes her an apology.

"Beth and I are getting evicted from our apartment," Adam says in a low tone because he's afraid of Beth bursting out of the bedroom and gesturing for him to not say anything to his mom. Something tells him she's listening anyway.

"Oh my," his mom says. "Why? What happened?"

"The landlord wants to sell the place, so we have sixty days to move out. Well, now it's, like, five days probably." He chuckles, but his mom doesn't reciprocate it.

"Do you have anywhere else to go? Have you already found another apartment?" his mom asks.

Adam contemplates lying to her, just so she won't worry. He knows she'll see right through him, though. She can tell when he's lying just based on the inflection of his voice, so he kills the idea before it blooms properly.

"No," he says. "We're still looking, but everything is either too expensive, too far, or a dump. Normally, I wouldn't have been picky like that, but we have to think about..." *We have to think about the baby,* he almost says before cutting himself off. "We have to think about our future here."

"I understand. You can't just move into any apartment, especially because of your work and all. You need to have something that's close."

Adam licks his lips. "About that. Something else happened." He waits a moment, but when his mom says nothing, he continues, "I got fired from the university."

There's an extended moment of silence before his mom speaks up, "Oh, Addy. What happened?"

"They had mass layoffs, and I happened to be caught by the wave. Unlucky, I guess."

He tries to make it sound like it's not a big deal, but he can hear the concern in his mom's voice.

"I'm looking for a job right now, but it's... to be honest, it's not looking too optimistic," he says.

He was supposed to dispel his mom's worry. Instead, he seems to be opening up to her about his feelings more than he has to Beth. He doesn't realize how stressed he is about the whole thing until it starts pouring out of him like a broken dam.

His mom takes a moment to respond. "Addy, do you and Bethany need money?"

The question takes him by surprise. If his mom were here, he would have hugged her tight and apologized over and over for treating her badly.

He contemplates whether to accept money from his mom. He and Beth really could use it, but even if he says yes, how much money can his mom give him? Not enough to help him and Beth pay the rent, for sure. Maybe just enough to cover a week's worth of groceries, but that's just about all.

"No, absolutely not, Mom. I could never ask that from you," Adam says.

"If things go bad, I'm always here to help. You know that, right? Whatever you and Bethany need, I'll always be here to help you."

And that's when Adam gets an idea. His mind screams at him not to say it aloud, but it's already too late. He'll worry about the consequences later.

"Actually, Mom, I think you might be able to help us."

Nineteen

"You must be out of your mind!" Beth says.

"Beth, just listen to me. I'm not suggesting we stay there for long. Just until we get back on our feet," Adam says.

Beth is fuming. Her face is red, and Adam knows that can't be good. He's not just playing with fire. He's stoking it with gasoline.

"I'm not moving in with your mom, no way in hell," she says.

"Beth, come on. We really have no choice here. We can't find an apartment, and I'm still jobless. We're lucky enough that you can work remotely so that we can move in with her."

"Do you not remember the way things went the last time we all lived together?"

"I know, but things will be different this time."

"Yeah. She'll be able to bully me more, and I won't be able to do anything about it."

Adam remembers all the fights, all the tension between him and Beth, all the problems that triangulated between the three of them.

The way your mom hit Beth over the head with a frying pan.

He had completely forgotten about it, and now that he remembers, he gets angry again, but only for a moment. His mom's willingness to help far overshadows everything bad.

"It's going to be different this time," he repeats. "It's a big house. We'll have our own room. If you don't feel like communicating with anyone, you can isolate yourself to a few rooms and spend an entire day without ever running into another person."

"Have you even talked to her about it? What makes you think she'd want me in the house?"

"I already asked her. She said we can stay as long as we want. She plans on leaving the house to us after she dies anyway, so we don't need to behave like we're guests there."

"We *are* guests there, Adam, and I don't want you to think we will be anything else because, the moment you start to get comfortable, we'll never get out of there. Just remember what happened last time."

"I know, and I'm sorry, but I'll protect you this time."

"I'm not talking about that, Adam. I'm talking about you not wanting your mom to leave. You knew she was okay, but you didn't urge her to leave."

Adam presses his lips together. A part of him knew Beth knew he had been postponing his mom's departure, but she never said anything until now.

"This is going to help us. Once we're back on our feet, we're out of there, and we can go back to living our normal lives. Just you, me, and our baby."

Beth puts her hands on her temples as if she's suffering from a huge headache. She turns away from Adam and chants, "No, this can't be happening. This is a dream. A freaking nightmare. It has to be."

Adam approaches her. He lays one finger on her shoulder. When she doesn't break away from him or tell him to leave her alone, he puts his entire hand there.

"Beth, I know you don't like this. I don't like it either," he says.

"Oh yeah? Because it looks to me like you're pretty happy about it." Beth whirls around to face him.

"Come on, Beth. Do you really think I'd be happy to move back in with my mom in my late twenties when we're supposed to be having a family of our own? I'm not. I'm heartbroken because I feel like I've failed us and we're now starting from scratch again."

Tears are blurring his vision. But even as he says that, it's not just heartbreak he's experiencing. There's something good there, too, contrary to what he's told Beth. There's a feeling of hopefulness and relief. Moving in with his mom will take away certain responsibilities. He's a child again, and his mom is here to save him from the problem that the world has created for him.

Juvenile thinking, maybe, but right now, he needs it before he's ready to face the cruel reality once again. One day, he will be a father, and his child might be in the same situation as he is today. He wants to be able to sacrifice everything to ensure that child's future is bright, just as his mom sacrificed herself for him.

Beth puts a hand on Adam's cheek. "You can't blame yourself, Adam. You haven't failed anything. It's just circumstances."

Her words make him want to cry with sadness but also relief. It's like he's said before: He doesn't care where he is, as long as he's with Beth.

"Maybe if I had worked harder at the university..." he starts.

"No. We talked about this, honey. We said you wouldn't go back to the past. There's nothing you can change there."

"Yeah. Right."

"Let's just look to the future for now. What exactly are our options here because we're almost out of time?"

"Well, if we get really lucky and find a good apartment, we'll be good a couple more weeks. And that's when my severance stops coming in, so... I'd need to find a job as well."

"Are you waiting for any of the employers to call you back?"

"A couple, but I don't think they will. I don't meet the qualifications for the only positions they had available. This all sucks."

"We *could* survive off of my paycheck for a while."

"Maybe, but we would need to use up our savings."

Beth frowns with a pensive expression. "We can get a loan from the bank if things go bad."

Adam shakes his head. "It'll wreck our credit score. Besides, I thought we wanted to buy a house."

"So what you're saying is, our only option is to live with your mom?"

"Just for a little bit, until I find a job and we find an apartment. Maybe we can even pay off some of our debt while we're living there because there's gonna be no rent. We might even save some money. It's really going to help us."

"But what about the baby?" Beth asks.

Adam takes Beth's hands into his, kisses them, and says, "We'll keep working on that. I don't want this setback to stop us. If we put our plans on hold every time something minor happens, we'll never have a child."

Beth sighs. "How do people do this?"

"Survive financially, you mean?"

"I mean all of this. Balance work and private life and become parents of not one but more kids. It just seems impossible."

"That's the thing, Beth. They deal with things as they come. Not a lot of people are fortunate enough to plan parenthood. It just happens, and they make it work as they go."

"It seems selfish to do that to a child."

"Maybe. But for some parents, it's the only way to make it happen."

Beth paces around the room, her gaze glued to her feet. She's thinking hard of another solution, something that won't involve moving in with his mom.

Finally, she looks at him and says, "If we do this... If we move in with your mom, we need to lay down some ground rules I'm going to need us to stick to, and I won't put up with any compromises this time."

"Okay, sure."

"I'm not going to sit around and let her insult me like she did last time. If she does that, I'm going to give you a fair warning about it, and if it persists, I'm going to move out."

Adam nods. "That's fair."

Beth sits on the bed. She eyes Adam up and down as if to decide if he's agreeing with her just because she wants to hear that or because he plans on supporting her.

"And I want to have my privacy. You know how important that is to me," she says.

"It's a big house. You can use my dad's reading room as your office. I think you'll like it there."

"I don't know if your mom is going to appreciate me using your dad's office."

"She is. I'm going to talk to her and make sure she understands we won't tolerate certain things."

"And what makes you think she's going to listen this time?"

The truth is Adam doesn't know if his mom is going to respect their boundaries this time. All he can do is hope everything will be okay. If his mom gives Beth trouble, he's going to have a stern talk with her. And if even that doesn't work, then they're going to move out, even if it has to be into a ramshackle one-bedroom studio apartment.

"So, are we doing this?" Adam asks.

He should be despondent because this is a step back, but he isn't. He feels like they're finally going to be able to catch a break, at least, for a little while. Every adult needs a break from adulting from time to time. Adam is lucky enough that his mom allows him to experience that.

The same can't be said for Beth. Talking to her mother even for just a few minutes puts her in a foul mood. Adam can't imagine having to move in with them. He wouldn't ever allow Beth to stoop so low. It's enough that her parents mistreated her so badly when she was a kid. He wouldn't allow them to do the same now that she's an adult.

"Beth. Baby, you're the most important person to me. I'm never going to let anyone hurt you. Not even my mom," he says.

He embraces her in a tight hug. She believes his words.

The problem is… he's not sure if he does.

Twenty

The move from the apartment is filled with rushing and sadness. Every now and again, Beth unearths an item she'd completely forgotten about for years. Once it's out, so are the emotions attached to it, and it's impossible to stop Beth from being sentimental.

Adam isn't indifferent about those little mementos either. Although unimportant at the time of obtaining, they now bear a much greater significance because they harbor memories of time spent in the apartment they're about to leave forever.

Adam finds a plushie that resembles a frog in a leather jacket. He'd won that for Beth from a crane machine at a carnival one summer.

He finds a booklet that contains his and Beth's pictures and their story that unfolds in the form of a text on each page. Beth had gifted that to him for their first anniversary.

Beth uncovers a golden rose still encased in its box. An old doll filled with wool and stitched clumsily

"Oh my God. I'd totally forgotten about this," Beth says, teary-eyed. She hugs the doll to her chest.

The doll's name is Fiona. Beth had a similar one in her childhood, but she lost it during a fire alarm. Her childhood friend, Sarah, who had been in the same cult as Beth, made that for her when they were teenagers.

"Oh, Sarah. Where are you now?" Beth sobs quietly.

The two of them got separated at one point during their teen years when Sarah was sent off to be educated by the cult elsewhere. They never told their members where their friends would be going.

"We'll keep it safe this time, baby," Adam says.

It takes Beth a long time to compose herself and continue packing.

When everything is packed up in cardboard boxes that are meticulously marked, Adam and Beth stand in the foyer and stare at the unrecognizable place that was once their home. Adam doesn't realize how much he'd grown attached to the apartment until he sees it in its current state. The coziness and hominess are gone, replaced by a void that the new owner will fill.

Adam gets irrationally angry at that. One day, maybe very soon, someone will move into the apartment. They'll look at the empty rooms, and they'll smile. Where Beth and Adam see memories thrown out, the buyer will see room to make new ones.

One person's sadness is another person's happiness.

"I can't believe we have to leave after all these years." Beth's voice trembles, and she puts a hand over her mouth.

Adam puts an arm around her shoulders. He wishes he could offer some words of consolation to say they're moving on to bigger and better things, but that's not the case. They're taking steps back for now.

Adam makes a silent promise to not allow Beth to find herself in this situation again in the future. If he has to bust his rear working to provide for her and their future kid, he will, but he will never again allow himself to see Beth hurt like this.

Just then, someone rings on the intercom, and Adam knows right away that it's the guys from the moving company. He unlocks the building entrance for them and says, "Let's head downstairs. We should let the moving guys take care of stuff here."

"Can we stay just a minute longer?" Beth gives him a puppy-eyes look.

How can he say no to that?

"Sure, babe. Whatever you want." He smiles.

And so they stand there and watch their old home together until the movers come.

****

Beth is quiet for the entire duration of the flight, except when she lets out a small sob.

"What's wrong, baby?" Adam asks. "Are you sad about us moving?"

Tears are trickling down Beth's face. She gasps, wipes her tears, and nods.

"Come here," Adam says as he reels her close to him. "It's all a shock for now. Once we get adjusted, you'll see that things will be a lot better for us."

She doesn't say anything. She just silently cries in his arms while he caresses her shoulder and back.

By the time they land, she's at least stopped crying. She's still quiet and lethargic like a zombie. Adam thinks she might be lost and forgot to take something important, so he runs a checklist in his mind and decides to take the lead, but to his surprise, Beth is perfectly lucid.

She knows exactly what they need to do, where they need to go, and what they brought with them. They take an Uber to his mom's home because the car isn't here yet. They paid someone to drive the car to their new (temporary) home, but he hasn't arrived yet.

Adam stares out the window of the Uber at the familiar streets from his childhood. He hadn't paid attention to any of it the last time they were here, when his mom was at the hospital, but now there's no rush and no sense of urgency. He's able to take it all in, and he hates it.

He wonders how many people his age are still in Casper, Wyoming. He hopes he won't run into any of them because he's not particularly fond of any of them. He didn't have any negative experiences in school. He wasn't bullied like Four-Eyed Michael, as the bullies called him, but he wasn't popular either. He stayed in limbo, neither here nor there, which ultimately led to him being a forgettable school individual.

Sometimes, we feel a need to prove ourselves in front of people from our past, especially classmates. It's a second chance to prove we're worth something and that, despite not exceeding in high school, we made it in life.

When Adam looks at Beth, he realizes how proud of himself he is for having such a kind, loving, and beautiful wife. He doesn't need a job next to a person who holds him dear like he's the last drop of water on earth.

He knows it's shallow, but he would at least love to brag with her in front of his old classmates and watch their jaws drop to the floor at the sight of Beth. That would further cause envy in them when she told them what she does for a living.

When the driver drops them off in front of the house, his mom is already on the porch, waiting for them patiently with a wide smile on her face. As soon as they step out of the car, she rushes down the driveway to greet them.

"Hello, hello!" she says enthusiastically.

She approaches Adam first and embraces him in a tight hug. In that moment, Adam knows everything is okay and the past has been forgotten. When she pulls away, she gives him a proper look as if making sure he's well-fed, healthy, and okay.

She then moves on to Beth and gives her an equally tight hug. Up until then, Beth has retained a rigid expression on her face, not knowing what to expect from his mom, given how their last interaction went, but when they hug, Beth goes with the flow.

She does give Adam a confused glance from the side, but she doesn't say anything. She's probably as glad to avoid conflict as Adam is.

"Bethany, you don't look so good. Are you sick?" his mom asks.

"No, ma'am. Just tired." Beth forces a dry-lipped smile.

"I'm not buying it. You need to get into bed as soon as you eat some of the soup that I made. Don't worry, it's not greasy." A shrill laugh erupts from her mouth, and she looks at Adam.

Adam doesn't even stop to consider whether that comment was passive-aggressive. Right now, the world seems right again, and he'll be damned if he's going to ruin it by questioning whether his mom's intentions are altruistic or not.

"Addy, I cleaned up your old room so you and Bethany can stay there," his mom says when they enter the house.

"Thanks, Mom. We really appreciate it," Adam says.

When his mom notices Adam and Beth standing in the foyer, she throws her hands up and says, "Oh, don't you act like you're strangers in this house. Come on in. Come on."

Adam takes Beth by the hand and is surprised at how stiff it is. Gradually, her fingers ease into his, and he leads her into the living room.

"I'm so sorry that the house isn't as clean as I wanted it to be. I've been cleaning for days, but this place is big," his mom says.

The house looks spotless, just as it always did, but his mom is the kind of person who's never happy with the tidiness and cleanliness of the place she's living in.

"You really don't need to bust yourself working so hard because of us, Mom. Your hip..." Adam says.

"Don't be silly, sweetheart. My hip is as good as new. And you two are my world. I'm going to make sure you're as comfortable here as you can possibly be. And don't worry; you'll have your space and privacy. You won't even notice I'm living with you."

The words make Adam ticklish with emotions. The guilt from treating her the way he did the last time they saw each other is now radiating brightly. He's overcome by the urge to apologize to her because of it, but he doesn't want to reopen old wounds. His mom has apparently forgotten about it, and he's too afraid of mentioning it out of fear of seeing some residual resentment on her side.

"I'm gonna set the table. You two must be starving," his mom says.

The warm feeling of nostalgia is polluted by the memory of Beth and his mom's conflicts regarding food. Rather than think about it, he smiles and watches his mom stride out of the living room.

When Adam turns to face Beth and asks her how she's feeling, he notices her standing in the middle of the living room, scanning the room inch by inch.

"What do you think about all this, Beth?" Adam asks.

He gets closer to her and caresses her cheek because he feels like that's what she needs at this moment.

"I... am not sure," she says.

"Any negative emotions about this?"

"I don't know."

She's confused because there are too many emotions swirling in her mind right now. She needs time until they crystalize. Until that happens, both she and Adam are going to be on edge. If she's feeling bad about something, Adam is, too. He can't be happy if Beth isn't happy.

"Come on, you two!" his mom yells from the kitchen. "You can worry about unpacking later."

"Coming, Mom!" As soon as Adam says that, he feels like he's seven years old again, playing video games in his living room, and his mom is shouting that lunch is ready.

"Adam, if you don't mind, I'm gonna lie down for a bit," Beth says.

"Yeah, sure." He nods. "You know which room is mine, right?"

She nods. As she turns to leave, Adam grabs her by the hand. When their eyes meet, he asks, "Baby, you know we're not trapped here, right? Give it a day or two for the impressions to settle down, and if you really hate it, we'll go someplace else, okay?"

She gives a grateful smile before climbing upstairs.

Adam is torn. On the one hand, he's happy that he gets to spend some more time with his mom. It gives him not only a chance to catch up with her but to patch up the holes between them. On the other hand, he doesn't want his wife to be miserable, and that's why he's praying to God that this works out, just until he and Beth are able to stand on their own two feet.

"Come on, kids!" his mom shouts.

A pleasant smell wafts from the kitchen. Home cooking that Adam doesn't recognize. After everything he's been through with getting fired and evicted, he decides he's going to allow himself to be a kid without responsibility today.

"Coming, Mom," he says again before sauntering into the kitchen.

Twenty-One

Days later, Beth seems to be herself again. If any doubts or negative emotions linger over her and Adam having to move in with his mom, she's not showing them... yet.

Yet.

Adam doesn't like that word because it always implies something that hasn't happened yet will happen in the future. Maybe not in the near future, but it will happen. It's only a matter of time.

In this case, he's on edge because he's expecting Beth and his mom to get into a fight again. If one happens, it's going to escalate into a chain reaction of many fights. Adam is like a pair of sharpened shears. As soon as a seedling of an incoming fight sprouts, he's going to snip it clean.

There's no need for that these days, though.

Yet.

Beth is working from his dad's old reading room, which is essentially an office with a comfortable chair, an oak desk, and a bunch of books stacked on shelves. Most mornings, when Adam walks by the reading room, he can hear typing on the keyboard. He doesn't enter because he doesn't want to disturb her. He knows how much focus programmers need when they're coding.

The bed in Adam's room and the one in his parents' bedroom have been swapped. His mom is now sleeping on Adam's old bed while he and Beth get to use the large bed. It fits awkwardly in Adam's old room, and he has no idea how his mom managed to drag such a heavy thing from one room to another, but he prefers not to think about it.

Adam and Beth have added their personal touch to the house because of that. *Please, this house is yours as much as it is mine. I want you to be as comfortable as you can,* his mom had said.

Adam has decorated his old room with trinkets from their previous apartment. Beth has placed Fiona the doll on the desk of the reading room. Since she's sort of a minimalist, it's the only thing she's taken out of the moving boxes.

Beth wakes up before him most days. As a former physics teacher, he used to wake up at 7 to make it to his 8 a.m. classes. Beth usually stayed in bed until well after 9 a.m. Nowadays, Adam wakes up at 8, and Beth is already up and working by then.

Adam had expected things to grow cold between them, but the opposite seems to be true. Beth is just as affectionate as she'd been in their old apartment. His mom isn't stressing her out, and he knows that for sure because he's monitoring the both of them like a hawk.

Maybe his mom has learned the lesson from last time. She hasn't acknowledged her mistake, and knowing her, she isn't the kind of person to apologize for something she did wrong, but Adam is just so glad that things are going okay that he doesn't give a damn about an apology.

To make things better, the rooms in this house are very nicely isolated, so he and Beth don't need to whisper to each other out of fear of being heard. That also means they're able to do other things without having to stifle the sounds coming from their mouths.

Even though it's only been weeks, Adam doesn't talk to John anymore. They exchanged a few messages after he got fired, and that trickled to a stop. Their friendship had been held together by the one thing they had in common—work. Without that adhesive, there was nothing to stop them from drifting apart.

It's a shame because he really likes John. He's a good guy, and Adam considered him more than a coworker. Distance and a lack of common interests wreck most friendships, though. Only the strongest ones survive.

Even though Adam and Beth have been living with his mom for a short time, they're already noticing a difference in their financial situation. Although Beth insists they help with groceries, his mom refuses to accept any money. Even for things like bills, she refuses to take money from them.

"But Mom, there's three of us now. Your bills are way higher. Just let us pitch in a little bit," Adam says.

"No." His mom shakes her head. "While you're here, you're under my care. When you move out to live on your own, you'll have plenty of bills to worry about."

It also helps that they have meals ready, three times a day plus snacks. The food is no longer greasy.

"See? I bought this frying pan that lets me cook food without the use of oil since you said my food has too much fat," his mom says.

It's another one of those comments that Adam can't decipher whether it's passive-aggressive or not, so he chooses to think it's of an innocuous nature.

"Well, at least let us help you somehow," Adam says, reverting to the previous topic.

"Well, if you really want to help me, then throw out that dusty, old abomination that's sitting on your dad's desk."

"You mean Fiona? Beth's doll?"

"You named that grotesque thing?"

"It was given to Beth by someone during her time at..." He doesn't finish the sentence because he hopes his mom will be able to pick up on the hint.

"Oh." His mom raises her eyebrows. "Okay. Well, in that case..." She doesn't finish her sentence, either, but just leaves the room to do her things.

For the first few weeks, Adam and Beth hardly leave the house. Beth is enthralled by her work, and Adam is looking for jobs. After they settle in, Adam suggests they go out more before they start suffering from cabin fever.

They begin taking regular walks at the nearby park every day, and they resume their weekly date nights. The perk of coming back to Casper is the fact that Adam gets to show Beth all the cool places she hasn't seen yet. He enjoys the way her eyes glow when he tells her this was where he went to elementary school, and this is where he bought his first car, and this is where he played with his best friend as a kid.

They did run into one of Adam's old classmates—a guy named Phil who passed middle school with Cs and Ds and often got sent to the principal's office—but they only said hi to each other in passing. No need to stop and pretend they're glad to see each other after all that time, thank God.

When Adam sees in the distance a few more people he recognizes, he starts to feel suffocated by the fact that he and Beth are living there. Not so much that they're living with his mom as that they're living in his hometown.

Casper, Wyoming is one of those places where rumors circulate fast, and if someone gets branded a certain way, they stay that way in the eyes of others until the day they die. There's also a sense of shame over staying in your hometown, at least in Adam's eyes.

Everyone dreams big when they're young. They think about moving away from the familiar and diving into something big and grandiose. Of course, life isn't that kind to many people, and some of them choose to stay surrounded by the things they've known their entire lives.

Still, when Adam sees someone he knew as a kid still living in Casper now that they're an adult, he instinctively wonders what went wrong with them to have to stay.

Were they unable to get a job? Did they care about their future so little that they were okay with working a minimum-wage job and smoking weed every day in their parents' basement? Did something prevent them from leaving, something that may or may not have been within their control?

That's why he inevitably feels embarrassed about himself, too. He's an unemployed former physics teacher living with his mom. There's something far more shameful in going out into the big world and then having to return than never leaving in the first place.

He never tells Beth about any of this. She seems to really like the place. If Adam didn't know any better, he'd think Beth prefers living in the suburbs, close to a smaller city, which is contrary to what he believed about her all these years.

"Do you miss the busy city life?" he asks one day.

She gives him a look of disapproval. "Miss what, exactly? Getting stuck in traffic? High crime rates? Not going five seconds without someone yelling or honking? Besides, I hardly left the apartment anyway, except to buy groceries or take a walk."

"It's really peaceful here, that's for sure. Especially in this neighborhood. I guess I never really paid attention to it when I was a kid because it was the norm. I yearned for the hustle and bustle of cities like New York."

"And did living in the big city fulfill your expectations?"

"It's as terrible as I imagined it to be. And now that I'm getting older and we're preparing to have our own baby, the suburbs are starting to look more and more appealing."

Beth tilts her head. "Are you suggesting what I think you are?"

"I'm not suggesting we stay in this house, don't worry." Adam laughs.

"Maybe living here someday wouldn't be a bad idea. I can see us as a family here. Not just yet, though. Maybe when... maybe in the future."

Adam can read between the lines. *Maybe after your mother dies*, Beth wanted to say. Either way, Adam wouldn't want to live in this house, especially not after his mom is gone. The last thing he wants is for everything to remind him of her. He also doesn't want to stay in his hometown.

When Adam and Beth lived in Portland, life was hectic and rushed, sure, but there was something beautiful about it, too. With such a huge population and the perpetually fast pace, individuals like Adam remained generally invisible in the streets. That translucency made Adam feel less vulnerable. He could watch, but he himself never felt like he was observed under a magnifying glass.

That also meant there was room for mistakes without forever being labeled in any way. If he were single, he could go out to a nightclub every week and approach a dozen different women without worrying about them spreading rumors of his incompetence talking to the opposite sex. He could get blackout drunk and fall asleep in a dumpster with his pants stained with urine and feces and passersby wouldn't bat an eye. He could enter a café and no one would turn their heads, expecting to see someone familiar.

He had his own world, just like every other person in the city had theirs, and everyone minded their own business. That's the kind of environment Adam wants to raise his kid in.

Sure, the child would lose out on the friendliness that comes with the suburbs, but that's what kindergartens, schools, and playgrounds are for.

"I don't think I'd like to live here, Beth," Adam says.

"Wait, really? Why not? I thought you liked it here." Beth looks surprised.

"I like this kind of neighborhood, but not *this* particular one. If we move to a less crowded neighborhood, I want it to be away from this city. A place where we can start with a clean slate."

She smiles. "But you no longer want to live in the city where everything is close?"

"No. I don't think that's a good environment for a child. What about you?"

She shrugs. "It's convenient being close to everything but also frustrating. It's loud, dirty, and the air quality is questionable."

"So you're warming up to the suburbs more and more?"

"Yeah, and if we both want it, it's a good thing because houses in the suburbs are cheaper than apartments in the cities."

"I guess we can agree that we're both changing our views. Maybe it's a good thing we're sitting on the idea of buying a house. Who knows what we'll want a year from now."

"We can go wherever you want to go, babe."

In that moment, he loves her even more for being so understanding. How did he get so lucky with such a loving wife?

He can't keep his hands to himself. He feels as if he's going to implode if he doesn't channel the sudden love he feels so profoundly for her. His mom happens to be out drinking tea with a neighbor, and she'll be gone for hours.

That means Beth and Adam get the whole house to themselves.

****

A week from then, Adam gets a call from an unknown number. He answers, hoping it's one of the schools.

And it is.

"Am I speaking to Adam?" a deep voice on the line asks.

"Yes, that's me."

"I'm Principal Reiner, and I'm calling from Rosewood High School."

Rosewood High School?!

He's applied to dozens of schools and universities since moving in with his mom, and a few of them emailed him back to schedule an online call. The interviews went well, but none of them called back yet.

Just keep applying. One of them is bound to recognize your quality, Beth had told him.

And someone did recognize his potential, it would seem, but Adam is anything but happy. He never applied to Rosewood High, which is the first thing that worries him.

The second thing that worries him is the fact that it's the high school he attended in his hometown when he was a teen.

"We're really impressed with your LinkedIn profile and would like to schedule an interview next week," Principal Reiner says.

Adam remembers Reiner. Even back when he went to school, the principal was an old man. Scrawny, a head so bald it glistened, and thick-rimmed glasses that made his eyes look insectoid. How is it possible that he's still not retired after all this time?

"Are you still there?" Reiner asks, and that prompts Adam to realize he's been silent for some time now.

"I'm sorry, I'm a little surprised is all. I didn't expect to get a call from Rosewood High, especially given how I never applied there," Adam says.

"I apologize for catching you off guard, Adam." *Adam.* Already on a first-name basis. "I remember your name from back when you attended Rosewood, and I noticed you're living in town again. We're in desperate need of a physics teacher, and I always give priority to our own."

He says *our own* as if Adam is already a part of some big cult where everyone watches each other's backs. He's not, and he never will be. He used to attend Rosewood, and that's it.

"You want to hire me to work at the school?" Adam asks. Filler words mostly, just to buy himself time while he thinks about what to say next.

"Yes. And we're willing to negotiate a higher salary than what we usually offer. How does eighty thousand sound? It probably isn't as hefty as your salary as a professor at a university, but given that we're a high school, we can't offer more."

Eighty thousand?!

That's barely below what he got as a professor. He's poised to shout *yes!* to Reiner, but he subdues himself before he can make such a rash decision. The pay is nice, but there are so many caveats here.

First of all, he isn't even looking for a job in this area. He's just staying here for a little bit. Secondly, working at a university, he would be able to get pay raises and earn well over six figures eventually. Thirdly, teaching college students is a lot easier than high school teenagers pumped up on hormones. The pay would be nice, but would it be worth the hassle?

Having been a student of Rosewood High, Adam knows there are many problematic individuals there.

"Mr. Reiner, I am only temporarily in the area. I'm afraid I wouldn't be a good fit for your school," Adam says.

"I see. What if I offered eighty-five thousand?"

Jesus.

It was becoming harder and harder to say no. He couldn't make this decision now. He feels that Beth at least needs to know about it before he says no.

"I have to think about it, Mr. Reiner."

"How long would you need?"

An employer who's rushing for a decision is never good news. It means he's desperate to close a deal before the employee can see the red flags. But Adam knows all about Rosewood High's flaws.

"A few days," Adam says.

"Is until Monday okay?"

What choice does Adam have? If he says no, Reiner will continue pestering him.

"Monday's fine," Adam says.

"Perfect. Thank you, and I'll talk to you on Monday."

The call ends. Adam's head is spinning. Eighty-five thousand as a high school teacher is good. It's better than good. Still, it's all for nothing if he doesn't plan on staying here.

He walks up to the bedroom where Beth is sitting on the bed. Her knees are pressed together, her hands in her lap. She's staring up at Adam.

"Beth, I just got a call from a school and... What's going on?" he asks.

It's not until then that he notices the pregnancy test in her hand. She stands up and hands it over to him. His hands are trembling violently as he takes it from her and looks at the results.

"Babe?" he asks, his voice shaking.

He looks up, and tears are glistening in her eyes. Her lower lip is quivering, and she lets out a sob. Adam hugs her and they both weep, but they are tears of happiness.

Because the test is positive.

Twenty-Two

His mom is ecstatic when she hears the news. She says she'll help even more from now on since Beth needs to take it easy. Beth and Adam decide to celebrate by reserving a fancy restaurant for Friday night. There will be no wine for Beth, unfortunately, but that's the least of everyone's worries.

Adam still can't believe it. He's going to be a dad! Strange as it is, he hasn't thought about parenthood beyond the point of cradling a baby in his arms.

What gender would he like the baby to be? If he has a son, he can do all the things with him that his dad did with Adam. Somehow, he's leaning more toward having a daughter. Someone like Beth. Gentle, kind, and loving. Someone he can raise the way Beth should have been raised so that the child inherits everything good from Beth minus the trauma and baggage.

Beth, on the other hand, wants a boy. She's already talking about the kind of traits she wants him to have, and of course, they're Adam's traits. She wants him to be clumsy like him, but also to be interested in physics and math, and to always look for a solution to a seemingly unsolvable problem.

She's already constructed scenarios in which the boy is a nerd, and he talks to Beth about his favorite cartoons and superheroes. She talks about how, rather than shaming him for his interests as her parents shamed her, she would indulge him and let him be whatever he wants.

They're in the car when she talks about it, and she starts crying. Adam hugs her and asks her why she's so emotional about it.

"It's just, we're gonna have a baby. And we're gonna be better parents than our parents were to us."

It's hard for Adam not to be hit by that statement. He doesn't consider his parents bad. Sure, his mom has her antics, but he thinks she did an excellent job raising him as a capable adult and a gentleman. His dad was a good man, too, and he probably would have complemented Adam's growth as a person if he hadn't died from a heart attack so quickly.

Luckily, Beth doesn't notice Adam's pause, and he's glad because he really doesn't want to get into this discussion. Not now, not later, not ever. If he does, he's going to justify that his parents did nothing wrong, and Beth is going to become defensive, and he strongly wants to avoid any unnecessary drama and anything that will put stress on her and the baby.

When they step out of the car, Adam says, "Hey, I know you can't drink wine tonight, but you can now start eating more food."

"We'll have to check with the doctor and see what he says. Because of my hypertension and all that," Beth says.

"Sure. We have an appointment scheduled for Monday anyway."

Adam suddenly remembers Principal Reiner. He has the weekend to think over his decision. He'd thought he already knew the answer he was going to give him, but after his conversation with Beth, doubts swirl in his mind.

It's only going to be temporary, and it's going to help us save up more money, she had told him.

He had been sure she'd shrug and tell him not to accept the job, so her response took him by surprise. Then again, he should have seen it coming. Now that she's pregnant, they need to get all the help they can, financially and otherwise.

Even his mom told him he should accept the job, but he isn't sure if she's giving him an emotional response or not. For her, it would be perfect because Beth and Adam would be right here.

No more once-a-year visits for the holidays. Instead, they could see each other whenever. On the one hand, Adam would like to be able to let his kid see his grandma once a week, but on the other hand, he doesn't want to stay here.

Both Adam and Beth want to provide their child with the best possible life they can, but if he does accept the job, where's the limit? How long is he going to be working at Rosewood High before they decide it's enough?

When will Beth and Adam sit to go through their finances and say, "Yes, we finally have enough money"? The longer he works for Rosewood High, the more he and Beth are going to stray from the initial goal until it fades out of existence.

Being a high school teacher at Rosewood High will no longer be a temporary job, and moving into a house far away will be forgotten. That's the trap he fears.

The clock is ticking, though. He only has a couple of days remaining. Principal Reiner has made it clear he's in a hurry to hire a teacher, but something tells Adam that, even if he doesn't give him the final answer on Monday, the job opening will still be here for him.

He's trying not to think about it too much. Not now, because he doesn't want his indecision to overshadow the euphoria surrounding Beth's pregnancy, and because the two of them are going to celebrate tonight in the restaurant Adam reserved.

"By the way, I'm thinking of going all in for tonight. I'm going to wear that one fancy dress I wore to Kayla's wedding," Beth says as they climb up onto the porch.

Adam smiles. "I love that dress. It really brings out your bodily features."

"I know you do. Enjoy it while you can because, pretty soon, I won't be able to fit into it anymore."

"I'm fine with that weight gain."

They open the door, and Adam immediately becomes aware of something that causes the smile to drop from his face.

"What's that smell? Is your mom cooking something?" Beth asks.

His mom must have heard them because she waltzes out of the kitchen. She's holding a sauce-stained wooden spoon in her hand. "Hello, children. I hope you're hungry because I'm making spaghetti. It'll be ready in ten minutes."

Adam and Beth exchange a look. Beth gives him a *you tell her* expression.

"Mom, Beth and I are eating out at a restaurant tonight, remember?" Adam asks.

"Really?" his mom asks.

Adam nods, but in his mind, he's wondering how she could not know this when they literally told her yesterday. He'd made the reservations and then went to tell his mom not to make dinner the following day. She even asked him what restaurant they're going to be eating at.

A jab of worry suddenly hits Adam. What if his mom is becoming senile? Maybe everything that had happened back when she lived with them in their apartment wasn't malice but forgetfulness due to old age. Maybe even the broken hip somehow impacted her cognitive capabilities.

"Yes, Mom. I told you about it yesterday," Adam says.

"Oh." The hand that holds the wooden spoon drops to her side. "I already made spaghetti for all three of us. I even made Beth's favorite dessert," she says.

There's a sadness to her voice. Adam suddenly feels sorry for her. He looks at Beth, trying to read her face for a possible solution to this dilemma. Do they bring his mom with them? No, that's not how tonight is supposed to go. Tonight is supposed to be just for Beth and Adam.

"It's all right. I guess I'll put everything away and we can reheat the spaghetti tomorrow." His mom turns to head back into the kitchen, and she suddenly looks a lot more haggard, defeated.

"Sorry, Mom," Adam says.

"No, no. Nothing to be sorry about. I don't want to be a burden to anyone, anyway."

Beth and Adam exchange glances. Adam bites his lip but doesn't say anything. It's Beth who breaks the silence.

"No, wait. We'll eat dinner at home," she says.

His mom turns around. All eyes are now pointed at Beth. Even Adam is surprised.

"No, sweetheart. I don't want to get in the way of your plans," his mom says.

"No, it's fine. We'll call off the reservations. Right, Adam?" Beth looks at Adam for support.

He hesitates before agreeing. "Right."

Although he selfishly wanted tonight to be just for the two of them, he wants to kiss Beth hard for being so considerate. Even if he doesn't agree with Beth, it's already too late to take it back anyway, because his mom has become too excited.

"Really?" she asks. "That's wonderful! I'll set the table."

She turns around but then swivels to face them again.

"Oh, Adam? I went into the reading room, and there's an ugly, old doll in there that we should throw out."

Beth's face turns sour.

"That was a gift from Beth's friend," Adam coldly says.

"It's just collecting dust. You should consider throwing it out," his mom continues, not aware that she might have offended Beth.

It's not the blatant rudeness that bothers Adam. It's the fact that he's already had this conversation with his mom, and now they're having it again as if it's the first time. He once again worries she's becoming senile, but those thoughts are swept away by the continuation of the conversation.

"If it's bothering you, I'll put it back in our bedroom," Beth interjects.

"No," Adam says. "It doesn't bother her. You're the only one who's using the reading room, so no one's going to be bothered by a doll that means the world to you. Besides, my mom said we should make ourselves feel at home."

He looks at his mom for approval. She smiles but doesn't say anything. She disappears into the kitchen, the discussion over. Adam and Beth head upstairs into their room, and Adam asks, "Why'd you do that?"

"I felt sorry for her being all alone," Beth says.

"I just thought tonight was supposed to be about us." Adam is trying to be careful with his words so that he doesn't make Beth feel like what she did is not being appreciated.

He's partly disappointed that they won't get to have a romantic dinner, but he's also glad they'll include his mom. After everything she's done for them, it's the least they can do.

"I know, but she's already made dinner. How about we make it about ourselves tomorrow instead?" Beth asks.

"Okay. I'll call the restaurant," Adam says.

"Did you notice what she said about Fiona?" Beth asks.

"Yeah. I guess she doesn't realize it means a lot to you."

"This is, like, the third time she's mentioned I should throw it out. Only, this time, she was talking to you."

Adam frowns. "Really?"

Beth nods.

"Don't worry about it. As I said, the reading room is yours, babe."

"Adam, maybe your mom doesn't appreciate me using your dad's old room."

"And why would she give a damn about that?"

"Because it's sort of like a memory of your dad."

"I'll talk to her, but she would have said something if it bothered her."

"Okay. But can you please make sure to talk to her, though? I'd hate to come home someday and see that she's thrown Fiona out."

"I will. I promise."

Since they're not going out, Beth doesn't wear the fancy dress, much to Adam's disappointment, which makes him wonder whether they should have gone out after all. This doubt is further exacerbated when he calls the restaurant to cancel the reservation and they tell him they have no available tables for tomorrow. He decides he'll call them back when he speaks with Beth to see what she wants to do.

"Babe, the restaurant is all booked up for tomorrow," he says. "Is there any place else you'd like us to go?"

"Hm. Let's figure it out tomorrow," she says.

When they head downstairs, the table is already set. His mom pulls out a chair to help Beth sit.

"You don't have to do that," Beth says.

His mom waves her off and goes to put spaghetti onto their plates. "Nonsense. You need to be taken care of like a princess. I wish I would have had such a tolerant mother-in-law. But no, Adam's grandmother was very critical of everything I did. I always felt like I had to walk on eggshells with her around."

Adam catches Beth smiling at his mom, but the muscles in her cheeks are too stiff, the upper lip pulled just a little too high. When his mom puts spaghetti on Beth's plate, that facial feature turns into disgust she can't hide.

The oil from the sauce is spreading all over the pasta in a steady trickle of orange. His mom hasn't made anything greasy ever since they moved in, so this is a terrible time to start doing it.

Adam is about to protest, but Beth kicks him under the table. She must be trying to avoid stress, so she's looking for every opportunity where she can skip getting into a conflict.

"Thank you. It looks good," Beth says with a grin.

"Well, you better eat up. Now that you're pregnant, you're going to need to give that baby strength. This is so exciting! Grandma's going to spoil that child to kingdom come."

"Mom..."

"Don't worry, I'm just joking, sweetie. I'll do everything I can to help raise him right. You two still have so much to learn about that, and I'll be here to correct your parenting."

Beth looks horrified at that, and it's as if she and Adam have a moment of telepathic communication. They both want his mom to let them raise their child the way they think is right, and not the way she thinks it is. Adam doesn't correct his mom because he wants to believe she simply misspoke.

No one says anything for a few minutes while they eat. Adam can see Beth moving the meat away and eating the pasta that's not stained too much with sauce grease. He tries to catch her gaze, but even if he does so, how will he communicate to her that she doesn't need to eat his mom's dinner and that they can order something?

"That job offer at Rosewood High couldn't have come at a better time, right?" his mom asks. "It might be rough working there at the start, but you'll manage."

Adam has jabbed the fork into the plate and is spinning it to reel in the spaghetti. He looks up at his mom to read her expression. She's not smirking as he hoped she would, which means she's serious.

"I haven't decided yet whether I'm going to accept the job," Adam says.

"Don't be silly, Adam. Your wife is pregnant, and you're unemployed. Of course you're going to accept the job. It's the mature thing to do. You're going to be a father soon, so you have to start behaving like an adult."

The tone of her voice conveys politeness, but the words couldn't be ruder. Adam waits to see if she's going to correct herself. When she doesn't, he opens his mouth to give her a piece of his mind, but Beth kicks him under the table again.

When he looks at her, he's on the verge of losing his temper. He clenches his jaw so tightly it feels like his teeth are going to break.

"So, how is your hip?" Beth asks his mom, a weak and obvious attempt at changing the topic.

And it works.

His mom starts talking about her visits to the doctors and later on hops to a completely different topic, away from the pregnancy, away from raising Beth and Adam's child, away from Adam's job offer.

Adam is still hung up on what she said earlier, though, and it makes him see something with a sudden clairvoyance that shines through everything.

Living with his mom for too long is going to be impossible.

Twenty-Three

"That's excellent news, Adam. I'm so glad to hear it. You've made the right decision," Principal Reiner says over the phone.

Adam doesn't share in the principal's enthusiasm. He's not sure he's made the right decision. His logic tells him he needs the money, but his gut tells him to stay away from Rosewood High.

"Mr. Reiner, I want to reiterate one thing. I don't intend on working here for too long. I hope you're aware of that. My wife is currently pregnant..."

"Congratulations."

"...and I need to think of what's best for my family. So, if a better opportunity arises, I want you to be aware that I could accept it."

He would never say that to a regular job offer. A part of him is hoping that his antagonistic words will cause Reiner to rethink the offer, effectively taking the choice out of Adam's hands. The principal does no such thing.

"Perfectly understandable, Adam. You've made it clear that you don't intend to stay in Casper for too long. I do want to ask you to at least give us ample time to find a substitute teacher before you give your notice."

"Mr. Reiner, Rosewood High has gone without a physics teacher for how long now? Three months? If it can survive for that long without a substitute, then it can survive when I give my two weeks' notice."

The principal remains silent on the line. Adam is loving this. For the first time in life, he's able to say exactly what's on his mind without the fear of being reprimanded by his superior. Reiner needs him, and that means Adam can bend some rules.

"I'll see you at school tomorrow," the principal says.

That's what I thought.

When the call ends, Adam approaches the reading room and knocks gently on the door. The muffled typing inside stops, and Beth shouts, "Come in!"

Adam opens the door to see Beth sitting at his dad's desk. For a second, he sees not Beth but his dad sitting there, and Adam is no longer an adult but a kid once again. The desk lamp is on, pointed at the open pages of the book he's reading. He used to love reading everything nonfiction: economy, psychology, biographies, etc.

He takes off his glasses, grins at Adam, and says, "Hey, champ. What's up?"

Then Adam blinks, and the flashback is over, and it's Beth sitting at the desk once more. He has to admit she looks elegant in his dad's seat. Maybe a little incongruous with the laptop and the modern clothes because they contrast the antiquated surroundings, but still elegant.

Adam wishes Beth could have met his dad. He would have loved her. He always wanted to have another kid besides Adam. A daughter, his mom had told Adam.

"What's up?" Beth asks, an eerily similar greeting to what his dad would say.

It makes Adam wonder if she's somehow taken on his old man's spirit by being in the office for too long.

"Well, I accepted the job at the high school," he says.

Beth's mouth stretches into a smile. She gets up and approaches Adam. "Baby, that's great!" She hugs him and plants a kiss on his lips. "Wait, just like that? No interview?"

Adam shrugs. "I guess they're desperate to hire someone as soon as possible."

"I'm so proud of you, Adam."

But Adam doesn't reciprocate that. He should be happy that he got a job, but his gut won't stop doing somersaults. Everything about this feels very, very wrong.

Adam puts his hands on Beth's shoulders and gently pushes himself away from her embrace. She looks like she can't conceive why he's pushing her away.

"What's wrong?" she asks.

"I need you to promise me something."

"Okay." Beth gives him a tentative nod.

"If I'm still working at Rosewood High in six months, and if I get too comfortable, I need you to force me to look for something else."

"Babe, why would that be—"

"Beth, please. I really need you to do this. One of us needs to be sober here, and it's gonna be hard for me to be that person. I'm gonna do everything I can to take care of you and the baby. But you need to promise not to let me slide into a routine. I don't want to stay at Rosewood High. I'm... I'm scared of it."

Beth takes a step closer to him. When she sees he won't push her away, she presses her body against his and gently touches his cheek. "Babe, we both want the same thing. I wouldn't want you to be a high school teacher forever, either. Especially not here. This is just temporary until we figure things out."

How many times has Adam heard that sentence? He feels like he might hear those same words six months from now when the deadline he's set for himself expires.

It's only temporary. And then when the child is born, *It's only temporary.*

And that's going to continue indefinitely.

"In exactly six months, we'll see where we stand, and if you're still in Rosewood High, we'll work on something else."

"You promise?"

"I'll set the alarm on my calendar."

The conversation makes Adam feel a lot better about everything. Now that he knows Beth wants—or rather doesn't want—the same thing as him, he can give himself some breathing room. He doesn't need to be in such a cramp about working at Rosewood High.

Not yet, anyway.

He knows quitting is going to be a problem, though. Whether it happens tomorrow, in four weeks, or in six months, it's going to be a tough hurdle to surpass because, not only will he have to worry again about finding a job, but he'll also need to explain to his mom why he no longer wants to work at the high school.

He's being very careful around her, stopping himself from saying anything that might make her think he and Beth are going to stay with her indefinitely. He has a feeling she's got her hopes up about it.

No, having her hopes up isn't the right expression. *Made up her mind* fits it more.

To make matters worse, it isn't long before strife is formed between Beth and his mom again.

Twenty-Four

It starts gradually.

The cooking first. Adam constantly has to remind his mom not to make the food greasy. She apologizes, says it won't happen again, then turns right around and does it anyway.

She criticizes Beth again about her lifestyle and how it's bad for her health and the baby's.

You should go out more. You shouldn't be sitting in the office that long. Your posture is bad. You need more of this food or that. You should be more physically active because it's good for the baby. You need to throw out all your old clothes because you're a married woman.

Although she never outright says it, there's an undertone to her words that clearly sends the message she thinks Beth is mentally weak. She'll do it by asking her if she went to the psychiatrist and if she considered booking an appointment just to make sure everything is okay with the baby.

At least, there's no criticism about her not doing anything around the house this time. Adam wants to talk to his mom a few times, but Beth stops him. Whenever he's about to do it, she retracts what she said and tries to convince Adam she isn't bothered by his mom's comments.

That's not true, and it's visible even at a distance because Beth soon starts asking Adam how much longer they're going to be living with his mom. He tells her he's still waiting for employers from other schools to call him back, and she keeps reminding him that they can't live with his mom when the baby is born.

He knows that, of course, but his hands are tied. Right now, he doesn't want to live in the same house as his mom any more than she does.

Then, one day, after work at Rosewood High (He has been working there for the past three weeks), he stops at a shop to buy a beret for Beth. Even though she never mentioned she wanted it, he saw her eyeing it whenever they walked past the shop.

When Adam returns home, he hears cooking in the kitchen. He assumes Beth is working upstairs, so he heads up to the reading room. He doesn't hear typing on the keyboard, but he knocks nonetheless. There's no response.

Adam opens the door, but Beth isn't there, and the laptop sits open on the desk. He approaches the bedroom and is about to open the door when he hears something that makes him freeze.

A whimper.

Immediately, he thinks of the worst possible thing. Something has happened to the baby. A miscarriage maybe? Some complications? Oh God, what are they going to do if the baby has died?

Despite the irresistible urge to barge inside and demand answers, he gently opens the door so as to not startle Beth. She's sitting on the bed, wiping her tears with crumpled paper tissues. The excitement that had held Adam up until then about showing Beth the beret fades out of existence.

"Beth?" Adam softly calls out.

She only just then becomes aware of his presence and quickly wipes her tears.

"Oh... I didn't hear you come in," she says as if pretending everything's okay would make the problems go away.

Adam sits next to Beth. He puts one hand on her back, the other on her thigh. "What happened, babe? Is it the baby?"

He doesn't mean to sound so impatient, but it comes out of him before he can stop himself.

Beth shakes her head. A stone falls off of Adam's chest. *Oh, thank God.* If it's not the baby, then whatever it is can't be as bad. He feels ashamed for thinking that way, but ever since Beth got pregnant, his top priority has been ensuring that Beth and the baby are okay. Everything else is secondary.

Beth's lips quiver. She lets out a sob, and Adam starts stroking her back with more vigor. He doesn't ask her what's wrong. She needs a moment to compose herself, and then she'll tell him.

She blows her nose and stares ahead of herself. Her eyes are red-rimmed, her cheeks puffy. She doesn't move or say anything for well over a minute. During that time, Adam sits with her in silence, gently running his hand up and down her thigh and back.

"What happened, Beth?" he asks again.

She turns her head toward him. Her lip trembles again, but she manages to utter one sentence.

"She threw Fiona out."

For a moment, Adam enters a vacuum. He doesn't feel a thing, and he doesn't know what he's supposed to feel. Beth is crying as if a living person has died when it's just a stupid doll. A part of him wants to say to Beth not to scare him like this again.

It all lasts for merely a modicum of a second before he comes to his senses. Beth is crying because, number one: her hormones are spiked because of the pregnancy, and number two: that doll meant a lot to her. It was a special gift from Sarah during the darkest period of her life.

And now, she's gone. Adam can't help but feel like a small part of Beth is gone with it, too.

The relief that had manifested for the briefest moment has disappeared, replaced by irritation and a strong desire for answers.

"My mom? She threw Fiona out?" Adam asks.

He finds it strange how both he and Beth are referring to the doll by her name as if it were a real person.

Beth nods.

"When did this happen?" Adam asks.

"When I went into the office today to start working, I noticed Fiona wasn't there. I looked around the floor and she wasn't there, so I went to ask your mom about it, and she..." Beth's voice trails into a high-pitched octave before she continues, "She said she threw it out."

"She threw it in the trash?"

Beth nods.

Adam stands up. "Okay. I'll just go look for it in the garbage. I'll find her, Beth."

"You can't," Beth says. "She threw it out last night, and the garbage truck already took the trash away."

She buries her face into her hands and sobs. Adam returns to the bed and holds his wife while she cries. The entire time, he's angry, though. He's already planning a speech in his mind that he's going to deliver to his mom. He's going to make sure this never happens again.

"Why don't you get some sleep, Beth? You need some rest," Adam says.

"I'm not tired," Beth says.

"Just lie down for a few minutes, okay? I'll be here in a bit."

"You're going to talk to your mom, aren't you?"

He doesn't know if he should lie or not. He's fast-forwarding both options in his head. If he tells her the truth, she might try to dissuade him from talking to his mom and causing a problem. If he says no, Beth might see through his lie and get angry that he's being dishonest with her.

"Yes. I'm going to talk to her," he says.

Surprisingly, she doesn't complain about that. She just says *okay* and lays her head on the pillow. He plants a kiss on her forehead, pulls the covers over her, and when he exits the bedroom and closes the door behind him, Beth's crying resumes.

****

"Mom, can I talk to you for a moment?" Adam asks.

His mom is in the kitchen, running from one end of the counter to another as she chops vegetables, seasons the meat that's cooking, and stirs the potatoes in boiling water.

"Sure, sweetie. What is it?"

Adam sighs. He had an entire dialogue planned out in his mind, counter-arguments included, but that was when he was angry. Right now, all he feels is an eerily familiar sense of tension as he fumbles to find the right words that won't offend his mom.

"You made Beth cry," he finally says.

"Oh?" His mom gives him one brief, compulsory glance before turning her attention back to the kitchen.

The fact that she's doing all of that when he wants to have a conversation with her is causing that rage to stir inside him once again.

"Why did you throw out... the doll?" He almost said Fiona before correcting himself.

"That tattered old thing? Honey, it was dirty, and it was collecting dust. Do you know how bad that is for one pregnant woman? I did Beth a favor."

"That's beside the point, Mom. That doll meant the world to Beth. It held memories that she cherished. And you went behind her back and you threw it out after she specifically asked you not to."

"I don't remember that."

"Yes, you do. You can't keep playing that card forever, Mom. I know you think you know best, but you make mistakes, too."

His mom glances at him briefly, but if she agrees with him on any of the points he's made, she's not showing it. The reticent stare tells Adam he's talking to a wall, and that only further angers him.

"Mom," he insists. "There's no way of fixing what you did here, but I want you to apologize to Beth."

His voice is drowned out by the sound of onions being cut on the chopping board.

"If Beth feels sad, she should probably go to the doctor. It's not good for the baby to be under stress," she says coldly.

The reason why she's stressed in the first place is because of you! Adam wants to scream, but he stops himself.

No matter how wrong his mom is, she's his mom, and he and Beth are in her house. She took them in when they had nowhere to go. But does that mean they have to put up with her crap?

Absolutely not.

"Mom, don't do this, please."

Not again.

"Honey, I really have a lot of work to do right now. Can we please talk about this another time?"

His mom couldn't care less. A sense of déjà vu overcomes Adam, causing his stomach to twist into knots.

"Fine," he angrily says as he strides out of the kitchen.

But there won't be another time because, just like with his job, he's setting clear goals. The next time something like this happens, he's going to pack his and Beth's things, and they're going into a motel.

Twenty-Five

Classes are slow today. Adam is teaching inertia and is writing down formulae on the blackboard, but it feels like he's talking to a wall.

The only reason the classroom is not booming with murmurs of inattention is because Adam has taught the students there will be consequences for talking. As a teacher, it's very important to set yourself as a figure of authority but also someone who's there to help. Overextend the kindness, and it's bound to be abused.

It's something that constantly needs to be refreshed, unfortunately, because high schoolers are perpetually testing those limits. Luckily, Adam has a simple method that he learned from his own physics teacher back when he was in high school.

When the students start talking too much, he raises a hand and starts furling finger by finger as a countdown. Someone in the classroom always picks up on it and tells the others to be quiet. He's never reached less than two fingers.

He does have a plan in case the countdown ever reaches zero. He would randomly pick one student for an impromptu oral presentation to make an example of them. Harsh? Maybe, but high schoolers sometimes need a little brute force.

Funny enough, Adam never had to use the countdown method at the university. Unlike high school, there's no obligation in college. If you want to sleep in and skip the classes, it's your right to do so. You're the one paying for college, and that itself is a big enough incentive for most students. The voluntary attendance also eliminates the chances of rebellion.

Adam misses teaching at his old job. Not only did he get to teach the things he actually loves teaching, but the students were a lot more interested in the subject.

Not only that, but they also appreciated his effort a lot more than high schoolers. Students would often approach him after class with additional questions and to thank him for the comprehensive explanation. A few times, female freshmen were flirtatious with him. Of course, he never responded to such remarks, but the gesture inflated his ego.

After he got fired from the university, he received a bevy of emails from students expressing their sadness that he'd no longer be teaching there. These ungrateful high schoolers never would have done that. If he got killed, they'd celebrate it.

Once the bell rings, the students start packing their bags and hurriedly rushing out of the classroom. Adam gives them one final reminder that there's a test due on Monday, but only a few of them are listening—the ones who are sitting in the front row and religiously taking notes on everything.

Those are the students that carry the weight of the entire class, Adam thinks. They remind the others what's for homework and when the next assignment is due, and they're the first ones to raise their hands and answer the teacher's questions correctly.

Adam heads into the break room to get coffee and eat a bagel. He sits, and just when he's about to take the first bite, his phone starts ringing.

Frustrated, he answers.

And the conversation has him sitting on the edge of his seat.

****

Adam comes home from work to hear screaming even before he opens the door. The moment he steps inside, his eardrums hurt from Beth's shouting. She's standing in the middle of the living room, gesturing vigorously with her arms while screaming profanities. His mom is staring at her with a cold face, shaking her head.

"What's going on?" Adam asks. He hardly hears his own voice over Beth's shouting.

Beth hadn't noticed him until then. When she sees him, she doesn't stop yelling at his mom.

"You're a horrible fucking human being! You're disgusting!"

"Beth. Beth!" Adam puts a hand on Beth's shoulder.

He knows it's a risky move right now, but it's the only thing he can think of to calm Beth down.

She's completely red in the face. Tears are streaking her cheeks, and despite the volcanic anger, her voice is shaking, and her gasps are audible. Adam has never seen her like this.

He and Beth have had their share of fights, but the worst it's ever gotten was Beth snapping at Adam by raising her voice a little and calming back down right after. Most commonly, if she gets angry at him, she does so in a slow-cooking way: She gives him the cold shoulder and refuses to talk to him.

The Beth standing in front of him right now is one who's yelling so hard that thick veins on her neck are bulging like snakes, and her voice sounds like it's going to go hoarse from all the strain...

His mom, on the other hand, looks cool as a cucumber. She's shaking her head at Beth in disagreement, occasionally uttering a word like "no" or "honey," but she's not losing her temper. That's at least one person Adam doesn't have to worry about.

Never having been in that situation, Adam doesn't know how to react or what to do, but his instinct tells him to talk to the one who's lost control of herself.

"Beth!" he shouts and squeezes her shoulder.

Finally, Beth seems to become aware of Adam's presence. She ends her shouting marathon with a final "you goddamn bitch" before turning away from his mom and storming upstairs, slamming the door shut behind her.

Awkward silence fills the house. It's so deafeningly quiet that Adam becomes aware of the heartbeat drumming in his chest.

He looks at his mom and asks, "What happened, Mom?"

His mom shakes her head. "Oh, Addy. She just lost it all of a sudden. It's a good thing you arrived when you did."

Adam is waiting for the rest of the explanation, but it doesn't come. His mom is just staring at him with that same calm expression on her face as if what just happened was nothing more than a minor inconvenience.

She has just upset his pregnant wife and is acting indifferent about it. The day that had started so well can quickly turn sour, but he's determined not to allow that to happen.

"When you say she lost it, what exactly do you mean by it?" Adam asks.

She shrugs. "I mean just that. She lost it."

There's something his mom is not telling him. He knows it all too well from prior experience. Adam knows that, the longer he stands here talking to his mom, the more time he's losing with Beth. He should be in there, consoling her.

He still wants to hear his mom's side, though. He has to know what she'll say versus what Beth will tell him. He's already made up his mind, though. He's going to take Beth's side.

"Mom, Beth doesn't just *lose it* out of nowhere. You must have said something to her that upset her."

He knows it sounds accusatory, but the spur of the moment is carrying him, and he doesn't care about tiptoeing around his mom right now.

"I think she's just sensitive these days. Pregnancy and all that. Hormones can make a woman crazy." She chuckles.

The way she says it all makes it seem like the fight with Beth didn't happen just seconds ago.

"Mom. Beth is pregnant. She doesn't need the stress," Adam says.

"Then tell her not to stress," his mom says as if it's the most obvious solution in the world.

Adam doesn't have time to argue with his mom right now. Beth is probably crying, and if he doesn't go up there to console her, she's going to remember it as the time he chose his mom over his wife—when she was pregnant.

Without saying another word, Adam climbs upstairs and enters the bedroom. He closes the door and locks it. Beth is sitting on the bed, her face buried in her hands, her shoulders shuddering. He's never seen her like this. He's seen her cry, and it was always soft crying: Tears silently sliding down her cheeks and an occasional sniffle.

Whatever this is, it's unprecedented, and Adam can only hope he knows his wife enough to be able to make her feel better.

"Baby…" he says as he sits next to her.

He doesn't behave around her like she's a wild animal that requires caution. Instead, he pulls her into a hug and holds her tightly. She lets him.

Good.

"Shhh," Adam says as he's stroking her back.

She cries harder, her shoulders bouncing with each gasp. He runs his fingers through her hair, pulling it back from her face wet with tears.

"It's okay, baby," he coos.

As much as he wants to know her side of the story, now's not the time. His plans to ask Beth about it once she's calmed down go down the drain when she suddenly pulls away from him. He's able to look at her face for the first time since entering the bedroom. It's ruddy, her eyes glistening with tears.

"I can't do this anymore, Adam. I can't." Her voice is shrill.

Adam puts a hand on her thigh. "Tell me what happened, honey."

Beth wipes the tears from her face, sniffles, and takes some time to regain her composure. Adam doesn't urge her. His eyes keep drifting sneakily to the door. He dreads hearing his mom knocking on the door or saying something like *dinner's ready*.

"She started insulting me again," Beth says with a cracked voice.

"Okay. Why don't you tell me more about it?"

Beth takes another moment to collect her thoughts. "She just always has these comments about me. She's stopped saying I'm lazy, but now she keeps telling me how I'm going to need to change in order to become a better mother."

"And what did she tell you today that upset you so much?"

Beth hesitates for a moment. "She said she's worried about the baby."

"Why?"

"Because... because of my past. She thinks the baby might not be right because of what I've been through and... that we should be worried about the baby being mentally sick like me."

Adam's eyes widen. "She said that?"

"Yes, Adam. In those words. She's hinted at it many times in the past, but this is the first time she's actually called me mentally sick. I can't go through this again, Adam. Not now when I'm pregnant."

"I know. I know. That's why I need you to be patient for just a little longer."

"How much longer?"

"Just a little longer, until we find an apartment in Portland, because I got a job there."

Beth looks at him in confusion. When she sees his smile, her own lips stretch into a beam.

"Baby, congratulations!" She hugs and kisses him.

They spend a few minutes rejoicing, and then Adam says, "We just need to survive with my mom until we can find an apartment. Can you do that for me and our baby?"

Beth nods vigorously. "I'll start looking right away."

"Good. And I'm gonna go have a talk with my mom."

Beth doesn't stop him this time. She's probably as fed up with her as Adam is. Beth's emotions have always been important to Adam, but now they're even more pivotal because everything that Beth experiences, the baby is going to experience, too.

Twenty-Six

"You're moving back?" his mom asks.

She's sitting in the living room. Adam is standing close by with his hands in his pockets, mostly just to prevent fiddling with things when the conversation becomes too awkward.

"Yeah," Adam says.

His mom stares at the screen of the TV a while longer, but he knows she isn't seeing anything on it.

"And you're going to quit your job at Rosewood High?" she asks.

"Yes."

"I don't think that's a good idea. You have a stable job here. Why would you squander it all by going into something that might not be as safe?"

"The college I'll be working at will be paying me six figures. Besides, I already talked to the principal at Rosewood about it and gave him my two weeks."

"You'll be spending more money there since it's a bigger city. Aren't you and Bethany happy that you're able to save up money living here?"

Adam frowns. He didn't expect this conversation to happen so soon, and he hasn't prepared for it. Talking to his mom about quitting at Rosewood High is harder than talking to Principal Reiner.

His mom's facial expression tells him everything. Despite constantly reminding her he and Beth would be moving out, she somehow convinced herself that they'd stay with her. A foolish thing to believe in, but his mom never listened to anyone but herself anyway.

"Mom, you knew this was going to happen. We talked about this. Remember?" Adam asks.

"I know, Addy. I guess I just didn't think it would happen so soon," she says. "I got used to having company, and I guess I'll need time to get used to living alone again."

Oh no. The victim card isn't going to work this time. Adam saw it coming a mile away. He's been preparing specifically for it and chose the best possible response he could think of.

Ignoring.

"Beth and I are going to start looking for apartments today. I don't know how long it's going to take, but I start working next month, so we have until then."

His mom doesn't say anything else, and he feels like it's a bad time to scold her about Beth, so he turns around to leave.

"You're becoming more and more like your father, Addy," she says.

Adam has climbed one step of the stairs, but he turns around when his mom says that.

"What?" he asks.

She's watching the TV. "Nothing."

Adam walks back into the living room. "No, what did you mean by that?"

His mom ignores him. He's about to repeat the question when she grabs the remote and turns off the TV. She crosses her arms and looks at Adam.

"He was making lots of bad financial decisions back when he was your age."

The sentence hits Adam out of the blue, so he spends a moment processing what she said. He finally asks, "What?"

"I was pregnant with you, and your dad was investing in all these supposedly promising businesses that failed, one after another. He was well on his way to depleting our entire savings account."

"Mom, what are you talking about? What Dad did is nothing like what I'm doing here. I'm creating a better life for my family."

"He thought he was doing the same."

"I work at a university as a physics professor. Dad splurged your money on shady businesses that promised easy cash. You can't even begin to compare the two."

One side of his mom's mouth twists into a lopsided smile. "He, too, was really stubborn."

Adam can see the words bouncing off of his mom, no matter how logical his answer is. She brings up a discussion without any intention of listening to the other person's points.

And how dare she? How *fucking* dare she bring his dad into this? Adam's dad may not have been a perfect man, but he was the best father Adam could have asked for. He was a better father than she's ever going to be a mother.

If he were here now, he'd not only support Adam's decision to move but also give them some money to get started on their new life, even if it was the last $100 he had.

His mom is the polar opposite. Instead of supporting his plans and dreams, she's holding him back just so she won't be alone.

Since arguing will make no difference, Adam decides to change gears. "I'm sorry, what exactly are you trying to do here, Mom? Why are you mentioning this? Why bring Dad into all of this?"

"Why are you getting so upset, Adam?" his mom asks.

Adam lets his emotions take over. "No, you don't get to do this. You don't get to say something hurtful and then pretend like I'm the crazy one for getting upset."

"Who says I do that?"

"You do, Mom. You did it to me all my life, and you're doing it to Beth. You can't just go around saying whatever the fuck you want to say without considering the implications of your words."

The F word causes his mom to squint momentarily. "Adam! Language!"

Despite the seriousness of the conversation, cussing is what she's concerned about the most.

"Beth is my wife. And I won't let you bully her," Adam says.

"I never said anything to Bethany." Denial, once again.

"You called her mentally sick. You told her we should be concerned about our child being like her."

"I never said that."

But Adam isn't listening. "What the fuck is wrong with you to say something like that? Beth is pregnant. Do you think she needs that stress right now?"

"I think Bethany is overreacting."

Adam exhales. He stares at his mom for a prolonged moment. He's waiting to see if she's going to start laughing, to indicate this is all just a bad joke.

She doesn't.

"You're unbelievable, you know that?" he asks.

"You know what I think? I think you and Bethany are two ungrateful brats. That's what I think."

Adam freezes. He can't believe she just said that.

"I take you into my home when you need it the most, and this is how you repay me. You should be ashamed of yourselves."

"Mom, we're grateful that you let us stay with you, but that doesn't give you the right to treat us like animals."

"Everything I do is for you and Bethany, and you treat me like I'm some kind of a monster. That's the thanks I get for helping you out?"

It's no use. Now that she's become defensive, it's going to be even harder to talk to her. There's only one thing Adam can do, and it's something he should have started doing a long time ago. He shuts himself off to become emotionally unavailable to his mom. If he does that, her words won't be able to hurt him.

He can't end the conversation without telling her one final thing, though. Something that, he hopes, is going to at least give her food for thought.

"I want you to understand one thing, Mom. You are not my main family anymore. My main family is Beth and the baby we're going to have. I know you don't like that, but I have a life of my own to build now. You need to learn to do the same for yourself without being so attached to me."

She doesn't answer, which gives him ample time to leave the room. Despite the guilt, he can't help but feel good about saying those things.

Twenty-Seven

It isn't long before Beth finds a suitable apartment for her and Adam. It's close to the university where Adam will be working. Finally, things are falling into place.

When Adam tells his mom about it, she seems neither disappointed nor happy. She goes into the kitchen, and a few minutes later, she announces they should host a baby shower before they move back to Portland. Beth and Adam are dumbstruck. They tell her it's still too early for a baby shower and that they want to do it right by inviting everyone they care about, but as usual, she shakes her head and dismisses their wishes.

"It's not going to be a shower. It's just a little party to announce Beth's pregnancy and to give her some gifts and well wishes," she says.

"That's literally the definition of a baby shower," Adam says, but his words fall on deaf ears. That doesn't stop him from trying. "Beth's comfort is the most important thing here, Mom. If she doesn't want to attend a party, we shouldn't make her. Stress is bad for the baby; you said so yourself."

"Nonsense. Everyone loves parties and being the center of attention. Bethany's going to love it," his mom says.

"Mom, we just told you we don't want this. Why can't you just listen to us for once?"

"She's going to change her mind when she meets some of the people at the party. It was like that for me."

"Beth isn't like you, Mom."

"Addy, I have to make a call to your Aunt Gertrude to let her know about the party. We'll talk later." She's already placed the phone up to her ear and, before Adam can say anything, his mom says, "Gertrude? Hi! How are you?"

Adam leaves the living room and climbs up the stairs. It occurs to him that he and Beth don't even need to show up to the party. That would be a very nice middle finger to everyone, but especially his mom. That might be exactly what they need to do so she would understand how much they don't want the party.

Adam remembers how his mom forced him to go to prom night even though he begged her not to go.

It's something that happens only once in your life, Addy. You have to see it through to the end, she had told him.

Adam ended up going, and since he went alone, he also left earlier. Pretty much as soon as the dancing started, he was out of there. When the school delivered the CD with the recorded event burnt into it, he tossed it into the fireplace because that's how much he hated remembering going there.

It was his mom's desire for him to go there, not his, and she allowed herself to be carried by the skepticism of what the townsfolk would say about Adam when they found out he was the only one who didn't go.

Years later, he kept mentioning in passing how he hated prom night and how, despite his mom's warnings that he would regret not going, he regretted obeying her.

He never received an apology from her.

Right now, skipping the baby shower is his own desire, but he knows Beth would want the same thing. At the same time, something is stopping him from doing so. Even with all his bitterness at the memory of prom night, he doesn't want to hurt his mom or leave a bad impression on the relatives.

He wonders if it's just indoctrination.

Either way, his wife's well-being far outweighs the opinions of his mom's relatives. That's why he plans on asking Beth what she would do if there weren't any consequences to their actions.

And then they're going to do exactly that.

****

"Beth, are you sure?" Adam asks.

Beth nods. "It's just going to be a small party. How many people could there possibly be?"

"You have no idea how many relatives my mom has. I'm surprised we don't have to attend all those birthdays like John. And yet somehow, none of them showed up when she broke her hip and needed help. Some family."

Beth lays her head in Adam's lap. "You worry too much about me, babe. I'll be okay."

"I'm just trying to protect you."

"Me or the baby?"

"Both. Listen, you really don't need to go to the party if you don't want to. Who cares what others will say? It's not like we'll ever see them again."

"Sure, but it will mean the world to your mom."

"What she wants is irrelevant, Beth. What *you* want is the only thing that matters."

He's staring down at her, admiring her beauty. He can't tell if he loves her more now that he knows she's carrying his child or if pregnancy has somehow done wonders to her skin.

"I want to go to the party," Beth says.

Adam sighs. "If that's what you really want, we'll do that. But you have to promise you won't be a people pleaser there. If at any point you start to feel uncomfortable, you have to tell me, and I'll kick them all out."

Beth laughs. "It'll be okay. I'm sure these people know they need to be gentle with a pregnant woman."

"Fine," Adam says, but he's not happy with Beth's answer one bit, mostly because he doesn't want his mother to have her way like she's had her entire life.

****

More people showed up to the party than Adam would have expected. He recognizes some of the people from his childhood. The unfamiliar ones come to him and present themselves as aunt this or neighbor that, and he pretends he remembers them just to end the conversation.

The house is booming with the voices of the guests who are cheerfully chatting with each other while holding drinks in their hands. Beth and Adam stand isolated in the corner of the living room. She has a glass of apple juice in her hand. Adam is drinking OJ to make her feel more included.

Although Beth is the star of the show, Adam feels as though she's utterly invisible, save for the few guests who would approach to congratulate her. Really, the true star of the show tonight is his mom. Everyone seems to be buzzing around her as if she's the one who's going to give birth and not Beth, and Adam wonders if the main purpose of this party is so that his mom can feel important.

Is she at least bragging about being a future grandmother? That's supposed to be the whole point of the party, isn't it?

Adam looks at Beth every now and again, trying to determine if she wants to leave the party. They can go to their room, sure, but these guests are too loud for privacy, despite the house being so big. If they want to ditch the party, they'll have to get out of the house entirely and stay out until the commotion's over.

At one point, he openly asks her if she's still okay, to which she nods.

"Your mom really seems to be enjoying herself," Beth says.

His mom is standing in the middle of the living room with a glass of wine in her hand, jovially talking about something while surrounded by other women. It's mostly women at the party.

"I think I'm gonna get some cake," Beth says.

She leaves just in time, too, because a few moments later, Adam sees an overweight woman with garishly red lips waddling toward him. She's staring right at him, grinning with a set of teeth so white they practically glow. She has a large wine glass filled almost to the brim.

Since their eyes have met, he can't pretend he doesn't see her and run out of the room to avoid a conversation. So, he just stands there, waiting for the large woman to cross the distance and talk about how she used to pinch his cheeks when he was a toddler.

"Oh, hello, Adam," she says. "Do you remember me?"

Now that she's this close, he can hardly breathe because of the perfume that emanates from her.

"Uh..." He wants to say yes just so he can skip that part, but if she tests him, it's going to be an awkward situation. "No, I don't."

"It's Isabella." She says it with such passion that Adam thinks he's expected to go *Oh, Isabella! Of course I remember you!*

"Sorry." He shakes his head.

The woman takes a huge sip of red wine. Lipstick coats the rim of the glass. "I visited your family a few times when I was flying out from Germany. You were still a baby back then."

Adam has no idea how Isabella expects him to remember her when he was a baby when he last saw her. He nods, but he's looking toward Beth, who's standing in front of the table with the array of cakes on it. Two women jostle past her while chatting like she isn't even there while they're talking to each other.

"I used to bring lots of presents just for you. Lots of clothes, lots of toys. You were the cutest little baby ever, you know that?" Isabella keeps chirping between slurps.

Adam nods and smiles, but he doesn't know what to say. A spark of a lighter in the middle of the living room catches his attention. He turns his head in time to see his mom lighting up a cigarette.

His eyes widen. Isabella's voice fades into the background, and his mom's obnoxious laughter increases in volume until it's the only thing he can hear. Seeing how the host of the party has lit up a cigarette, the women around her follow her example and do the same.

Meanwhile, Isabella's voice is still drumming, her meaty hands gesturing vigorously while she's talking between almost compulsive sips. Adam brushes past her while she's still talking, not bothering to apologize for the rude interruption.

His eyes are fixated on his mom as he strides across the living room. When he reaches her, he snatches the cigarette from her hand while she's mid-conversation. Her sentence is interrupted, and she turns her head to Adam in surprise.

Adam's initial plan was to slap her hand so hard the cigarette fell out of it, but he didn't want to cause a bigger scene than needed.

"Addy," his mom says in pure shock.

Adam has picked up a cake-stained plate that's been sitting on the table nearby and proceeds to crush the cigarette into it. He doesn't even need to take the cigarettes from the other women. Presenting the plate is enough for them to start stubbing their smokes themselves.

When all the cigarettes are snuffed out, he puts the plate back down and whirls around to face his mom.

"What the hell do you think you're doing?!" he asks furiously.

Gasps fill the room. His mom blinks. She looks taken aback.

"Smoking when Beth is pregnant? Really? What the hell is wrong with you?"

"It's just one cigarette, Adam. The house is big," his mom says.

The women around join in to support his mom.

"A little smoke won't hurt the baby."

"I smoked all the time when I was pregnant, and look at my Jimmy. He's just fine."

"We're keeping an eye on the smoke so it doesn't go in Beth's direction."

It isn't until Adam shouts, "Stay out of this!" that the women go quiet and he's able to focus on his mom.

"You're overreacting, Addy." His mom shakes her head and even adds a wave of the hand to the sentence to complete the dismissal.

Even now, when she's caught red-handed doing something she shouldn't, she's dismissive about it and refuses to take responsibility. This may be her house, but he's not going to tolerate this kind of behavior, especially since it is endangering his wife and child.

He's about to announce the party's over and everyone can go home when Aunt Gertrude says, "Honey, why don't you relax?" Her voice is like a broken siren. "Why don't you have some of your mom's cake? The almond cake is absolutely amazing."

Adam opens his mouth, but his words die on his tongue because of Aunt Gertrude's last sentence. His eyes dart to the plate in her hand. The cake she's eating is almost entirely gone, but he can see the leftovers. There's no way to tell what kind of cake it is because the colors are too uniformly brown.

Everything seems to play out in slow motion as his head snaps toward the cake table. Beth isn't there. He jerks his head to the spot where they stood just moments ago, and there she is, holding a plate. She's stabbing a piece of cake on the fork and bringing it to her mouth.

Adam breaks into a sprint across the room. His shoulder whacks into one of the ladies, and she falls over with a shrill cry. Beth sees Adam running right at her, and her face contorts into one of confusion. The fork with the piece of cake is lowered onto the plate.

He doesn't take the plate from her or tell her not to eat it. The moment he's close enough, he slaps the plate so hard the impact makes him think he broke a finger. The plate flies across the room, right toward Isabella, who's standing near the drinks table and refilling her glass. She never sees the plate coming.

Cake spatters her white dress, a brown splotch appearing right in the middle of her round belly. She drops both the wine glass and bottle with a loud gasp. They shatter on the floor and spill red liquid everywhere.

More loud gasps of shock. Although he's not looking at her right now, Adam can imagine his mom's shocked facial expression. He knows right away that these crones will be talking about this for years to come. There's something satisfactory about it.

"Adam!" his mom shouts. "Oh, Isabella."

Isabella is still standing flabbergasted, staring at the stain on her dress. She looks like she's about to start crying. His mom and the other women rush in to assess the damage like Isabella's a toddler who just fell off a bike.

Aunt Gertrude starts wiping the stain with a napkin. It does nothing but further smear it. His mom gives Adam a stern look, but he's not sorry, and he's doing his best to let her know that with his facial expression.

After the initial few gasps and murmurs about the stain coming off with a good wash and some baking soda, there's a deafening silence in the room. The stillness gives way to a sense of victory. Crisis averted, day saved.

That moment is short-lived when Beth calls out to him.

"Adam..." Beth says, and the single word sounds stifled.

He turns to her to see her face twisting in pain. She's growing red in the face.

"I'm not..." she starts before getting interrupted by a coughing fit.

"Oh shit." Adam runs up to his wife.

The women are now starting to question what's wrong with Beth and if she's okay.

"Oh, Bethany is fine. She's just overreacting." His mom waves dismissively and turns back to the stain on Isabella's dress.

But Beth doesn't look good at all. She's turning red in the face, her eyes filling with tears.

She opens her mouth and manages to utter one sentence in a quick breath. "I'm not feeling well."

That's when she starts gasping and clawing at her throat.

Twenty-Eight

"Hold on, Beth! Just hold on!" The words have become a mantra in the past few minutes of speeding down the road.

Beth is in the passenger's seat, gasping for air. Adam is glancing at the road every couple of seconds, just long enough so that they don't crash. He's keeping an eye on Beth's worsening condition.

The gasps have become shallower, less vigorous. At one point, she looks like she's about to fall asleep.

"Beth, stay with me!" Adam says. "Please, baby. Please be okay. Please, please, please. I don't want you to..."

The word *die* is in his mind, but he refuses to entertain it.

He must have run every red light in the town before pulling up in front of the ER. Beth has stopped gasping for air. Her head is slumping forward, her eyes closed.

No, no, no, no!

Even before he opens the door on his side, paramedics are pouring out of the building to see what's going on.

"My wife's having an allergic reaction!" he shouts the moment he steps out.

It's all them from here. They get Beth out of the car, put her on a stretcher, and rush her inside while talking in medical terms to each other.

Adam runs after them, trying to follow the conversations, but he doesn't understand much of it. He hears the word "pregnant," and he doesn't know how they know about it. He must have been lucid enough to tell them at one point, but he doesn't remember when.

When they rush her inside one of the rooms, he's stopped from following.

"Sir. We'll do what we can for your wife, but you need to let us do our job," one of the medics says.

Adam is too distraught to argue. He nods passively and takes a seat in the waiting room per the instruction of the medic.

Minutes pass, and the adrenaline that had held its clutches firmly on him starts to subside, making room for the terrible thoughts that had been masked by the survival instinct.

What if Beth dies? What if this is the end for her? It can't be. Their life is just about to begin with their baby.

The last moments of the party replay in his mind over and over, forcing him to relive it as his own, personal hell.

Beth, standing in the isolated spot of the living room, the plate of cake in her hand. A confused expression as she watches Adam sprinting at her. Her face growing increasingly red as she starts choking. The horrified looks on everyone's faces as he rushes Beth out of the house and toward the car.

But not all faces were horrified. Now that he replays it for the millionth time, he knows that. One face remained unchanged the entire time. One person he thought he knew so well, only to be very, very wrong about her.

His mom never uttered any anguished cries or offered to help. She just stood there, watching with a reticent stare as Adam and Beth ran out of the house, and in this moment, he hates his mom. He hates her so much that he wants to pulverize that blasé face. He wants to do all sorts of unimaginably violent things to her until she's no longer able to keep that serious expression on her face.

Staff members hurriedly walk up and down the hallway. Every time someone walks past him, Adam's thoughts freeze in anticipation of news. Not all of them are focused on Beth, of course. The ER must be filled with cases like Beth's. All the time.

The way their eyes don't even flick in Adam's direction for a second shows how utterly desensitized they've become to the whole thing.

Then one of them does talk to Adam.

"You're her husband, right?"

Adam is on his feet and facing the doctor standing in front of him.

"Yes. Is she okay? Please tell me she's okay," Adam blurts, all words sounding blended.

The doctor makes a somber face, and Adam knows the news is going to be bad. He feels something icy crashing over him from head to toe.

"Your wife is okay. She's going to be fine," the doctor says.

"Oh thank God." Adam feels like he's going to pass out because he's been holding his breath for too long.

"I'm afraid I have some bad news, though."

"What? What is it?"

And then it hits him even before the doctor says it.

****

When Adam enters the room, Beth is in bed, staring catatonically at the ceiling. She's pale, her lips dry, and her cheeks look eerily sunken under the pale light. She has an IV attached to her arm.

"Hey, babe," Adam says in a low tone as he steps closer to her.

He sits at her bedside and takes her hand. Her fingers are stiff, unresponsive to his touch. Her eyes are red-rimmed, an indication she's been crying.

Adam has never felt such a mixture of relief and sadness at the same time. He will never tell Beth this, but if he had to choose between her and the baby, he'd rather save her. The whole point of having a baby was so that the two of them would raise it together. If she dies, then...

He doesn't want to think about it. He doesn't know how he kept a clear enough head to drive Beth to the hospital, but now that everything's over and the danger is no longer in the vicinity, realization of just how close she'd come to dying crashes over him. He suddenly feels like vomiting.

"Beth?" he asks.

Beth's head slowly turns toward him. She looks furious, and Adam braces himself for a flurry of insults. But then her lips start quivering, the corners of her eyebrows arch upward, and she breaks down sobbing. They hold each other in a tight embrace.

Adam cries, too. It seems to last forever, just the two of them crying in silence. Their entire world has just fallen apart, and they don't know where they would even begin to pick up the shattered remains.

Twenty-Nine

Beth is discharged from the hospital the same night. Adam treats her like a delicate flower. He guides her to the car and opens the door for her, closing it once she's inside.

On the way back to the house—not home, house—he drives slowly. He's shocked by the fact that he hadn't been pulled over by a police cruiser while getting Beth to the hospital. He wonders if any cameras or radars caught him and, if so, when the ticket is going to arrive and how expensive it's going to be.

Just another headache to add to the platter.

Beth is quiet in the car the entire time. She looks frail, broken, merely a shadow of the person she was less than two hours ago. Every now and again, a small whimper escapes her mouth. Adam doesn't know what to say to make her feel better. He doesn't think there are any words that can do that right now, so he puts his hand on her thigh to silently console her.

When they arrive back at his mom's house, all the people are gone. The mess in the living room remains though. Adam's eyes drift to the cake table. The uneaten desserts are still there. The spilled wine and broken glass have been cleaned.

His mom's priorities, it seems.

Adam had checked his phone once since taking Beth to the hospital. He had three missed calls from his mom, two of which he missed, and one that he refused to answer out of fear that he'd lose control and yell obscenities in the middle of the ER.

When Adam closes the front door, footsteps approach the living room. His mom appears in the kitchen doorway and smiles. "Oh, you're back. Is everything all right?"

The nonchalant way in which she asks it makes it seem as though it was a simple check-up at the doctor, and not a life-threatening situation.

A life-threatening situation caused by his mom. The same person who now seems to not care about almost killing Beth.

Adam looks at Beth and sees her face slowly contorting into something. It's hate, he realizes, just in time to step in and de-escalate the situation. He stops in front of Beth and puts both hands on her shoulders. He leans in and whispers, "Go pack your things."

That seems to defuse her. She looks at him in confusion and then nods in understanding. Without another word, she strides upstairs, leaving Adam alone with his mom in the living room. He waits until he can no longer see Beth or hear the sound of her footsteps.

"Addy, is everything okay?" his mom asks.

Adam slowly turns to face his mom. He has a million insults ready to let loose, but he knows he can only use one properly. He decides to savor the moment. For now.

"Beth lost the baby," he says.

His mom's face goes through multiple expressions and colors, all in the span of a few seconds. "Oh."

It's like she's come to more than just the realization of what Adam has done. It's like the almond cake was planned all along; only she hadn't planned on it going that far.

"What happened?" she asks.

Is she joking right now? "She went into anaphylactic shock because of her nut allergy. That combined with her high blood levels caused the miscarriage." He doesn't say his mom's cooking contributed to the miscarriage. He wants her to realize that on her own so that it doesn't sound like he's blaming her.

"Well, why didn't she monitor her blood? Really, someone who's pregnant should know better, Adam. And I've seen all the desserts she eats on the side."

Adam is biting his tongue in order to prevent himself from having an outburst. It's not worth it.

"Beth and I are leaving tonight," he says.

"Addy, don't be ridiculous. Why would you leave in the middle of the night?"

"Because I will be damned if I spend another *goddamn* minute under the same roof as you." He's practically hissing the words through his teeth.

His mom pulls her head back in surprise. She wasn't expecting those words from Adam. Oh, she better brace herself because the things he's about to say are going to drive her into the grave. And he's going to enjoy it. He hadn't planned on doing it up until a few seconds ago. Now, he's going to let hell loose.

He steps closer to her and says, "We're going to pack our things, and we're going to find a place to stay in the upcoming days before the apartment is ready for renting. And you and I are done. We are never going to see each other again because you're dead to me."

His mom looks like she's trying to process his words. "Addy, what are you saying?"

Adam chuckles. "I don't know how you want me to make it any more understandable than this. You killed my child. I want you to think about that. You. Killed. It."

His mom's jaw drops, and her eyes widen. "Where's this coming from?"

Did she really just ask him that? She's delusional. Still, that doesn't stop Adam from trying to make her see the truth. He needs her to see it. He wants her to feel guilty. What's done is already done, and nothing about it can be changed, but solace can be found in making those responsible feel guilty.

Adam wants his mom to see what she did wrong. He wants her to wake up every morning with regret and know that her pettiness was what caused her not only to kill her grandchild but to alienate her only son, too.

"You tried to kill Beth!" Adam shouts.

"Adam, don't be silly."

"You made almond cake even though you knew she was deathly allergic!"

"I didn't force her to eat the cake, Addy," she says with a wry smile.

"You *made* almond cake, and you didn't say anything about it. I should call the police on you for attempted murder."

She pauses, and for a moment, Adam thinks she's finally understanding his words, but then she says, "Adam, did Beth tell you to say all of this to me? I know how much she hates me. If you two want me out of your life, all you have to do is say so. I'm not going to be a burden to anyone."

It's no use. It doesn't matter what he says. His mom is deflecting everything expertly, and the bullets that Adam is shooting are ricocheting back, hurting only him.

He turns around to leave, but his mom, being his mom, has to have the last word. It doesn't matter whether she's right or wrong. She's the mom, and in her head, that always makes her right and superior.

"I've done nothing but good things for you. I gave my life for you, let you in when you needed it, and this is how you repay me. The only person who should be blamed here is Beth."

A loud crack fills the room. Adam blinks to see his mom holding a hand over her cheek, eyes wide and filled with tears. The stinging in his palm tells him he's just slapped his mom, but it happened so fast that he hasn't even registered it.

It feels so good to see her sober up like that. He'd like to slap her again just for good measure.

His mom's face goes from discombobulated to that of pure, unadulterated anger. Adam doesn't remember the last time he's seen her look like that.

Good. If he can't make her budge with words, then he's going to do it by using brute force. He doesn't care how primitive it is. Some people only understand the language of violence.

"You ungrateful little shit!" she hisses.

By then, Adam turns around to leave. Now is the right moment to do so. He's made her angry, and leaving now is only going to make her even angrier. Despite everything—the fury and the heartbreak—there's a smile on his face as he climbs the stairs, ignoring his mom's insults.

Even when he closes the bedroom door, he can still hear her screaming at him from the living room downstairs.

Thirty

Beth and Adam pack in a hurry. His mom stopped shouting some time ago, and now the house is eerily silent. It gives Adam a foreboding feeling, like waiting for a jumpscare in a horror movie. His ears are perked up for any movement outside the bedroom, and a silly part of him keeps expecting to see the door swing open and his mom standing in it with a steak knife raised above her head.

"You don't need to pack everything, babe," Adam says to Beth. "Just grab the essentials, and I'll pick up everything else another time."

Beth shakes her head. "I don't want you coming back here."

"All our things won't fit in the car."

"Then leave them."

"No. I'm not going to let her have any of them," he says.

Adam knows he should be agreeing with Beth right now, given her vulnerable state, but he refuses to do so. He wants her to know that his mother is not this omnipotent being that Beth has made her out to be. She's just a rotten woman, and Adam is not going to allow her to control their lives.

"Then don't come back here alone," Beth says.

Her responses are curt, barely a few words for each sentence. It's probably all she's capable of right now. Adam wants to reach out to her, to tell her she had been right all along and that they shouldn't have moved in with his mom.

He's not ready to open that door yet because he knows there's going to be a lot of blame shifted in his direction—

and rightfully so. After all, he's the one who suggested they go live with his mom, despite the red flags that had been present while she stayed with them.

He can already see Beth shutting down, and there's nothing he can do about it. He knows that, the more he tries to reach out to her now, the further she's going to slip away, like soap in a bathtub.

It's going to take her a few days to even start opening up to Adam, and that's when all their problems are going to start surfacing. Not just the things that culminated in the loss of the child but everything prior that had been swept under the rug.

All the times Adam chose not to take Beth's side when she fought with his mom, the times he didn't support her working so hard, the times she kept everything inside her instead of telling him because she didn't want to hurt him, the times he canceled date night, the times he wasn't as excited about her new dress as she hoped he would be.

Watching Beth now, Adam sees the face of a stranger, and he's afraid because he doesn't know how close they are to the precipice of the end. For all he knows, they've already crossed it, and they're past the point of no return.

When they're finished packing, Adam cracks open the door and peeks out into the hallway. He can't believe he's afraid for his and Beth's safety—from his own mom, no less. Two hours ago, he wouldn't have believed the woman capable of doing anything to harm others, and now his and Beth's baby is dead.

Dead.

That word doesn't sit well with him. It's the finality it conveys that makes his stomach flip.

His own child, dead. His first child. Killed by almond cake.

No, killed by his damn mother. That damned bitch. That malicious, evil, selfish, petty bitch.

Anger pounds against Adam's skull again. He hopes he and Beth won't run into her on their way out of the house because he isn't sure if he's going to be able to control himself.

"Come on, Beth," Adam says.

He takes his wife by the hand and looks back at her. She looks hesitant.

"Are you ready? I'll keep you safe, I promise," he says.

He's already made that promise once, and he broke it. Beth has no right to believe him, and yet, from what he sees, she does.

She nods her head and lets him lead the way. They tiptoe down the hallway, descend the stairs, and after taking a peek to make sure the living room is clear, they get out of the house. Adam ushers Beth to the car and packs everything into the trunk. The entire time, he's keeping an eye on the house.

He can't shake the feeling that he and Beth are being watched and that, by slapping his mom, he's crossed into a very dangerous territory.

"Adam! My laptop!" Beth exclaims as soon as Adam opens the door.

Shit.

"You left it in the reading room?" he asks.

"Yes."

"Stay right here. I'll go get it."

He's about to slam the door shut when Beth calls out to him. "No, wait!" He pauses while Beth thinks about what to say. "We should probably send the police instead."

"No, I'll go get it," Adam says.

"Adam..."

"I'll be fine. I promise." Another promise he doesn't know if he can keep. "Stay inside, and if you see her come out, lock the doors and drive away, okay?"

She wants to argue. He can see it on her face. But at the last moment, she nods and says, "Be careful."

Adam closes the car door and looks at the house. The living room lights are on. The rest of the house is engulfed in darkness. Walking up the driveway, Adam feels like he's stepping inside a zoo cage with a dangerous animal inside. When he grabs the doorknob, he needs a moment to brace himself.

She's just an old woman. You're a man, and you're younger and stronger than her. She can't hurt you.

Oh, but she can hurt him. If she sneaks up behind him with a kitchen knife, he could be dead before he even gets a chance to fight back. Would his mom even be capable of doing that? It feels so strange to think about her as this dangerous individual, and yet, it somehow feels natural after tonight.

Adam steps inside the living room. The mess from the party is like an echo of what happened. Just a few hours prior, he and Beth were getting dressed in their bedroom, talking about the party and how they couldn't wait for it to be over. It was supposed to be just a nuisance that would last a few hours tops.

That's what unnerved Adam about it the most: the fact that most tragedies happen when the victims least expect them.

No one expects to get into a fatal car crash on the drive home from work or to get robbed at gunpoint on a walk in the park or to get a call about their loved ones suddenly passing away. In their heads, they plan dinner and play music and think about that coffee they're going to grab with their friend next week, and before they know it, all of it is interrupted in an instant.

The party was such an insignificant thing in Adam and Beth's lives that their minds skipped over it and focused on what they considered more important—until the party became something they'll probably replay in their minds over and over and over.

It will be something that will haunt them whenever they join a celebration or see someone eating cake or go to the doctor's office while someone is being rushed into the emergency room, or see a woman with a bulging belly on the street.

How had everything changed so fast?

More importantly, where's his mom? He finds it difficult to believe she'd just retreat after their altercation. She had been screaming stuff at him like a banshee, and now she's gone.

The longer Adam lingers in the living room, the more likely that he's going to run into her. He ambles upstairs, peeking around every corner. When he opens the door to his dad's reading room, he can't see a thing due to the darkness. He flips the light switch on and, a click later, the blackness is dispersed.

The laptop is sitting right there on the desk. Adam snatches it, unplugs the charger from the wall, and clumsily reels both things to his chest. He turns around and—

A small scream escapes his mouth at the figure standing in the doorway.

His mom is blocking the way, staring at him. He's unable to see her facial expression because of the darkness in the hallway. Instinctively, he looks at her hands in an attempt to see if she's holding any weapons.

He wonders how she was able to hide the sound of her jewelry. All his life, Adam has heard those things even when he was two rooms away, and now she somehow managed to sneak up on him without so much as a muffled tone.

For what feels like a small eternity, neither of them moves or talks. When Adam can no longer take it, he forces a word out of his throat.

"Mom."

She makes a microscopic flinch at that. It could have been missed easily in the blink of an eye.

Then, just like that, she turns and walks away. Adam doesn't move. He's listening for any movement in the house. He can't detect any.

A noise blares so loudly in the room that he feels like he's going to jump out of his skin. He reaches into his pocket and pulls out his cellphone. Beth's calling him.

"Hello?" He presses the phone to his ear.

"Are you okay in there?" she asks.

"Yeah. I'm good."

"What's taking you so long?"

"Nothing. I'll be out there in a moment."

He hangs up and finally forces his feet to unroot themselves from the floor. Peeking out into the hallway, he doesn't see his mom anywhere. The house is too quiet. It's never been this quiet before.

Adam reaches the stairs. The front door is so close that he thinks he can make a run for it. So, that's exactly what he does.

He doesn't look to see whether his mom is in the living room or waiting around a corner. He just runs for the door, yanks it open, and runs outside. Only when he jumps off the porch does he turn around to look at the house.

Nothing is moving. Nothing is making noise.

He suddenly feels foolish for behaving like this, but he thinks that's the part of the brain that still refuses to accept reality. His mom, whom he thought all his life was a saint, is actually a monster. He knew that all along, of course, ever since John told him about the two types of rude people. He knew it, but he chose not to believe it because it was the easier thing to do than admit his mother is a bad person.

It's going to take him time to get used to that idea.

And the idea that he's never going to see her again.

Adam walks back up onto the porch and grabs the doorknob. He takes one final look inside the living room, a part of him hoping he'll see his mom standing somewhere so he can at least say a proper goodbye, and then he closes the door and returns to the car.

Thirty-One

Adam drives all night long. He doesn't care that his lower back is starting to hurt. He doesn't care that he's sleepy. He just wants them to move into their new apartment.

While in the car, Beth calls the new landlord and asks if it's okay for them to move in earlier though she knows they aren't supposed to be in Portland for another week but that they really, really need it, and she offers to pay the one week at a higher price if necessary.

The landlord is understanding enough to agree to meet up with them and give them the keys. Not only that, but he also says they don't need to pay for the one week that's going to be off the record. Beth thanks him a dozen times before the call ends.

Good thing they don't need to stay at a motel.

Adam feels like he's in a living nightmare that he can't wake up from. His mind refuses to accept the knowledge that the baby is dead. It can't be. Not like this. He and Beth didn't even think of a name. They didn't even find out if it was a boy or a girl. There were so many things they planned. A life the baby was supposed to have...

Adam stifles a sob. Next to him, Beth does the same but less successfully. In his pain, Adam feels drawn to Beth. He needs to be close to the one person who can commiserate with him.

When he takes her hand, she doesn't resist. She eagerly accepts it, and he knows they're going to get through this somehow because they're going to stick together.

The interaction with his mom goes through his head like a slideshow. He keeps hearing the whipcrack of his palm slapping her across the face. It's so satisfying to think about it but insufficient. He wants to do it again and again until she starts begging for mercy, until she admits that this was all her fault, until she admits that, yes, she's the one who killed the baby because of her stubborn behavior.

Almond cake...

Adam keeps going back to it, trying to find a logical reason behind its existence. In life, whenever something terrible happens, we look for a reason behind it.

Why did it have to happen this way? Why did it have to happen to me? Why now?

Since we can't go back in time and fix it, finding answers is the only thing that can give us a shred of solace. The problem is the reason isn't always there. It's left to our own imagination to interpret it how we see fit.

Life can be unfair sometimes.

At around 5 a.m., when Adam's eyelids start to close, he knows it's time to take a nap. Strange how the echoes of his fatherly instincts still kick in and the first thing he considers is Beth and the baby's safety.

He stops the car at a gas station off the interstate. He and Beth pull their seats down, and they don't speak another word. They don't have to because the noise in Adam's head is deafening.

The fight with his mom plays in his head even after he falls asleep, the dreams distorted and nonsensical. In them, his mom is knocking on the window of his car with a long nail. Her smiling face is so close to the glass her breaths are fogging it up.

Adam gets out and slaps her, but something is different. Instead of the satisfying crack, his hand sinks into her cheek like it's a fluffy pillow, and his mom doesn't flinch or yelp. He tries hitting her over and over, but the results are the same.

Meanwhile, Beth is casually walking toward the gas station entrance while holding her hands on her belly, and she's saying they can fix her baby in there.

When Adam turns to face his mom again, she no longer looks like the gentle woman he's used to seeing, but her eyes are bulging, the skin on her face sunken and dark, and her teeth are sharp.

She doesn't attack him like he expects her to. She just stands there, staring at him. Where he moves, she follows him with her gaze. He somehow knows that, if he turns around, she's going to attack him, so he keeps her in his sights. He fumbles for the car door, but his hand is grasping at thin air. He makes the mistake of turning his head to see where his car is, and that's when he hears a shrill cry, and his mom jumps on top of him.

Adam wakes up with a start. He instinctively looks at the glass on his side, expecting to see his mom's face there, but there's nothing. He breathes a sigh of relief until he looks at the passenger's side. Beth isn't there.

Adam raises himself into a ramrod sitting position and whips his head around. The momentary scare disperses when he sees Beth exiting the gas station and approaching the car with snacks and water in her hands.

"Got you this," she says when she enters the car.

She proceeds to hand him a bunch of sweets and a can of energy drink—all his favorites. Even now when she's so absorbed in her pain, she doesn't forget to buy the small things that make Adam happy.

"You're the best, babe," he says.

They eat in silence for a few minutes before Adam says, "Ready to go?"

Beth looks at him. "What about sleep?"

"I took a short nap. I feel fresh," he lies.

The truth is he knows he's not going to be able to fall asleep and, if he does, he's afraid of the nightmares that are going to plague him. Right now, his dreams match the dolor of reality.

"Are you sure you're up for it?" Beth asks.

"Yes. I'll be fine driving. Besides, don't you want to sleep in our new bed instead?" He smiles at her.

She doesn't smile back. There's nothing to smile about.

The drive continues. At around 7 a.m., they arrive in Portland. At 7:30, they are in front of their new apartment. At 8 a.m., the landlord arrives to give the keys to them and show them inside the apartment.

Adam and Beth had not seen the apartment in person until now. The beauty of it is marred by the tragedy that envelops them. The landlord's words are an echo coming from the bottom of a deep barrel. Adam feels like his brain suffered a short circuit, and he's no longer able to focus on anything.

It's Beth who does all the talking with the landlord. Adam doesn't hear much of anything except *thank you*, so he instinctively thanks the landlord, too, even though he's not following the conversation. The whole interaction passes in a blur, and before Adam knows it, it's just him and Beth in the apartment.

Moving to their new apartment was supposed to be promising. Their new lives were supposed to start here. They're supposed to be admiring their new place. Beth is supposed to go from room to room and let out gasps of awe at the pristine kitchen, the spacious living room, the tidy bedroom...

Instead, they're standing in the middle of the apartment like they're in a graveyard.

"Sleep?" Adam asks.

Beth nods slowly. Her eyelids are half closed, and whenever she blinks, her eyes have trouble opening. The two strip out of their clothes and slink under the covers of the new bed. It's big and very soft, or maybe it just feels like that because Adam has spent all night driving.

As per his routine, he puts his phone on the nightstand, but he makes sure to check for notifications first. He doesn't know why, but he half-expects a message or a missed call from his mom. If she does try to call him, he's going to answer, only so he can shout all sorts of terrible things to her over the phone. He's had plenty of time in the car to think about the insults that would make her feel like crap.

Even as he closes his eyes and drifts into dreamland, he wishes things could have been different.

Thirty-Two

Adam starts working at the university soon. He likes it here even more than his previous university. It helps him a lot because he doesn't have as much time to think about the baby. Beth, too, immerses herself in her work. She starts going to the office a lot more often and stays until late.

They hardly talk to each other, and when they do, it's a cold and sterile conversation. In the bedroom, there's no intimacy, but sometimes they hold each other while sleeping. They are two recluse strangers living as roommates.

Adam wishes he could talk to someone about it. His mom is no longer in the picture, not that he would ever entrust her with any information again. John was his only other friend, and he hasn't spoken to him in months, so it would be weird for him to trauma dump on him out of nowhere.

What happened to all the friends Adam had when he was younger? When he was in high school and in college, he had so many friends he could hardly keep up with seeing all of them. As the years went by, those numbers dwindled.

Most of them got snatched by life. Some got married; some got jobs in different states; some tragically died; some just stopped responding to messages. They all disappeared one by one in such a gradual manner that he didn't even realize it until he needed them to hear him out.

People grow in different paces and ways, and their paths often diverge. After college, it's no longer all about having a good laugh and going out to get drunk on a Friday night.

With maturity comes a solidified need for peace while everything else is rejected. For Adam, that rejection encompassed most of his college friends, whom he found he no longer had common interests with.

Growing up, Adam thought he'd find his best friend in school or in college and that the friendship would survive hell and high water. In a sense, he found his best friend in Beth. The problem is he can't talk to Beth about everything.

Like right now.

He wants to rekindle with Beth, but he doesn't know how to approach her, and she doesn't seem willing to let him. The elephant in the room remains unaddressed, and that only amplifies the tension.

It isn't going to be long before they have to talk about what happened. The baby, his mom, all of it will have to be discussed, and that's when the real marital problems are going to start. Adam expects a lot of blaming, a lot of yelling, and crying. He just hopes he and Beth can weather that wave.

It feels like their marriage is slowly reaching the point of no return. Until it suddenly starts to change for the better one day. They start talking more. Beth laughs once. Then twice. Then a month after the tragedy, she's her old, buoyant self once again. She still has bouts of depression, but they're not perpetual like before.

Then she and Adam share a fiery night of intimacy. Adam thinks things will start to fall back into place after that, but he's wrong. The passion they share is a channel for their grief, and things only resume the way they'd been going up until then.

They still haven't talked about the *thing*. Until they address it, they won't know what their future is going to be like. Do they start trying for a baby again? When? How soon is too soon? How does Adam even broach the subject when he doesn't even know how Beth feels about it?

For all he knows, she's had a complete emotional shutdown regarding that, and any attempt to talk about it will cause all the buried stuff to pour out. If there's anything that really is buried, then it will have to come out sooner or later, and better sooner while the dirt is still fresh and easy to scoop out.

And yet, whenever Adam wants to sit Beth down to talk to her about it, he can't. Something stops him from opening that old wound. Maybe he himself has had a shutdown and he doesn't even realize it. He does find it odd how he was able to overcome the pain of his loss so fast. Maybe he hasn't overcome it at all. Just suppressed it so that he doesn't need to deal with it.

And that's when strange things start to happen.

Adam starts to think he's being stalked by someone. It begins small. He feels like he's being watched, only for the feeling to disappear as soon as it arrives. He can't tell why he feels that. Even though he looks around and sees nobody, it's like an invisible pair of eyes is watching him.

Then, he actually sees someone across the street, peeking at him from behind the corner of a building. The silhouette is gone in the blink of an eye, and Adam looks around to see if anyone else saw it. If they did, they're too enthralled in the hustle and bustle of their own lives to pay attention.

It slowly progresses to the point that it's difficult to ignore it. He'll see a car tailing him. As soon as he becomes aware of it, the car takes a sharp turn and gets away as if realizing Adam has spotted it. He'll look out the window at the street below and see a figure staring up among the passersby. As soon as he notices it, the figure expertly merges with the crowd and disappears out of sight.

He doesn't tell Beth anything about it. He doesn't want to worry her any more than she's already worried. He tries calling the police, but without concrete information or evidence, there's nothing they can do about it.

Then one day, he almost catches the figure. He notices it in his peripheral vision but doesn't look directly at it. He knows the moment he does that, the person will flee. So, he pretends to be doing his own thing while slowly getting closer.

When he thinks he's sufficiently close, he jerks his head up and breaks into a sprint toward the stalker. The figure is much faster. By the time Adam rounds the corner, the person is gone, and he's left spinning in circles with his hands on his hips.

Dammit.

He has managed to catch a glimpse of the figure for the first time, though. He was clad in black and wore a plain blank mask with two slits where the eyes should be.

****

He arrives home the same day to find Beth sitting in the living room. A bottle of wine and two full glasses sit on the table. She's drinking from one glass.

It's not a romantic occasion. Beth isn't dressed up and wearing makeup, and the atmosphere in the apartment is anything but amorous. This is stress-drinking, Adam realizes.

"Beth? Everything okay?" he asks.

Beth takes a sip of wine. Her hair is bedraggled as if she hasn't washed it in days. The only times Beth takes care of herself these days is when she goes to work at the office. Adam dislikes it, but he doesn't say anything because he wants to believe Beth is going to get back to her old self once the grieving period passes.

"Yeah. Just unwinding a little bit," she says as she takes another big gulp, downing a quarter of the glass.

Adam sits on the couch next to her and brushes her hair behind her ear. She remains unresponsive to his touch.

It's one of those days, it seems.

"I assume the second glass is for me?" Adam asks.

Beth nods. "Or I can drink it. it's all the same to me."

Adam has no intention of letting her drink so much. He takes the glass and brings it to his mouth. The smell is intoxicating, and he realizes how much he needs to get drunk. The stress that he's been bottling up is now finally starting to seep out, and he feels that alcohol might make the transition easier.

The first sip slides smoothly down his throat, and he instantly feels the tension in his muscles abating.

"Do you want to talk about it, babe?" he asks.

"Nothing to talk about. It's just been a bad day, and I'm miserable, that's all."

Adam takes that personally because it makes him feel like he's failed as a husband. It's his job to make his wife happy, and he's unable to do that.

"How was your day?" Beth asks.

Adam wants to tell Beth about the stalker situation. He thinks about the black mask with the slits for eyes, and the black clothes.

He weighs whether it's a good idea to tell her or not. She's already worried about a lot, so maybe it's best to keep it to himself. Then again, if someone really is stalking them, Beth might be in danger as much as Adam.

In fact, Adam thinks Beth is in more danger than him because he knows who the stalker is.

"Nothing special. Just another work day." He shrugs, but he's still not one hundred percent sure if he wants to keep the information from her or not. In his head, he's thinking of a way to tell her without making her panic.

"How's everything at the university in general?" Beth asks as she takes another sip.

"Fine. I feel kind of excluded, though." He takes another gulp.

"How so?"

"I don't know. I guess I…" He starts losing his train of thought. The wine must be getting to him already. "I don't have any friends here like I had back at the other place. Even at Rosewood, I met some cool people. Too bad the school sucked."

"Yeah."

Adam already feels lightheaded.

"What about you?"

Beth shakes her head. "Nothing special to report on my end."

"I feel like there's so much we should be talking about, but we don't." He wouldn't have said that normally, but the wine must be getting things out of him.

"I just need time. I'm still feeling this intense hate for your mom, and I don't think it's ever going to pass." She stares pensively ahead, looks down at the tattoo on her wrist, and then says, "You know, I thought I was done with all of this."

"What, exactly?"

"These emotions that I had all the time in the *family*." She's always referred to the cult as "family." Adam never asked if that was the official name, or if they just called themselves that. "Every morning I woke up, I knew I had another miserable day ahead of me. Yelling, beatings, disparaging. We were constantly told that we would never be good enough no matter how hard we tried to be perfect. It was their way of keeping us in check. I used to dream of getting away from the *family* someday, meeting a wonderful man, and having a family of my own. One where I wouldn't be made to feel like I'm worthless."

"You're not worthless. You know that," Adam says.

Beth nods. "I know. But being with your mom... it all brought me back to those days. The girls in the *family* were educated to believe they were only meant to give birth to future *family* followers. When I talked to your mom... At moments, I swear I felt like she was one of the elders, that I was just a little girl again, and that I had no power over anything she said."

Adam inches closer to Beth. "You're right to hate her. I hate her, too. What she did is unforgivable. But we can't keep living like that. We have to focus on our own lives."

Beth takes a sip. Adam mimics her.

"I know. And we will. We're going to buy our house when we're able to. And we're going to try for a baby again. I just need more time."

"Take as long as you need, but don't beat yourself up. It's not your fault."

"I know it's not *my* fault. It's your mom's." Her timbre changes to a more hostile octave.

Even though she clearly blames his mom, Adam can't help but wonder if he's missing something from between the lines. Is she perhaps blaming him as much as she's blaming his mom?

Adam is ready to take the blame stoically. In the past weeks since the miscarriage, he's had intense feelings of guilt over what happened. He thinks about the things he should have done differently: How they never should have moved in with his mom, how he should have been firmer with her, how he should have made sure the party cakes—*that damn almond cake*—were removed so that Beth wouldn't accidentally eat them.

"I wish I could take it all back, Beth," Adam says.

Beth shakes her head. "It wasn't your fault. It was all her. We should have pressed charges."

Despite hating his mom from the bottom of his heart, Adam can't imagine going down that path, mostly because it's still a shock for him to consider that their relationship went from perfect to hostile pretty much overnight.

He has to keep reminding himself that it was never perfect. His mom has only made him believe in that while conveniently making him forget about the bad things.

"How do I fix this?" Adam asks.

"*We* are going to fix this together," Beth says.

That sentence gives him some solace, no matter how small. It encourages him to try to get closer to Beth.

The wine is hitting him hard. His thoughts are swimming, but he's grasping onto one of them firmly.

"I miss you, Beth," he says before the thought gets away.

She looks at him blankly. For a second, he thinks she's going to look away, unable to reciprocate his emotions. She puts a hand on his cheek and gives him a longing look.

Adam doesn't think he can stand to be away from her any longer. He lunges toward her without thinking whether she wants the same thing or not. He'll think about that if the rejection happens. When he kisses her, she doesn't fight.

He leans toward her, gently pushing her into a lying position. He runs his hand down her hip, her thigh, kisses her neck, her clavicle, explores her body like it's their first time again. She gasps as she runs her fingers through his hair, pulling his face closer to her chest.

He grabs the neckline of her blouse, and he doesn't care whether she likes that one or not. He tears it open. The buttons pop off, and Beth's pert breasts are revealed. He still sometimes admires her breasts, even after all these years.

The bulge in his pants is begging to be released. Beth is already undoing his belt and unzipping his jeans. The moment she reaches into his underwear and grabs his rod, he feels like he's going to explode, and he can no longer wait.

He pulls her pants off and doesn't bother with the panties. He pushes them aside before sliding into her. Beth lets out a shrill moan as he enters her with his full length. She wraps her arms and legs around him and pulls him closer.

It's the best sex they've had in a long time, and the first sex in their new apartment. When they're done, they fall asleep on the couch in each other's arms.

Adam wakes up to a shiver caressing his exposed skin. He tries to get up to put some clothes on, but his wrists refuse to budge. There's a coinciding clink as he moves.

When he opens his eyes, he's no longer on his couch but in a cold and dark warehouse, handcuffed to a pipe.

Thirty-Three

Oh shit oh shit oh shit oh shit.

Panic isn't just setting in. It has exploded inside Adam's skull, spreading fallout everywhere. He's unable to inhale deeply. His head is spinning, and he feels like he's going to pass out. A million thoughts race through his mind.

Where am I? How did I get here? Why am I cuffed? How the fuck did I get here? Why does my head hurt so much? Where's Beth?

That last one exacerbates his already present inability to take a deep breath. He's hyperventilating now, each gasp for air that of a drowning man, his constricted throat unwilling to cooperate.

He tugs at his binds for minutes, slamming the chains against the pipe in hopes of breaking the links, but it's no use. He may as well try to flip a truck, and all he's managed to do is make his wrists burn from the cold metal that bites into them. He doesn't even register the pain until his strength is fully depleted and he's left panting with exhaustion, a film of cold sweat coating his skin.

"Help!" he lets out a scream he wasn't even aware he was capable of. "Help me, please!"

He continues to scream like that for well over a minute. His voice echoes in the spaciousness of the warehouse. He screams until his throat feels like he swallowed a strip of sandpaper. When he goes silent, the warehouse falls silent, too.

Please, God, please let Beth be safe. Please don't let anything happen to her. Please please please please.

Adam's head is killing him, and he's sure it's from the lack of oxygen getting to his brain. He closes his eyes and focuses on his breathing. Deep inhales through his nose, deep exhales through his mouth. The breaths are shallow at first, but gradually, the cramp in his throat and lungs lets up, and he's able to breathe more freely.

His heart is thudding against his chest, and now that the initial wave of panic is subsiding, cold is beginning to envelop his body. He's wearing only his underwear, and the concrete he's sitting on is painfully icy.

With rational thinking finally kicking in, Adam starts to look for a way out.

His eyes are well-adjusted to the dark, and scanning the dark warehouse, he sees old crates and rotting pallets. He doesn't see a way out, and there's nothing close to him that would let him break free of his binds.

He slides the chain of the handcuffs up and down the pipe he's bound to, testing to see if there's perhaps a gap. No dice.

Adam plants his feet on the floor and props himself into a standing position. His legs quiver, and it takes lots of effort to do that. For some reason, he's feeling really weak. Even standing for a few seconds makes him dizzy, so he quickly slides back down to a sitting position.

Nausea forms in his stomach, and he thinks he might throw up before the sickness subsides. With the physical pain gone, he once again finds himself in panic mode.

Morbid thoughts run rampant in his head. What happened to Beth? Where is she? How did this happen? Who did this to him?

He's starting to hyperventilate again, so he focuses on telling himself Beth's okay. She has to be. If something happened to her, then...

No. Don't think about it. Don't think about it. Think of something positive.

But thinking of something positive is a little hard to do, especially when everything around him is dark and damp. All he can do is wonder what happened to Beth and what's going to happen to him. He tries to tell himself that there's a reason he's not dead yet, but then he remembers that a lot of serial killers kidnap their victims so they can do things to them before offing them.

In fact, the more he thinks about it, the less he can see any scenario where he's likely to walk free from this. Whoever kidnapped him did so with the intention of killing him.

The question is: Why?

For the next hour, he goes through bouts of panic, screaming, tugging at the cuffs, and looking for a way out, only to fall back into the exhausted state of despair. He doesn't have much strength left. He's freezing, he's hungry, and he's sleepy.

If only he could die before his kidnapper shows up so that he doesn't need to suffer. No, he still needs to find out what happened to Beth. He has to know. He just has to.

Suddenly, a door squeals open and then slams shut somewhere. Footsteps echo in the air.

Adam raises his head, his breath held in his throat as the footfall approaches. Each step sounds like a gavel being brought down on the block. Then, a figure emerges from behind one of the pallet stacks.

It's the masked figure who has been stalking him for the past few weeks. At the back of his mind, he knew the masked figure was responsible for his kidnapping the moment he woke up. His brain just didn't have time to process it properly with everything that had been running through his head.

Adam wants to yell insults at the person, but he can't seem to find the courage. With each step the kidnapper draws closer, Adam's fear grows.

He's carrying a heavy duffel bag in his hand. When he's around ten steps to Adam, he stops. The featureless mask is terrifying, but what's even more terrifying is the fact that Adam can see a semblance of eyes inside the slits.

They're human eyes, and yet, they're devoid of everything that makes them human. They're the eyes of a killer.

They're boring into Adam with a coldness that makes Adam's entire body stiff with tension. The kidnapper doesn't look at Adam like he's a human being. He looks at him the way Adam would look at a mess that needs to be cleaned up.

No passion. No emotions. Just annoyance at the job in front of him.

"Why are you doing this to me?" Adam asks.

His voice is cracked and meek. The kidnapper stares at him wordlessly for a moment longer. Adam has the urge to look away, but he doesn't. He doesn't want to show how scared he is even though his bladder is pretty much ready to burst.

The kidnapper turns perpendicular to Adam, takes a few steps forward, and throws the duffel bag on the ground. It falls with a heavy thud, and something inside clinks. Adam doesn't like the sound of that. The kidnapper squats, slowly unzips the bag, and puts one hand inside.

Now that he's not looking at him, Adam gains a surge of courage to speak up.

"Where's my wife? What did you do to her?" he asks.

The kidnapper pulls out a handsaw and neatly places it next to the bag in plain sight for Adam to see.

Oh God. Adam's heart skips a beat. What does he plan to do with that?

He knows already; he's just in denial. His heart is hammering against his chest, and he feels like he's going to vomit. He feels like crying. He wishes to be away from here. Anywhere at all, just not here. Even his mom's house looks like heaven in his mind right now.

"What do you want from me? Money? I'll give you whatever you want. I'll do whatever you want, please."

The kidnapper pulls out a large combat knife. The blade looks long enough to cut off someone's head with enough effort. He places the knife next to the saw. He pulls out rolled-up trash bags and lines them up with the tools.

Oh, Jesus.

Adam has been in denial until now, but seeing those things, he knows what's about to happen. The kidnapper is going to kill him, and then he's going to slice him into pieces and put his body parts in the trash bag. He's going to dump his body parts somewhere, and Adam is going to end up as just another dead case on the news.

University professor discovered dismembered in a trash can.

Tears fill Adam's eyes, and his voice turns petulant. "Please! I'm begging you! Just tell me what you want, and I'll give it to you! Please, just don't hurt me!"

The kidnapper doesn't even turn his head to face Adam. He just continues pulling out things, one after another, each one worse than the previous.

"Answer me!" Adam demands. "Please, don't do this to me. Please. Please, please, please." The final word trails into a whisper where Adam continues to chant the mantra to himself.

Please, please, please. God, please, this can't be happening. Please.

Begging isn't going to help. He knows that much. No one kidnaps a person just to change their mind at the last moment. That still doesn't stop us from pleading, anyway. The human brain and body will resort to any desperate measure to keep themselves alive.

Think, Adam. Think. Think. What can you do?

He licks his painfully dry lips. One thing comes to his mind, but it's a long shot. He inhales as deeply as he can and, after a moment of holding his breath, he says a single word.

"Mom."

The kidnapper freezes. The hand inside the duffel bag stops rummaging. His mom slowly turns her head to face Adam. He can't see where she's looking, but he feels her gaze on him.

It's a start, one that Adam hasn't expected to get. Now he doesn't know what to say next, and he knows he must choose his words carefully because one wrong sentence will spell his demise.

"I know it's you. This is because of the way I treated you, isn't it?" Adam asks. "You want to make me suffer for what I did."

His mom stands. She turns to face Adam. He thinks he senses anger emanating from her. This is confirmed moments later when his mom bends down to pick up the combat knife and breaks into a stride toward Adam.

It's the most explosive motion she's done in the warehouse, and it makes Adam recoil with his back into the pipe because he knows he's going to be punished now for revealing he knows who she is.

He turns his head and squeezes his eyes shut in a futile attempt to hide from the knife. Just when the footsteps reach him, Adam lets out a whimper, his whole body tensing, but nothing happens. It takes him a few seconds to open his eyes and look in his mom's direction.

She's standing barely two feet away from him, dwarfing him. Her chest is heaving up and down with deep exhales, the hilt of the knife gripped firmly in the gloved hand. Adam's eyes are mostly stuck to the knife because he expects the blade to sink into his throat or stomach any second, but his eyes flitter to the expressionless mask every now and again.

"Mom, please," Adam says. "I'm so sorry. I'm sorry for everything. Please don't kill me."

Tears are sliding down his cheeks, and he's unable to stop himself from crying because—please God—he doesn't want to die. He wants to see his wife again, and he wants to have a baby with her, and he wants to continue teaching at the university, and he wants things to go back to the way they were between him and his mom.

His mom stops breathing heavily. Her shoulders relax. It's like he can almost hear her uttering, "Oh, Addy."

This is it. She's going to have mercy on him, he thinks.

His mom raises a hand and grabs the lower part of her mask. Slowly, she pulls it up, up, up, revealing her face. Adam can't even gasp from the shock because the person underneath the mask isn't his mom.

It's Beth.

Thirty-Four

For the first twenty seconds, Adam's mouth opens and closes, but he's unable to form any words. The impossibility of what he's seeing is hitting him like a haymaker to the nose. His mind is already churning out explanations about this whole situation.

Beth is being forced into this.

The person in front of Adam is not Beth.

None of this is real.

He wants to pinch himself to wake up, but he knows—he just knows—this is reality. He's not dreaming. He's not in a coma. He's not hallucinating. Beth is as real as the handcuffs holding him in place, as the burn in his wrists, as the shiver enveloping his naked body.

Beth is standing in front of him, staring down at him. She has that cold look that he knows all too well. Except, staring into her eyes now, he sees not a stranger but Beth for who she really is. Everything Adam knows about her is a lie.

The one with the black clothes, the mask, and the knife in her hand? That's the real Beth, and it always has been.

"B-Beth?" Adam stutters.

He's barely able to get the word out of his mouth. He's supposed to be able to speak to her freely, without fear or shame. It's his wife, after all. He feels exactly the opposite, though. He feels as though Beth is dead, and this monster standing in front of him is puppeteering her corpse.

"Beth," Adam says. Her name leaves his mouth more smoothly this time.

Beth's facial expression remains deadpan, as if she's staring at an inanimate object, and not a living being, not her husband who she's been with for years.

"Baby, what's going on?" he asks.

The look on her face is scaring him, but something else is scaring him even more. Her refusal to speak to him. If he could just hear her voice, he'd know it was her. He'd then have some kind of leverage, no matter how small.

He's surprised that he's already thinking in that direction, despite the person he loved and trusted the most in this world having betrayed him. Maybe the betrayal from his mom trained him to be ready for everything.

But Adam doesn't want to be ready for those things. No one should live expecting to get a knife stuck in their back, especially not from the people who mean the world to them.

He no longer has the strength to be angry or afraid. Fresh tears run down his cheeks as he breaks down sobbing. An immense sadness takes him over, unlike any he's ever experienced in his life. He thought he knew pain when his dad died and when his mom killed his and Beth's baby.

It's nothing compared to the betrayal he feels now. If there's one thing he'd never be able to take, it's losing Beth, and that's exactly what happened tonight. She's physically still here, but the Beth he loves is gone, so he cries like the day he found out his dad died.

He doesn't know how long passes before a soft, gloved hand touches his cheek. He winces and stops crying. He looks up at Beth and blinks the tears away. He thinks he sees some familiarity on Beth's face, a ghost of a look she used to give him.

As quickly as it appears, it fades into nothingness. Beth removes her hand from Adam's cheek, and the fragment of comfort that her touch gave him dissolves as well.

He sobs harder because that look on her face tells him things will never be the same between them again. However things end tonight, they will never have the closeness that they've had in the past few years.

"Why? Why?!" he begs through tears.

He doesn't expect an answer, and yet he gets one.

"This was always the plan," Beth coldly says.

It's Beth's voice, the one she has when she's angry at him. Her *real* voice. The buoyant one was a façade.

Adam stops crying once more and looks up at her. He waits for an explanation that never comes. She just stands there, the knife dangling from her hand. She's neither enjoying nor hating the moment. Or maybe she is, and he just can't tell.

He stops crying because he's determined to at least get answers, even if he won't survive the night.

"What? What does that mean?" he asks.

She looks away, her face contorted into something akin to sadness. Adam's initial reflex tells him to go hug her. A passing thought that disappears the moment his eyes fall on the knife in her hand.

"What are you talking ab—" And then it hits him.

His eyes widen in terror, and a fresh patina of cold sweat breaks out on his skin. His teeth start chattering, and he suddenly feels like such an idiot for not realizing sooner what's going on.

"You never left the cult," he says.

It's not a question; that's how sure he is of the sentence. Still, he's hoping she'll deny it. *Please, Beth, deny it. Give me a reason to keep loving you.*

She turns her head toward him. With a small shake of her head, she says, "No. I didn't."

There's a hint of pride in her tone.

"But why, Beth? Why?" Adam asks.

Beth spreads her arms before letting them fall to her sides. "Why would I? I have everything I need right there. An identity, a sense of belonging, even a family."

"I thought I was your family."

She scoffs and shakes her head. He can't be sure, but the gesture sounds like, *Don't be ridiculous.*

He's holding onto the hope of being able to convince her not to go through with whatever she plans on doing here. "Beth. Baby, let's talk about this. I want to help you. I love you."

She smiles. "I love you, too. And you will help me. You'll help me complete my initiation and join the ranks along with the rest of the honored members."

She theatrically raises her knife in demonstration. Adam flinches before Beth slowly lowers the knife.

"Initiation? Beth, I don't understand. Why? Why are you doing this? I thought this was all behind you."

Beth shakes her head. "Of course it's not behind me. That's just a little sob story I created when we met. You know how I "worked" from the office every Thursday? Well, I didn't. I had meetings with *them*. This right here is proof of my eternal loyalty to them."

She lifts her sleeve to show the tattoo on her wrist. She gently runs her finger across the symbol like it's a baby that needs nurturing.

Baby.

Adam needs a moment to collect himself before asking the next question. "What about our baby? What happened to it... Was it... Was it you?"

He's afraid Beth is going to let out a malicious laugh or shake her head again. He's afraid he'll see indifference in her eyes toward her child.

He doesn't know if he can take it. To know she was fake with him this entire time is one thing, but to know she was acting, even about the baby—something that's supposed to be the most sacred thing to every mother—terrifies Adam.

"Answer me," he says through his teeth.

Beth's face grows dark, and he notices pain behind her eyes. No matter how little he knows this woman, she's unable to hide pain from him.

"I'm sorry for what happened to our child, Adam. I truly am," Beth says.

Our child. Those words spark something inside Adam. His pain for the miscarriage is suddenly relit like a previously extinguished fire. He wants to hug Beth tightly so the two of them can share in the pain, but he's also afraid of her. It's the most conflicted Adam has felt in his entire life.

Maybe Beth killed the baby on purpose, maybe it was all an accident. Either way, it doesn't matter because it played out exactly the way Beth wanted it to. Unshackled by Adam or her future child, she's free to go back to the cult, to where she thinks she belongs.

He's suddenly furious. Beth knew all of this, and she lied to him about it. She deliberately deceived Adam for years and years, leading him on, wasting his time.

"You're a monster," he says.

He wants to break from his bonds and wrap his hands around Beth's neck. He wants to choke the life out of her for being like this.

"You're a fucking monster!" he shouts.

She continues staring at him calmly.

Adam reaches into the depths of his soul to pull out the most vicious, vile insult he can. "My mother was right about you. You're fucking insane. You're sick in the head, and that fucking cult has brainwashed you!"

He expects to see her face change. Anything but the vacuous expression she has right now. As her husband, he thought he knew exactly what he needed to say or do to push her buttons. It looks like that's not the case, because Beth remains untouched by his remark, or at least looks like it.

Adam leans forward to get as close to her as he can, but the handcuffs won't let him. His body's natural urge is telling him to start tearing at the bonds even though there's no physical way to reach Beth. The logical part of him knows it's going to be futile.

"Why wait so long?"

"If it's any consolation, I planned on killing you right at the time when your mom broke her hip. Everything went to hell when she moved in with us. Then I made the same plan when you kicked her out, but we got evicted, so I put those plans on hold again. That's why I decided I'm not going to wait any longer."

She drugged his wine. He now knows that. That's why he feels so weak and groggy and why his head hurts.

"You didn't answer my question, Beth," he says. "Why didn't you just kill me after we met? Why spend so many years with me? Was this your plan all along? To give me all those years of happiness with you only to take them away in the end? Is that how your fucking cult operates?"

"Look, I know you want answers, Adam. You think that's going to make it easier for you. It's not. You think I want to do this?" She raises her voice, and for the first time tonight, he starts to hear emotions in it. She's getting worked up talking about this. "I want to be able to have the best of both worlds. I want to devote my life to them, but I also want to have one with you."

She takes a step closer to Adam, and the hilt of the knife is now gripped firmly in her hand. Adam is almost out of time.

"Then why don't you?" he asks.

"Because it doesn't work that way. You can only have one, Adam." She takes another step.

She's crying. She doesn't want to kill Adam, but she feels like she has to. All because an insane cult put the idea inside her head.

"It's not too late. We can go back to our old lives, Beth. Things can be exactly how they were before all of this. Just you and me. And our baby," Adam says.

Beth lets out a sob. "No. It would never be the same again. You and I have crossed a boundary that was never meant to be crossed." She sniffles and composes herself. "There's no going back from that."

She raises the knife above her head.

This is it. Adam is out of time and words. He had his chance, and he blew it. With nothing left to do, he freezes. He doesn't look away. He doesn't beg for mercy. He knows what's coming, so he looks Beth in her eyes.

He read somewhere that staring someone in the eyes makes it harder for them to kill that person. He can't tell if the hesitation that Beth is displaying now is a result of that or the fact that she remembers her and Adam's life together.

She raises the knife higher, and this time, she's ready to bring it down, which Adam can tell from the way Beth sharply inhales.

Just when the knife is about to be brought down, something collides with Beth's head from the side with a dull thud. Beth lets out a clipped "ugh" as her head kicks to the side and she topples. The knife drops from her hand and clatters to the floor next to her.

It takes Adam a moment to process what's going on. He's staring at Beth on the floor and then at the rock that hit her in the head. Even Beth is confused as her head swivels in various directions, trying to find the source of the ambush.

And then, a voice comes from somewhere, the most beautiful voice Adam has ever heard in his life, accompanied by the all-too-familiar jingle that echoes in the spaciousness of the warehouse.

"Oh, Bethany. You've been up to no good, haven't you?"

Thirty-Five

From the shadows, she emerges, more elegant than ever. His mom strides with a confidence he didn't know she was capable of. She walks like she owns the warehouse, like her son's killer isn't right there.

"Mom!" Adam shouts.

His heart leaps into his throat. He doesn't have the words to describe how happy he is to see her. If she's here, then everything is going to be okay. He's not going to die! She's going to make everything right just like she always does.

His mom catches his gaze and smiles, only for the briefest moment. It's a smile that says, *Mom's here, no need to worry.*

"Addy, you'll catch a cold sitting there all naked," she says.

Adam blinks, unable to process what she just said. Too many things have happened tonight, and Adam finds it difficult to consider the fact that his mom is worried about him catching a cold when losing a life is at stake.

"What the fuck," Beth groans next to Adam.

She hops to her feet with surprising speed and picks up the dropped knife. There's a rivulet of blood trickling down her temple from where the rock hit her.

Beth wipes the spot and looks at the tips of her fingers. When she sees blood, her face grows wild. "You fucking bitch. You just have to interfere everywhere, don't you?"

"If by "everywhere" you mean places where my son's life is in danger, then yes. I have to interfere everywhere," his mom says.

She's calm. Too calm for a situation like this one. Adam can't take his eyes off the large blade in Beth's hand. That thing can easily kill a person with one properly placed stab. Even if a non-essential body part is hit, it could cause the person to bleed out pretty fast.

Adam jerks his head toward his mom. She looks unarmed. How does she plan to take down Beth? Beth is younger and probably stronger and a lot faster than his mom.

He's suddenly afraid for his mom's safety. He doesn't want to watch her die right in front of his eyes. The thought of her getting stabbed to death by Beth right in front of him makes him feel like he's going to vomit into his mouth.

"Mom, get out of here! Call the police!" he shouts.

His mom lets out a chuckle. "Addy, please. We don't need to bother them with this nonsense. They're too busy dealing with real problems."

Adam can't believe what he's hearing. Has she lost her mind? He wants to shout at her not to be stupid and to get out of here before Beth does something to her, but he's so dumbstruck he can't seem to speak the words.

"Bethany. Let's talk. We really need to discuss your manners," his mom says.

"You crazy, old bitch," Beth responds. "I don't know who you think you are, but I'm glad you're here because now I can finally give you payback for what you did."

His mom raises her eyebrows. "Payback? Payback for what? I've only ever treated you fairly, Bethany, like a member of the family. But when you go and do something like this..." She gestures to Adam. "I'm a very patient woman, Bethany, but even I have my limits."

"Oh, you'll get to find out what your limits are right now. I've had it with your bullshit."

Beth slightly bends her knees. She assumes a combat-ready stance, and Adam knows the fight is on. His mom sighs and rolls her eyes.

"Oh, all right. If you insist we do things this way." she says with a shrug.

She reaches behind her back and pulls out a steak knife. It's nowhere near as impressive as Beth's combat knife, but at least she has some sort of a weapon to defend herself.

Beth breaks into a sprint forward.

"Mom!" Adam shouts, but it's too late. The fight has already started.

Beth doesn't hesitate. Her knife swipes the air, right where his mom's head is. The blade would have slashed right across her face had his mom not ducked in the last second with a speed that belies her age and build.

Beth stumbles forward, carried by the momentum, before regaining her balance. She doesn't waste time swiping the knife across the air again, aiming at his mom's face. His mom evades backward—how is she able to do that with a barely healed hip?!—and sidesteps the next attack.

"Bethany, stop," his mom says.

Beth lets out an animalistic growl as she charges forward again. This time, his mom raises the knife and parries the attack, stepping aside and shoving Beth back with her palm. Each move she makes causes her jewelry to rattle loudly in the warehouse. Beth faceplants the floor, where she remains for a moment, unmoving.

Adam hopes she's unconscious, which will give his mom enough time to call the police and uncuff him. To his dismay, Beth plants her hands on the floor and clambers to her feet. She turns to face his mom, who's standing with her hands behind her back, the calm facial expression unwavering.

"What the hell are you?" Beth asks.

His mom shrugs. "What do you mean? I'm just a protective mom, that's all. Oh, and I may have taken a few Krav Maga classes here and there."

"You bitch!" Beth lunges again.

The tip of the knife is pointed at his mom. His mom spins into a pirouette to dodge the attack. Adam doesn't see it, but while she spins, she cuts Beth's arm. Beth yowls and drops the knife out of her hand. His mom doesn't stop there. She finishes the spin with an elbow to Beth's cheek.

Beth's head recoils as she falls over like a mannequin.

There's silence in the warehouse before Beth lets out a moan. Her hand reaches for the knife. Adam is internally screaming at his mom to stop her, but she does nothing. She just waits with her hands behind her back and watches Beth as she takes hold of the knife and gets up again.

"It's not too late to stop, Bethany," his mom says. "We won't call the police. Just take your things and get out of here."

Beth looks surprised, but only for a moment. Her features are carved in anger. It's an expression Adam has never seen before, even when Beth was the angriest he ever saw her.

"No. I have to do this. You're not going to stop me," she says.

"I'm trying to help you," his mom says.

"You're trying to ruin everything! You won't stop me from becoming a member!"

This time, she hesitates before attacking. When she thrusts the knife forward, his mom deflects it with ease. She kicks the back of Beth's knee, which causes her leg to buckle under her. His mom takes hold of Beth's wrist and twists her arm. Beth throws her head back and screams in pain as she drops the knife.

Her scream is cut short when his mom spins her and shoves her forward. Beth falls for what feels like the millionth time.

"I'm giving you a fair chance to get out of here, Bethany," his mom says.

Beth is panting as she crawls forward. With a terrifying realization, Adam sees that she's actually inching closer to the rest of the tools next to the duffel bag.

"Bethany," his mom says just as Beth closes her fingers around a wrench.

She chucks it in his mom's direction, and the woman barely bothers to dodge out of the way because there's no need. Beth is scrambling to her feet, taking hold of the saw. She's not focused on his mom this time.

Her eyes drift to Adam, and he can see the idea drawn all over her face.

She runs up to Adam, practically falling to her knees, and presses the blade of the saw against his throat. Adam pulls his head back as far as he can, but he can't escape the serrated teeth of the saw.

"I'll kill him! I swear I will!" Beth cries.

His mom shakes her head. "No, you won't. You already would have done so if you wanted to."

"What the hell do you know about me?!" The blade presses deeper into Adam's skin.

"I know you love my son," his mom says.

The hand that holds the saw trembles. Beth's breaths are shallow, and Adam is bracing himself to feel the blade cutting his jugular open. Then, the pressure on his neck loosens, and Beth breaks down sobbing.

The monster that had possessed her is gone, leaving the frail, wounded woman that Adam knows all too well. She may not have told him the truth all those times that she cried on his shoulder, but the tears were as real as the comfort he provided her with.

He begins crying again, too, because he doesn't want to go on living without her. She's the love of his life, his best friend, and the person with whom he wants to spend the rest of his life. A life without her would be hollow.

"I'm sorry," Beth says through tears.

Adam wants to hug her, but those blasted handcuffs are stopping him. As if reading his mind, Beth reaches into the pocket of her pants and pulls out a small key. She reaches behind Adam where his hands are bound and fumbles with the cuffs.

A click later, the metallic bite on his wrists is gone. He doesn't realize how much of a relief it is until he's able to rub the sore spot and move freely.

He thought he'd run up to her to embrace her in a hug, but everything inside him is urging him to get away from her. Even though she's crying, Adam scoots away and clambers to his feet. Meanwhile, Beth's face is buried in her hands as she weeps like a little child.

The urge to hold her is real because she's crying just like she did after the loss of their child. These tears are true pain.

Adam feels a hand on his shoulder.

"Let's leave, Addy," his mom says.

Adam looks at her and then back at Beth.

What about her, he wants to ask, but the words don't come. Beth stops crying, lowers her hands, and stares up at Adam.

"I loved you," Adam says with a cracked voice.

He wants to throw those words in her face, to rub them in and show her all the dedication and sacrifice he's put into this marriage.

Beth is on her knees, staring up at Adam, sobbing, but he can't tell why she's spilling the tears. Does she feel sorry that she threw away everything they had, or is she sorry she failed to kill him? Maybe it's both.

"Addy. We have to go," his mom says.

Adam hesitates. He doesn't move his eyes away from Beth because there's a need for him to hear her say something, to give him something to hold on to in the aftermath of all of this. To defend herself. To tell him she did what she did because she was scared or forced into it.

The regret on her face tells Adam it's not going to happen. She's taking responsibility for her actions.

"We should call the police," Adam says. "But we won't. You should spend the rest of your life in prison for what you did, but I can't do that to you because I'm too weak. You better use that to start a new life. Goodbye, Beth."

Adam forces himself to turn around, and he and his mom start walking in the opposite direction.

"No!" Beth screams after them.

Adam and his mom turn around. Beth is firmly clutching the hand saw. Her shoulders are rising and falling from her quickened breaths.

"This is the end of the line," Beth says.

Adam braces himself. Beth raises the saw, but instead of getting off her knees and charging at Adam and his mom, she brings the blade to her throat. Adam knows what's going to happen even before it does.

There's a moment where time freezes and Adam and Beth are staring at each other. Adam doesn't need to guess what she's thinking because he knows it. He's thinking the same thing.

They're remembering their lives together, from the moment they met all the way to Beth getting pregnant, and finally culminating in what happened tonight. There's happiness, sadness, but most of all, regret.

For a modicum of a second, Adam feels like they can come back from the precipice, like this can all be forgotten and they can continue living their lives like before. It's not too late.

Except it is because, in the next moment, Beth runs the serrated blade of the saw across her neck, and it's all over. Adam looks away and squeezes his eyes shut. He clamps his hands over his ears, but he can't block out the sound of Beth gurgling.

When everything goes quiet, Adam realizes he's crying again. He's also on his knees, and he doesn't realize when that has happened. His mom is helping him up to his feet and leading him out of the warehouse. He feels like his legs can't carry his weight anymore, so he sits on a stack of pallets close to the exit to regain his strength.

"Wait here. I'll bring you some clothes, Addy," his mom says.

As she turns around, he calls out to her. "Mom. I'm sorry for everything."

She smiles, an expression that tells him the past should stay in the past. "You are my son, Adam. There isn't a thing in this world a mother wouldn't do for her child. Even if it means giving my life for you."

With that, she turns around to exit the warehouse and find some clothes for Adam. Left alone in silence, Adam smiles to himself. He's lucky to have such a caring mother who would do everything to protect him.

He thought she was an evil person, but everything she did, she did it because she wanted to protect him. Her methods may not have been perfect, but her intentions were clear.

After all, mother knows best.

Epilogue

The room is filled with the shuffling of figures entering and taking up seats at the large, round table. No one speaks a word, and no one's face is seen, because everyone is clad in black robes, their heads cloaked and veiled in darkness.

One by one, the seats are taken as the members enter the room. The person sitting next to you or in front of you could be a stranger you've never seen in your life, or it could be someone you know very well: The neighbor across the street that invites you to barbecue on the weekends, a coworker, hell, maybe even a family member. When the meeting is over, you'll go back to your normal life, and you'll never know who was in the room with you, and neither will they.

When the final seat is taken, the room falls silent. There's a minute of adjustment as everyone grounds themselves and prepares for the meeting. Then, the main spokesperson stands, and everyone follows in his gesture like a wave.

"It is with great sadness that I announce we have lost a cherished member," the spokesperson says in a deep, gravelly voice. "Join me as we wish her a safe journey to the bridge of eternity."

Everyone puts their hands together and hangs their heads down. A choir starts playing from somewhere. The words are in a foreign language. None of the figures is moving while the song lasts. When it's over, the spokesperson gestures down, and everyone except him sits.

"We will be discussing her contributions later today. For now, we must see what went wrong."

Another person stands up and says, "Beth Miller, real name Zoe Caldwell, a proud member of our family for over ten years. She's made many contributions since joining and has shown great potential in growing. Unfortunately, the initiation was a failure, and she ended up taking her own life."

Murmurs fill the room as the person sits. The spokesperson raises his hand to silence the room. Cloaked heads are turned toward him, demanding an explanation. Outrage is brewing. Initiates die or get imprisoned all the time, but not so close or during the initiation itself, especially under such unclear circumstances.

"We will now begin to dissect what happened so we can improve on our recruitment and make sure this never happens again," the spokesperson says.

The first member on the spokesperson's left side stands and says, "No deviation in her behavior detected."

"Next," the spokesperson says.

The next one who stands up says the same.

"Next."

The third one says, "She often allowed her emotions to take control as observed during her training phase."

"No deviation in her behavior detected."

"She exceeded all expectations at recruitment and in the following years. There's no way to say what went wrong."

"She took too long to eliminate the designated target and lost the ample opportunity for it. Keep in mind that she had multiple openings."

"No deviation in her behavior detected."

"No deviation in her behavior detected."

"She allowed her pregnancy to cloud her judgment, and losing her baby made her impulsive."

One by one, the members offer their observations and opinions until they reach halfway around the table. That's when the spokesperson doesn't say *next* but stops so they can recap.

"So, from what we can tell, something went wrong during those final months leading up to the initiation. Something happened there, but no one seems to know what. Either Bethany was really good at hiding things from us, or... Someone was involved in her downfall."

More murmurs before the spokesperson silences the room.

"Next," he calls out.

"No deviation in her behavior detected."

"Next."

The person in line doesn't stand. Heads turn to the one whose turn it is, but no one says a word. This isn't a classroom where people can just start shouting at the oblivious students who are being called on by the teacher. The spokesperson is the only one who gets to do that.

"Next!" the spokesperson calls out again.

The cloaked figure's head doesn't snap up at attention to indicate they just realized they were being called. Instead, they calmly raise themselves like a wraith, and as they do so, something underneath their cloak creates a distinctive jingling sound.

"The initiate was unfit for the family," the woman under the cloak says.

There are gasps and more murmurs. Someone even shouts, "*How dare you?*" They don't take lightly to such accusations because it means that the decisions of all the members who had previously assessed the initiate are overridden.

The cloaked figure who made the statement doesn't flinch or even look around. She keeps staring ahead of her, directly at the spokesperson, even though he can't see her eyes.

The spokesperson raises his hand, but the room remains filled with outraged voices.

"Silence!" the spokesperson shouts, and that's when the peace returns to the chamber. He waits a moment longer to make sure everyone has settled down and then says, "Explain why you think the initiate was unfit for our family."

The woman takes a moment to respond. "As stated before, she took too long to eliminate her target. We all know that the longer we wait, the more likely something is going to go wrong. She has proven unable to improvise in situations that get in the way of plans. On top of that, she had developed emotions for the target. In the end, taking her own life doesn't come as a surprise to me."

More gasps, but the spokesperson silences them before the room can explode with interruptions.

"It doesn't come as a surprise to you? It sounds like you knew her well."

The cloaked figure remains quiet for a bit before saying, "I... observed her closely during the final months of her life."

"Observed and nothing more, I hope."

"That is correct."

"Because you know the punishment for interfering with initiates on their path to righteousness."

"I'm well aware of our laws."

The spokesperson stares at the cloaked woman, perhaps deciding whether he believes her or not. In the end, she's been with them for many years. Although no one knows who she is, the sound of her jingling jewelry underneath the cloaks has become her trademark in the meetings. If anyone is a trustworthy family member, it's her.

"Does the target know of our existence?" the spokesperson asks.

"No. He knows Bethany used to be in a cult, and that's it."

The room hangs in silence. The cloaked woman doesn't say anything else even though the spokesperson expects her to. Finally, he asks, "Does anyone else have anything of value to offer about the initiate?"

No one stands.

"Very well," the spokesperson says, and the cloaked figure takes it as a sign that she's free to sit.

Another loud jingle accompanies the gesture as she plops back into the chair.

The spokesperson says, "We will honor the fallen initiate after the meeting. As per our laws, her target will gain immunity for surviving the initiation."

There are complaints and disappointed gasps. Someone shouts something about him deserving to die.

"Silence!" the spokesperson shouts again. "Laws are laws. We are not going to break them, no matter how much we want to protect our family members. The initiate's death is unfortunate, but she went into it knowing full well what could happen. We don't punish the survivors. We reward them. Does anyone else have anything they would like to add?"

No one says anything.

"In that case, the topic is concluded. Bethany will be honored as a contributing member, and the target, Adam Miller, will be put on the list of people who are to be protected by the family. The meeting is adjourned."

Chairs start moving as all the members stand to leave the room. The cloaked woman with the jingling jewelry remains seated a moment longer.

No one can see it, but underneath the hood, she smiles.

THE END

Final Notes

Years ago, when I first started posting my stories online, I wrote a short horror story about a mother who was using black magic against her son. The idea was to make it look as though the mother wanted her son to be dependent on her for the rest of his life. It portrayed the selfishness that parents sometimes show when their child is about to leave the nest.

For many, taking care of their child has been a primary task throughout their lives, and they cannot imagine not having a child to take care of anymore. You take away that responsibility from them, and what are they left with?

Letting a child out into the hostile world is possibly the most difficult thing a parent has to do. I cannot say for sure, since I'm not a parent, but I would assume it would feel like losing a big part of ourselves.

This book had the goal to capture the essence of not just a parent's inability to let their child go, but also their undivided love and willingness for sacrifice. I think every parent who reads this book will agree they would do things the same way the mother in the book did.

If you, however, found yourself empathizing more with Beth, that is okay, too. I think many of us have experience with rude or unbearable mothers-in-law. This book is for you, too.

If you enjoyed reading *Mother Knows Best*, I would appreciate it if you left your review on Amazon. It only takes a minute, and it means a lot to small authors like me.

More Thrillers by the Author

1. Never Leave Me
2. Not My Husband
3. The House Across The Street
4. Mother Knows Best
5. Feel Free To Scream
6. Maria

Buy paperbacks at
www.borisbacic.com

Liked what you read? Subscribe to the author's newsletter and receive a free horror book.

Subscribe at
https://dl.bookfunnel.com/63a17lay5z

Made in the USA
Middletown, DE
10 June 2024

55544523R00188